Sam Hanna Bell was born in Glas
parents. On the death of his father, a
to Ireland at the age of seven to be re
of County Down, where his accla
December Bride (1951), is set. He worked during the 1950s, 19
1970s as a senior features producer with the BBC Northern Ireland Region, pioneering the collection and broadcasting of fast-vanishing folklore and folk music from remote country areas. He continued to write during this period and after retirement; his other novels are *A Man Flourishing* (1973) and *Across the Narrow Sea* (1987). In 1970 Queen's University Belfast awarded him the honorary degree of MA for achievements in the arts. He died in February 1990.

December Bride, A Man Flourishing and *Across the Narrow Sea* are all currently available from Blackstaff Press.

THE HOLLOW BALL

•

SAM HANNA BELL

THE
BLACKSTAFF
PRESS

BELFAST

First published in 1961 by
Cassell & Company Limited
This Blackstaff Press edition is a photolithographic facsimile of the first edition printed by Cox and Wyman Limited

This edition published in 1990 by
The Blackstaff Press
3 Galway Park, Dundonald, Belfast BT16 0AN, Northern Ireland
with the assistance of
The Arts Council of Northern Ireland

Printed by The Guernsey Press Company Limited

British Library Cataloguing in Publication Data
Bell, Sam Hanna, *1909–1990*
The hollow ball.
I. Title
823.914 [F]
ISBN 0-85640-452-7

TO

JOHN BOYD

AND

J. U. STEWART

Looking back rom some vantage point we delude ourselves that we can see a pattern in our lives; but we have been impelled to this stage by events with which we were powerless or afraid to interfere.

The Radical's Almanac

Part One

I

The Albert Memorial clock sounded the first stroke of nine as he pushed open the street door of Messrs Hamiltons' wholesale warehouse, crossed the floor of the Mantles Department and knocked at the door of Mr Hamilton's private office.

'Yes?'

He pulled off his cap, wiped his feet, and went in. After a moment Mr Hamilton raised his smooth, florid face with the tight peregrine nose in the middle of it. The thick gold ring on his finger, the gold-topped pen in his hand, the soft silver suit on his big body, was the uniform of a man who owned things and directed people.

'Well, boy, what is it?'

'I'm Minnis, sir—David Minnis.'

Gently Mr Hamilton allowed the desk pen to slip into its holder. He needed no longer than that to remember what David represented.

'Ah yes, Minnis, Readymades Department?'

'Yessir.'

Mr Hamilton pressed a button on his desk, withdrew the pen, and went on with his writing. Then he laid the pen down and looked at David.

'Mr Rankin, the agent, mentioned your name to me, didn't he?'

'Yessir.'

'I hope you'll like being with us, Minnis. We get on well here together. A big family. A big industrious family. You're now a member of it, Minnis.'

'Yessir. Thank you, sir.'

There was a tap at the door and a boy older than David entered.

'John, this boy is David Minnis. Take him up to Mr Whaley, Readymades Department.'

'Yes, Mr Clarence.'

The boy crooked a finger at David and David turned to thank Mr Hamilton again. But Mr Hamilton, his well-groomed fingers fanned out on a page of the company's chequebook, had noted David down, indexed him and stored him away against the unlikely eventuality of ever having to consider him again.

As they climbed the stairs to the Readymades Department David's escort studied him out of the corner of his eye. He noted the carefully brushed blue suit, the face a shade too good-looking, the long well-shaped head, the smooth fair hair. He didn't like what he saw. 'Just starting?' he asked with a sidelong glance at David's tie.

David answered with a quick smile. 'Yes. What department are you in?'

'I'm in no department,' the other said coldly. 'I'm a member of the office staff.'

The Readymades Department was on the first floor. The clerk led David around large hessian bales, between counters, among a scattering of customers who had arrived early in the warehouse. He paused, his hand raised to knock at the door of an office partitioned off in a corner of the large room. 'What's your name, again?'

'David Minnis.'

The clerk tapped at the door and opened it. 'Mr Clarence asked me to bring this boy to you, Mr Whaley. His name is David Minnis.'

Mr Whaley, in his shirtsleeves, was arranging small squares of cloth laid out on the leaf of a high desk. He nodded without looking up and the clerk left David to him. After much consideration, Mr Whaley laid each pattern down on one of several little heaps, as though he were playing a sort of woollen patience. Suddenly he straightened up with a satisfied 'Ah!' and clapped his hands together. Then he turned to David. 'You're David Minnis, eh?' He laid a firm hand on David's shoulder. 'What can we do with you? Yes, of course—the Trousers.' He turned David around. 'Up there to your left. Ask for Alec Roden. He'll give you something to start on'—and he clapped David on the shoulder.

'Yessir.'

As he walked away Mr Whaley called after him: 'Doesn't Mr Rankin live in your house?'

'Yes—yes, he does.'

'Thought so. Now off you go, boy, and get your coat and cap hung up.' And Mr Whaley returned to his patterns.

David walked back through the warehouse. A sliding fireproof door was pulled back from the entrance to a smaller room on his left. He went in. The room was filled from end to end with racks of women's coats in puce green and electric blue. As he turned to go he heard a noise from the corner of the room. Suspended by a thick rope which hung from a black aperture in the ceiling was a square hamper. It jerked in mid-air as if it were alive. Below the hamper was another opening dropping to God knew what depths. From the hamper came puffs of chaff and stifled cries.

Overcoming his fear he leaned over the wooden parapet around the open trapdoor and tapped the hamper. 'Is there anybody in there?' The voice stopped. There was a convulsive jerk of the hamper that left it hanging at a fearful angle in the rope. He stepped back, certain that he had seen the gleam of maddened eyes through the wickerwork. 'Wait till I get out, you wee bastard, and I'll fix you!' The prisoner wriggled again and the hamper slipped out of the loop another groaning inch.

'Don't move!' shouted David. 'Or you'll crash to the bottom!'

Motionless, the voice in the hamper considered the warning. Then, 'Who are you? Aren't you Fogarty?' it asked.

'My name's Minnis. I'm a new fella.'

'Well, don't stand there. Let the trapdoor down.'

David dropped the door below the hamper. 'Will I go and get somebody to let you out?'

'Not at all. What would you do that for? D'you know how to work a hoist?'

'I don't think so,' said David, peering into the opening above.

'D'you see two ropes hanging down the wall?'

He saw them.

'Well, pull on the one nearest you—easy, now!'

David pulled and the hamper rose in the air with a frightening slip and creak.

'The other rope, damn you—easy—'

A sharp jerk on the second rope brought the hamper crashing on the closed trapdoor. The looped rope, released from the drum above roared down on the prisoner struggling out of the hamper. He shook the rope off his head and shoulders, glared at David, and ran out of the storeroom.

David looked at the empty hamper and the coiled rope, the rows of mill-girls' coats, glanced back at the hamper and shrugged his shoulders. Serving an apprenticeship to the woollen trade mightn't be as dull as he had feared. A customer, trailed by an assistant, passed the doorway. 'Where are the Trousers?' asked David. The assistant jerked his thumb at a narrow flight of stairs beside the storeroom. 'Up there,' he said.

2

TITS FOGARTY stopped drumming the heels of his patent-leather shoes against the counter on which he sat, and listened. Except for a youth with his head and shoulders in a fixture at the end of the department, he was alone on this top floor that encircled the main well of the warehouse. At the sound of David's feet on the stairs he slid from the counter and ran silently into a small dark room off the main floor. From here he could look down the hoist. He saw the open and empty hamper on the floor below. He stepped back into the darkness and watched the stairs apprehensively. David rounded the last step and stood with his hand on the balustrade. Fogarty's face cleared. 'Customer for your department, Mr McFall!' he cried to the youth who had vanished into the fixture except for his backside and the soles of his shoes.

'Then serve 'm, Mr Fogarty!' came a wooden boom from the fixture.

Muttering, Fogarty came out of the room. David smiled. It wasn't returned.

'I'm a new fella. I'm starting to work here. I was sent to look for Mr Roden.'

Fogarty stopped, looked him over and chuckled. 'A new fella, eh?' He turned and shouted to the crouching figure at the end of the long floor: 'Hi, Boney, here's a new apprentice!'

They watched Boney withdraw his head and body from the fixture. 'Wassat?' he said putting his hand to his ear.

'Come here, stupid!' invited Fogarty. He turned to David. 'What d'they call you?'

'David Minnis.' This, he decided, wasn't the man he was looking for. 'Are you Mr Roden?'

Fogarty waved him to silence. He hummed a little tune and shuffled his dapper pointed feet like a comedian. 'Here's a new fella starting,' he said as Boney approached.

'Ah?' said Boney, stopping. He was tall and lanky and young, not much older than I am, thought David. He carried his jacket over his arm and while he considered David he drew it on and the square white wrists came too far out of the cuffs. He tucked a soiled string of a tie, a schoolboy's tie with horizontal stripes, into the top of his pullover. A soft fluff blurred the line of his jaw. David turned away to Fogarty's smart, ageless face, coloured vest, sharp, glittering shoes. They consoled him.

'So you're the new start?' said Boney. His voice was from the back streets, but slow and gentle.

'Our Boney misses nothing. Sharp as a pin,' said Fogarty, dancing a step in joy.

'Yes,' said David impatiently. Boney grinned and David forgot about his clothes. The wide mouth stretched into a crescent of warmth and friendship. It was irresistible. David giggled. Boney's smile widened. He stood there grinning, his pale, big-knuckled hands hanging by his sides, and David, swallowing a laugh, forgot his soiled clothes, starting ears, unkempt hair.

'I was sent to look for Mr Roden.'

'First year?' asked Fogarty.

David looked at him, puzzled.

'He means are you a first-year apprentice. Are you starting your time from the beginning?'

David nodded.

'What age are you?' asked Fogarty.

'Sixteen.'

Fogarty threw back his head and laughed. 'Tits, you're a late starter. You'll be more'n twenty before you're out of your time!'

David didn't laugh. 'I've been working since I was fourteen in a potato firm. They sacked me when—'

Fogarty slid over to the stairs and stood listening. '*Here's Roden!*' he hissed and melted into the dark small room.

The man in his middle twenties was humming a tune as he mounted the stairs. But when he came round the banister-head David could see no music in his face. He looked around suspiciously and sniffed. 'Loafing again, McFall!' he shouted. He plucked a bundle of boys' tweed knickers from under his arm and hurled them at Boney. 'Get those into a fixture and get on with your work!' He glared round the department with narrow-eyed malignity, and David, watching him, was uncertain whether or not he could sense an element of pantomime behind all this shouting and ferocity.

'You being attended to?' he demanded of David, all the time his eyes on business of their own.

'My name's Minnis—'

Fogarty, tiptoeing on his pointed shoes, tried to slip out and past, unseen. Without looking back Roden shot out a hand and grasped him cruelly, coat-lapel, shirt and tie gathered up into a handful. 'Ah, Alec!' squealed Fogarty, wrestling in the thick hairy grip.

Roden swung the dapper youth in front of him, staring into his shrinking face. 'Up loafing again? Smoking, no doubt?' And he glanced into the dark packing-room. 'No, I wasn't—my hand to God I wasn't—ah, you're tearing my shirt!' howled Fogarty.

'Don't use that expression in this department, Fogarty,' said Roden, thin-lipped. 'What were you doing then?'

'I was assisting Boney,' and David saw a furtive smile on his face.

Roden shook him again. 'To put Charlie Connif in a skep. And take that sarky grin off your face, Fogarty!'

'Aw, tits, Alec, I will, I will—I'm sorry,' moaned Fogarty as his shirt gave at the neckband.

Roden hurled him away. 'Get down below and stay down, and if Connif breaks your backside don't come girning to me.'

Fogarty retreated to the head of the stairs where he straightened his tie, slicked back his hair, and again David sensed the play-acting under the violence. 'Pity you had to make such an exhibition of yourself, Alec. That's the new fella—'

'Get back to your work!'

'God help him too!' shouted Fogarty, and they heard the swift drum of his feet as he raced downstairs.

'I'll put the bad language out of that one yet,' said Roden evenly. He looked David over. 'You're David Minnis?'

'Yessir.'

'You're to work up here with McFall and me. McFall will show you where the stock is. Boney, come here a minute. And there's one thing more, Minnis. When there's work to be done, stay in your own department and do it. This is Boney McFall—David Minnis.'

'I've met him,' said Boney.

'Well, show him where things are. And Boney, you stay up here unless your work takes you downstairs. I've told Connif if he goes looking for you or Fogarty or if you interfere with him I'll march the three of you up to Mr Whaley. And you know what that means.'

'Yes, Alec. Sorry.'

'Put David on to building in those Bedford cords and brushing down some fixtures. On you go,' and he waved them into the small room.

Boney switched on the light. A great fat bale stitched tightly in sacking lay on the floor. David wrinkled his nose. 'Blankets,' said Boney and lifted the lid of a large wooden bin. David turned away in disgust from the stench of the soft creamy blankets piled in it. 'I never thought blankets smelled like that!' he said.

'You get used to it,' said Boney. He kicked the bale lying on the floor. 'These are the riding-breeches Alec was talking about. You have to open it—like this.' He took a jacknife from his pocket and cut the taut cord that stitched the sacking together. The tight cover curled back like the rind of a fruit. It was pleasant to watch. Boney severed the corner strings and the cover peeled away and collapsed on the floor.

'Ah—Boney, there was a lot of cod in all that shouting and pushing between Alec Roden and that fella Fogarty, wasn't there?'

Boney smiled and grimaced. 'There was and there wasn't. Fogarty's always dodging customers. Alec's a senior assistant and he's trying to get married. He knows the fellas here don't give a damn about their work, but he has to keep his job, so he pushes them around, see?'

'Is Roden a decent fella?'

'If you take him the right way—by the throat.' David smiled politely at the familiar schoolboy treason.

Boney stripped off the sheets of packing and uncovered the breeches lumped and crushed together. To David they looked like sandwiches of new brown bread that had been tied too tightly. Boney stooped and lifted most of the pile. 'You bring the rest,' he said, and staggered out into the department. David took up his burden and followed him. With a grunt Boney heaved the breeches onto a counter below an empty fixture.

'Now,' he said, 'this is how you build them,' and he lifted a pair and shook them open to show David the label on the waistband. 'See, size eight—that's the biggest size. They go at the bottom of the fixture. Look at that gut, would you?' and he held the breeches against his waist.

David laughed at the voluminous waistband that could have gone twice round the other boy's body. 'No wonder they call you Boney.'

Boney shook his head. 'That's not why I'm called Boney. My name happens to be Bonar Law—Bonar Law McFall. My mother's that way inclined.'

'Who's isn't?'

'I knew you were a Protestant by the look of you. Now watch;

you lay the big sizes down first, heads to tails, and build them up like *that*, keeping a nice level front so that the dust won't get in. See if you can do it.'

After a time David's attention wandered and he became aware of the small noises that insinuated themselves into that long dim room. The roar of traffic from the street below crept through the dusty arched windows and was deadened by the walls of clothing around him. From the rectangular well that rose through the three floors of the warehouse came a murmurous hum from the other departments. When he had stowed away the breeches he leaned over the mahogany rail. The floor below him was also walled up to the ceiling with box-like fixtures filled with overcoats, suits and waterproofs; on the bustling ground floor customers and salesgirls wound through a maze of racks hung with furs, umbrellas, coats and dresses as bright as bottled sweets.

Boney tugged urgently at his sleeve. 'Come back outa that!'

'Why?'

'I'll tell you. You got this job because the fella that was here before you was sacked last month. D'you see those fitting-rooms?' Boney, peering cautiously down through the floriated metal under the rail, pointed to a row of glazed boxes that ran along one side of the ground floor. 'The Chairman got those roofed over about a week ago. This fella, Jimmie Cummings, was leaning over the rail here, doing nothing just like you, when a wee dame that was trying on a pair of corsets looked up and seen him. She let a squawk that brought the Chairman running out of his office. "There's a man upstairs looking at me!" she kept yelling. You've only met Mr Clarence, haven't you? Wait till you meet the Chairman. That's his uncle. Anyway, he hardly gave Cummings time to collect his cap and cards before he set him out on the street. What made Cummings mad was that he never seen this wee doll. But the Chairman wouldn't listen to him. See what I mean? One of those dames looks up and spots you—you're out!'

'Thanks for the tip, Boney.'

'Away and get your cap. It's time you went for your dinner.'

In High Street the noon sun was warm and comforting on his

back. He glanced up at the Albert clock and remembered that he had only an hour in which to get his lunch. An Ormeau Road tram was leaving the stop opposite the Queen's Hotel. If he had hurried across the road he could have caught it but he loitered deliberately until it had picked up speed. Then he went after it; three or four fleet paces down the pavement, then a long swerving run across and through the oncoming traffic that carried him behind the tramcar. He paced behind it for a few yards then accelerated and swung himself onto the footboard. The conductor who had watched his passage across the crowded street regarded him sourly. 'You'll get you neck set yet, me bucko,' he prophesied as he collected David's fare.

He smiled to himself as he took the ticket. Running was one thing he could do supremely well. He had not been a particularly good runner at school but as he reached adolescence his body, arms, legs and head had arrived at some happy co-ordination that gave him this fleetness of foot. At times he quivered with the impulse to race. Then he would go scudding down the street in what was to the neighbours an impressive but quite unnecessary explosion of speed.

After he left school and became more sensitive to what people thought of him he ceased to run the streets for the thrill of doing so. At school he had been a good footballer. But there everything had been free. Now he found it just a little too difficult to raise the few shillings for club subs, travel and gear. So he hadn't played football for the past two winters.

He alighted at the foot of Ormeau Road and turned down Colinvista Street, a thoroughfare of three-storeyed houses with startled eyebrows of yellow brick over the ground floor windows. At number eleven he put his hand into the letter-box and pulled a frayed string to open the door. The Minnises' hall was covered to elbow height with a brown embossed paper. The upper part of the walls was coloured a damp cinnamon. The fanlight over the door was crystal clear but the light from it and the dim glow that filtered from the casement on the first floor barely lit up the gloomy hall. The gloom seeped from a tall hallstand muffled under the dead shapes of coats. In the middle of the stand was a lidded receptacle which when opened emitted an odour of gloves and bibles.

In the left-hand wall of the hall were two doors. The first opened into the front room which Mr Rankin used as an office and where he ate his meals. The second door led into the kitchen, or, as his mother preferred to call it, the living-room.

There was a smell of cabbage and bacon in the hall and he sniffed it hungrily. He opened the living-room door. His mother and his young brother Freddie were seated at the table.

'You're early, aren't you?' said Mrs Minnis with a smile.

'They told me to go for my dinner at half-twelve.' He brought a chair to the table. She rose to get his meal. As a young woman she had been slender. Now she was spare, sinewy, her dark head flawed with grey. As she set down his plate she said, 'And how did you get on?'

'Oh, it looks all right. It's a quare big place, Hamiltons. I'm away up in the top of the house.'

'What are the other people like?'

He looked up from his plate. 'They seem decent enough. Why shouldn't they be?' He raised his brows and tried to keep the impatience from his voice.

'I only asked you a question,' she said in the calm, toneless voice he knew so well.

He kept silent for a moment, cutting his bacon into fragments with unnecessary vigour. 'They seem all right. I've only met the ones in the Readymades.'

For the first time Freddie's interest was engaged. His smudgy schoolboy face lit up with expectation. 'Is it good fun?' David turned to smile at his brother. Inexorably Mrs Minnis checked her elder son's affectionate sarcasm. 'What fun would there be in it?' she demanded.

The smile faded from his face and he continued with his dinner. He looked at his mother from under his brows, a woman giving her life for them, unstintingly, ungraciously. At Freddie, weaker and younger than himself. There should be someone there to protect all three of them, and he felt pity for them and a sick annoyance because he felt it.

'It's not bad, Freddie,' he said.

'It's better than school, anyway.'

'It's different.'

'Have they a football team?'

'I dunno. I didn't ask yet.'

'There's more important things than that,' she said in a hostile voice.

'I know—'

'You've got to make a better effort here than you did in the potato place—'

There was to be no truce between them. He blanched with anger and flung his fork noisily on the table. At that moment, Mr Rankin, wiping his lips with his napkin, tapped at the open door. 'The milk, please, Mrs Minnis,' he said, looking in.

'Oh, I'm sorry, Mr Rankin!' She jumped up and ran into the scullery.

'Well, David, how did things go this morning?' said Mr Rankin, smiling and leaning against the door.

'All right, thank you, Mr Rankin.'

'Think you'll like it?'

'Oh, yes, I'm sure I will.' He nodded energetically. Mrs Minnis came up from the scullery with a jug of milk. Mr Rankin took it from her, thanked her, frowned in mock warning at Freddie and closed the door.

'You might have thanked Mr Rankin,' said Mrs Minnis, but her voice was placatory, without reproach.

'Oh, but David did thank him, Mammy,' said Freddie.

He didn't speak, but tousled Freddie's hair and ordered him to comb it and get his cap. They left the house and walked up the street together. At the corner he put his hand in his pocket and gave his brother a threepenny bit he couldn't afford. Freddie took it in wide-eyed, polite astonishment. With a grin, David watched him dart joyfully away.

He was fond of his mother. Yes, she worked away at her sewing to keep them, and he was fond of her, but my God she drove him nearly daft with the things she said! Casting up to him about his last job like that! He grew angry again, striding through the crowded streets, sullen and shy. When he saw a pretty girl he stared straight ahead, a morose scowl on his face, then out of the corner of his eye he watched with mingled satisfaction and longing how she turned her head away in abrupt anger as they passed.

3

WHEN the clock in his office was precisely on the stroke of half-past five, Mr Clarence pressed a button on his desk and buzzers sounded in the Mantles, the Woollens, the Pattern Room, the Silks, the Readymades, the Trousers. Immediately there arose throughout the building the clatter of heavy scissors and yard-sticks thrown into fixtures, the sound of running feet and slamming doors. Bonar, who had been brushing down a pile of corduroys, tossed his stiff yellow whisk under the counter. 'Come on,' he said. 'Grab your cap. It's knocking-off time.'

As they left the warehouse entrance Bonar and he turned to the left. Bonar stopped. 'Where do you live?'

'Up the Ormeau,' said David.

'Do you? So do I. What street?'

'Colinvista Street.'

'I know it. I live in Majestic Street.'

David had a confused recollection of a skein ot cobbled working-class streets running from the Ormeau Road down to the Lagan. 'Down near the river?'

'That's right,' answered Bonar with a satisfied nod.

So that's where you live, he thought. He recollected with complacency the three-storeyed house in which he and his family lived.

'D'you know big Artie Twaddel that knocks round the Gas-works Bridge?' asked Bonar as they walked along High Street.

'Can't say I do.'

'Big Artie was a great footballer till he got on the booze. He played for Ireland once. D'you play?'

'I did when I was at school.'

'Were you any good?'

'Yes—very good.'

His answer was so flat and matter-of-fact that he didn't trouble to watch how it was received. Nevertheless he was rather surprised that his companion didn't jeer. They walked on for a time in silence.

'Well, if you were all that good why did you give it up?'

This time he didn't answer. He weighed whether he should tell Bonar the reason and decided against it. He saw his boots, small, cracked, sere, the studs worn askew, hanging in the outside lavatory. They had almost crippled him in the last two or three games.

'Ah, I got fed up.'

'You don't get fed up with something you're good at!'

'Don't you? I did. What does it matter anyway?'

'Nothing. Only the firm has a team. We play up at the Park. Alec Roden's captain. He'll be after you to play. We're in the Haberdashers Alliance. Finished at the foot of the table last year —and the year before.'

'Consistent, eh?' laughed David.

'Yes,' said Bonar, turning round in surprise at the word. 'That's us—consistent.' David noted the gesture and was pleased. Already, he felt, he had established a shade of ascendency.

In Cromac Street, Bonar paused and looked around as if in search of something. 'Did you see any of the Troubles?' he asked.

'Only a papish fruitshop burned out in the Dublin Road when I was a kid.'

'I saw a man shot dead—there.' Bonar pointed to the street corner opposite.

David was impressed. 'Where were you?'

'I was down a message for my mammy'—at the endearment David winced—'and just as I was crossing here I heard the shots. I bunked for a doorway and when I looked out there was the man down on his hands and knees coughing and three fellas running away down Eliza Street. The man fell on his face and two ould shawlies came out of a house and pulled him onto the pavement. After a minute I thought about going across to have a look at him, but a peeler came running up and when he'd looked at him, he took off his jacket and threw it over the fella's face.'

'He was dead?' asked David, his eyes wide.

'Stiff. Look, I'll show you something.' He drew David across the street and at the low window-sill of a shop took his hand and ran his fingers over the ledge. 'Feel it? That's where one of the bullets struck. It went right through him.'

'How d'you know?'

'I saw it. I saw the peelers digging it out of the wood. The ould lady in the shop got fed up with people coming and looking at the hole. At first she thought it would bring custom to her place but she only sold cooked pigs' feet and not everybody eats them. So she had the hole puttied up and painted over. She mighta left it. It was a sorta historical thing, wasn't it?'

David agreed doubtfully. He hadn't known that murderous death had been so close to Colinvista Street. 'Who was the man?'

'They said he was a rebel that squealed. That's why the peeler covered up his face. He probably deserved it. They never caught the three fellas.'

'How d'you know?'

'Because my da kept the papers for weeks after that. He searched every bit of them. There was no mention of the shooting at all.'

'A thing like that! Your d— your father might have missed it.'

'Not him! He said from the first thaւ the shooting would be kicked about till it was lost. He's always saying that the peelers do things like that when it suits them.'

What sort of father was this who criticized the police and how did he know that the police weren't what they seemed to be? You should never poke and pry and pursue after things that could hurt other people, but . . . with an ingenuous smile, inflecting his question as delicately as he was able, he asked, 'Why, has your father ever been in—trouble?'

Bonar laughed. 'The only trouble he ever has with the police is when the wind blows out his lamps. He's a boss night-watchman —when he's working. His trouble is that he's devoured three libraries, covers and all.'

He felt keenly disappointed. 'So he was only talking when he said that about the police—it wasn't true?'

'I dunno. He talks that much some of it's bound to be true.'

They swerved and dodged through the crowds, were separated at the outpourings of streets, met up again with a grin, got used to each other. On the broad, quieter pavements of Ormeau Road they walked for a time in silence. Then: 'You didn't say how you liked your first day at Hamiltons.'

'All right. Not bad. You're not killed with work.'

Bonar chuckled. 'It gets easier as you go on—I'm glad, Davie, that you're the fella got the job.'

Surprised and pleased, he turned to meet his companion's wide grin. 'Ah . . . thanks, Boney. Me too.'

They parted at the corner of Colinvista Street. 'Might see you here at twenty to nine in the morning?' Bonar called.

'I'll be here.' And he waved his companion goodnight.

His mother had potted half a dozen herrings for tea. He liked potted herrings and she knew it. She had taken special care with these fish. The flesh was baked with a pleasant crispness, the juice was bland and not too vinegary. There was a hint of mace. A fragrant clove was tucked into the rolled flesh of each fish. David clapped his hands and crowed over them. His mother laughed and said, 'They're making a hungry man out of you in that place!'

When the meal was finished and the dishes washed, she went upstairs as she had done at this time every evening since David could remember. As he sat glancing over the paper while Freddie finished his schoolwork the dull insistent throb of her sewing-machine started in the room above. It took possession of the walls, the floor, the ceiling, and set the electric light above them swaying slightly.

Shortly after ten o'clock he went into her room to bid her goodnight. He stood in the doorway watching her feed the silky material under the needle, turn it adroitly this way and that, draw it away and drop the finished article on a sheet of brown paper on the floor.

Her foot paused on the treadle of the machine. She looked up, nodded and smiled. 'Is there anything you want, David?'

He shook his head.

'Goodnight, son.'

'Goodnight, mother.' He closed the door and went up to his room. Long after he had fallen asleep the house still vibrated gently to the beat of the sewing-machine.

4

COLINVISTA STREET had still some justification for its name when Mrs Minnis had come there as a young bride twenty years before; looking across the city from her attic windows she could see a ridge of the mountain above the chimney tops. Then seven years later a ramshackle shirt and blouse factory was thrown up, blotting out her glimpse of the mountain. It was in that year and about that time that Pastor Minnis died, leaving her with two infant sons, a rented house half-furnished, a shelf of evangelical works and one hundred and fifty-three pounds in the Post Office. Had she been so disposed she might have seen an augury in the loss of her mountain view, for, from that time on, as Pastor Minnis' successor said with more accuracy than forbearance, her feet were destined to tread in lowly and difficult places.

There had been a deep affection between husband and wife, and in the first anguish of loss she felt that life might as well come to an end for her. She never spoke of this despair, but recollected it afterwards with humiliation and merciless self-reproach.

As the days passed in the company of her helpless children and as she responded to the warm and sensible sympathy of her neighbours and her friends at the Gospel Hall, her courage revived and she began to look around for some way to earn a living for herself and her family. To David, a child of barely six, the loss of his father meant little. There had been one or two tearful requests at bedtime, or he would stop in the middle of some play and shout on the absent man to disentangle a toy. But it was his mother's tears more than his father's death that lingered briefly with him. Soon the man's image and even the memory of him were forgotten by his son.

The sympathy that Mrs Minnis received was practical as well as liberal. The Gospel Hall where her husband had ministered granted her a pension of a pound a week and continued to do so until David left school at the age of fourteen. When Mrs Cassidy, who lived three doors below, heard that she had a machine she induced her to take in sewing. One morning Mrs Cassidy called for her and introduced her to the manageress of the tall factory that had blotted out the mountain. Mrs Minnis had never really cared for Mrs Cassidy, and even when the sewing, with Mr Rankin's board, became her main income, she refrained from anything more than a cordial greeting in the street.

Then one night during the Troubles the Cassidys had to leave their home hurriedly and fly to a sister's house in the Falls Road. Mrs Minnis took in two of the Cassidy children that night and made them up a bed on the kitchen sofa. Afterwards, when her neighbours congratulated her on her generosity, and indeed, her courage, her answer, calm and quietly spoken, was always the same, 'The woman was kind to me at once.'

When the Troubles flickered down again a number of people in the street were prepared to admit that the Cassidys had been human beings after all, and all agreed that Mrs Minnis' action was what might have been expected from a woman of character who had saved herself from destitution by her own efforts. And was she not, after all, the widow, in a manner of speaking, of a clergyman?

To Mrs Minnis, the good opinion of her neighbours, although they did not find it necessary to voice it so often as the years passed, was very precious. Deliberately she shaped her life and that of her sons to be worthy of other people's approval. The courageous effort by which she overcame her early loss was sustained until it became an obsession with keeping up appearances. She made a virtue out of necessity, and subordinated everything to that aspect of her existence; the routine of her home and the conduct of her children, equally.

Although her life had been difficult after the death of her

husband, it had its compensations. Mr Shrubsole, the new Pastor, came to her often for advice. David could still remember the afternoon when he first heard Mr Rankin's name mentioned. Mr Shrubsole was standing in the hall talking to his mother.

'It will help to keep things running, Mrs Minnis.'

'Yes, but—oh, I don't know what to say!'

'Once again, Mrs Minnis, you've nothing to worry about. Mr Rankin is a very fine man—a very fine man. All that is over—forgotten—' Mr Shrubsole's voice faded as he moved to the front door followed by Mrs Minnis, her hands clasped, an anxious frown on her face.

When Mr Shrubsole had gone, she came back into the front room where David was seated at the table finishing his schoolwork. 'I'm taking a boarder,' she announced. She ran her eye round the room. 'This'll be his sitting-room. He'll take his meals in here.'

He was angry. He didn't really care very much about the front room. The back living-room and his own bedroom were the parts of the house in which he spent most of his time. But a stranger was coming in to steal away part of their house and their privacy.

It turned out to be different from what David expected. Mr Rankin was all right. He had been brought to Mr Shrubsole's notice and care by some mysterious body of people whose identity was never made clear, at least to David and his brother. Because of this, Mr Rankin attended the Gospel Hall, or at least he did for about a year. Then he began to miss an occasional Sunday morning and eventually stopped going altogether.

Anyway, Mr Rankin was different somehow from the Hall people. His voice was quiet and he didn't say very much. Sometimes, when Harry Peebles, the coalman, or Mr Sinton, who owned a linoleum store on the Shankill Road, dropped in with their wives to see his mother, they would catch Mr Rankin before he could escape upstairs. The talk would always start about the finances of the Hall and then to Good Works and soon words and phrases like *atonement* or *redemption through our Lord Jesus Christ* or *working for the Lord* would go shuttling backwards and forwards across the room, all expressions as familiar as the taste of potatoes and salt in the mouths of the Peebles and the Sintons and his mother.

But David, peering curiously at Mr Rankin, saw that he became nervous and shy when the talk took this turn. He would sit with an uneasy smile coming and going on his face, clasping and unclasping his hands, all the time looking at the others with a furtive and incredulous surprise as though they were using words and toying with a profound and tremendous secret that they had agreed was not a matter for gossip.

Only once had he seen Mr Rankin angry after one of these evenings. He had risen abruptly in the midst of the talk and rushed out to the hall. David, filled with curiosity, followed him. Mr Rankin was struggling into his overcoat. He looked down into the boy's questioning face. 'I wonder do those people know what they're talking about?' he whispered, his lips quivering. Then, when he had pulled the front door open, he turned back and grasped David by the shoulder. 'Don't say anything. Don't say a word. They're good people!'

They were all standing up when he went back to the living-room and his mother was repeating, 'You don't think that he . . . ?' and Harry Peebles, who was angry, kept asking, 'Well, what *did* we say!' and Mr Sinton circled around slowly saying with an uneasy smile, 'Oh, come, come. I wouldn't worry. I think it'll be all right.' They drank their tea standing and hurried away leaving half the sandwiches and scones uneaten, which was unusual.

But Mr Sinton was right. Whatever they feared didn't happen. David was almost asleep when he heard the front door closing and a murmur of voices. Then Mr Rankin's step on the stairs and his voice, warm, friendly, saying, 'Well, goodnight, Mrs Minnis.' After that evening Mr Rankin didn't go to the Hall any more but Pastor Shrubsole still called in to see him when he visited Mrs Minnis.

Mr Rankin's personal possessions were few and well-worn, but good. When Mr Rankin was out and his mother busy elsewhere David used to slip into the man's room to look at them and touch them. Standing before the mirror he brushed his hair with the two silver-backed brushes and then hunted for long fair hairs caught in the bristles. He leafed over the collections of Kipling and Haggard that stood between book-ends of Irish marble. Sometimes he plucked the strings of the 'cello that stood in the corner and waited apprehensively for the deep quivering sound to die before his mother heard it.

But Mr Rankin was happy to share his books and music. When David was recovering from influenza he was given *Allan Quatermain* and *King Solomon's Mines* to read. And sometimes in the evenings they would hear Mr Rankin playing scales on the 'cello. He bowed with great feeling, always in the minor key, and always, it would seem, about to lip over into a melody.

In this fatherless house Mr Rankin was never too tired to chat and joke with David or take Freddie out to the park. He occasionally bought them books, and the Meccano that he had given to David and that had been passed on to Freddie had new parts added every Christmas. They couldn't always follow Mr Rankin's jokes, for sometimes he talked to himself as much as to the boys. But if David, as he listened and chuckled at whatever he understood, had been asked to name, out of his small experience, the person he most admired, he would have named Mr Rankin.

5

HE bent down and slid his hands and wrists under the bale. 'Gimme a lift up with this, Tits,' he said.

'Away t'hell,' said Fogarty, stretching his legs further along the counter and delicately tapping ash from his cigarette.

With a grunt David lifted the bundle and heaved it with his knee into the fixture. He felt a sudden snap and a disconcerting looseness in the middle of his back. He groped under the tail of his jacket and brought away a frayed loop of his braces.

'Damn you,' he said, aggrieved. 'Look at that, now!'

'They were done anyway,' said Fogarty.

'They wouldn't have bust if you had helped me.'

'What are you beefing about? Aren't there dozens and hundreds of pairs round you?'

'Even at cost price it's still going to be three bob out of my pocket!'

'Who said anything about paying for them?' Fogarty swung his feet onto the counter and stood up. 'Have a look at this, Minnis,' he said, jerking his thumb at the space between the top of the fixture and the ceiling. David clambered up beside him and peered into the dark crevice. All he could see was a tangle of dirty, tattered straps lying in a thick cushion of dust.

'Well, what about it?'

Fogarty hooked out a cluster of straps. They were broken braces. David stared at them. 'How did they get there?'

Fogarty swivelled on his heel, thrust one hand into the breast of his jacket and stretched the other across the silent department. 'Men who trod this floor before you threw them up there. Some are dead, some are in the Chamber of Commerce, but all observed the old wholesale custom of helping themselves to a pair when they needed 'em.'

'Outa stock?'

'That's right. All the boys do it.'

'What does Mr Whaley say?'

'Why don't you ask him when he comes back from his lunch?' sneered Fogarty. He unbuttoned David's jacket and snapped what was left of his braces. 'They're a disgrace to the firm. Take a new pair.' He climbed down and David dropped lightly on the floor beside him.

'Go on. How many hundreds of apprentices d'you think have been clodding their gallasses up there in the past fifty years?' Fogarty broke open a box of braces. 'There you are. The best. Stick them on you.'

He put out his hand. 'Wait a minute. That's a new box. I'll take them from a broken dozen.'

Fogarty grinned. 'You're learning,' he said.

David stripped off his jacket, slowly unbuttoned his braces, put on the new pair, and threw the old pair to the back of the fixture.

Fogarty climbed on the counter again, drew at his cigarette and beat the smoke away with the box lid.

'You know Maurice Rankin, don't you?'

'Maur—? Oh, sure. He lives in our house.'

'Nice fella, isn't he?'

'Yes.'

'Been there a long time?'

'About four years.'

'Ever wondered why he has his office in a private house instead of downtown like other agents?'

'I suppose it suits him that way. Why?'

'Oh, nothing. I just happen to know him. Did a lot of business here at one time.'

'He still does, doesn't he?'

'I said a *lot* of business. Before he went to gaol.'

David had been patching up the broken box. He let it slither through his fingers. 'What are you talking about—gaol?'

'I thought you knew? He was in gaol for three years—manslaughter—'

'You're a liar, Fogarty.'

Fogarty smiled bleakly. 'I could slap you across the kisser for that, Minnis, if you weren't so ignorant. Rankin was in clink for three years. He and two or three other fellas got a skinful of drink into them one night in Bangor and killed a girl on the way home. Rankin was driving.' He saw David's face and paused. 'You like him?'

'I told you!'

'So do I. That's the truth. He's the decentest man I know. Before he got into trouble he worked in his father's place, Moore, Rankin and Abernethy. Family gave him some money and booted him out.'

David was silent. A lot of things that had puzzled him suddenly became understandable. And he wished that he had never learned the truth. He looked at Fogarty with distaste. But Fogarty's eyes were now as innocent of malice as they could ever hope to be. 'God, Fogarty,' he said, finding an outlet for his seething dislike, 'I'd hate to trust you with any secrets of *my* life!'

Fogarty pressed out his cigarette on the sole of his shoe and tucked it carefully into his vest pocket. 'Aw, go t'hell,' he said.

He swung himself round the banister-head and went skipping lightly down the stairs.

6

THEY were walking homeward when Bonar said: 'I'm thinking of buying a motor bike.'

David stopped. 'You're not!'

'I am. There's a fella coming round with one tonight.'

He started to walk hurriedly. He was eaten up with envy. 'You're mad!' he shouted. 'Where'll you get the money?'

'I have it. Seven pounds saved up.'

'That'll get you a hairy motor bike!'

'Oh, I don't know,' said Bonar mildly. 'It'll be all right. The fella's bringing it round tonight—'

'So you said.'

'Would you like to come round and see it?'

He walked on in silence. Boney, with his damned calmness and honesty made you ashamed of yourself. 'All right,' he said. 'What time?'

'About half-seven. Remember, ninety-three Majestic Street.'

'I'll be there.'

After tea he helped his mother wash up, took a glance at the evening paper, and then, with a strange pricking at his heart, watched Freddie at his homework. His own schooldays seemed so distant and irretrievable now. But he kept moving about, going into the scullery for a drink of water, or leaning over Freddie's shoulder to read the problems, for he knew that if he were suddenly to get up and start preparing to go out she would ask questions. He wanted her to understand, without questioning, that he was going out. At a quarter-past seven he went into the scullery and polished his shoes, then he combed his hair at the mirror in the living-room.

She lowered the paper. 'You're as restless as a flea tonight.'

'Am I?' he smiled, studying her in the mirror.

'Are you going somewhere?'

He nodded slowly into the mirror. 'Yes, I'm going out,' he said. As she remained silent he turned and they looked into each other's eyes. We're on the lip of another quarrel, he thought. Freddie stirred apprehensively at the table. Mrs Minnis shrugged her shoulders and lifted the paper. 'You might have told a body.'

He swallowed and gave his hair a last touch with the comb. 'I'm going round to Majestic Street to see a fella I work with,' he said in a conciliatory voice.

'Majestic Street? That's on the other side of the road, down by the river?'

'That's right. Well, cheerio now. I won't be late.'

The warmth of the summer day still hung in the air and the residents of Colinvista Street, who wouldn't have been caught dead lounging in their doorways, stood their doors ajar in the hope that a cooler air might percolate through the houses. It was different in Majestic Street. There the heat had sucked the people into the open. The dwellings were so honeycombed together that the numbers seemed to mount in tens as he stepped adroitly over the sprawling children. Their fathers and mothers, a day's work or idleness over, roosted on the window-sills and shook their heads, bosoms, bellies, fingers across the street at each other. Old men and women with quilts over their knees sat in the doorways, chuckling, scowling, dozing, or staring out with wide eyes as if they had been plucked back from a long journey. Men gave him the slow nod for the stranger, fat women winked, girls laughed as he passed. A surf of laughter and talk lapped and slapped backwards and forwards across the narrow, bent street.

As he crossed over from the even to the odd side, he heard the erratic explosions of the engine. At the end of the street his friend and half a dozen others were gathered round the bike. The man in the saddle revved the engine and all except Bonar scattered, hallooing and shouting to each other and clapping their hands to their ears. The man dismounted and offered the quivering machine to Bonar. He hesitated for a moment and the engine gave a bang, a whoop and fell silent. David chuckled and saw with relish that it was a very old, tattered machine. Bonar handed it to its owner and the onlookers clustered again, David among them. Bonar saw him and nodded. His face was flushed. 'It seems the timing's a bit off,' he said.

'Your own timing's nothing to write home about, either!' a man called from the doorway of a house. Bonar scowled across at him. 'Shut up, Da!' he shouted.

The young man who owned the machine set the throttle-grip with care and once again threw himself frenziedly on the kick-starter. The engine broke into a roar. He fiddled with the controls until the turmoil settled to a steady beat. 'She's all right now,' he said, offering the handlebars to Bonar.

David, alarmed, stepped forward. 'What are you doing?' he hissed. 'Sure, you've no driving licence!'

Bonar glared at him distractedly. 'What's the good o' buying a licence when I dunno whether I'm gonna buy the bike?' He tossed himself into the saddle, lifted the clutch, urged in the reluctant gear lever and moved away down the street in a string of deafening explosions.

David watched him until he turned the corner at the end of the street. Then he looked across at Boney's father. This was the man who had devoured three libraries and didn't think much of the police. David didn't think much of him. He was in his shirt-sleeves. His small, thin chin was dark but he couldn't tell whether it was because of stubble or the shadow of his cloth cap. Apart from sharing the ribald amusement of the neighbours he showed no interest in his son's purchase. A strange father. Suddenly he was thrust aside vigorously and a young girl stood in the doorway.

Her chin tilted angrily, she looked right and left, paying not the slightest attention to anyone in the street. We might as well not exist, he thought in sharp annoyance.

'Who's away on that motor bike?' she demanded of Bonar's father. Recovering from his exaggerated stumble the man in shirtsleeves put his hand to his heart. 'My God!' he said. But she wasn't taken in. David noticed that she had clenched her fists, the thumbs straight, as women do.

'You can tell me, or—' she paused, 'you can tell m'mammy.'

'It's Bonar.'

She turned and hurried into the house.

They could follow Bonar's progress along the back street by the thuds of the machine's exhaust. The clamour grew louder and they turned and stared expectantly up Majestic Street. Bonar rounded the distant corner and made jerky progress towards them. He stopped in a dying whirr of machinery. His eyes were alight with excitement. 'She's great!' he shouted to David. 'Great!'

The owner stepped forward. 'Well?' he asked eagerly. Bonar eased himself out of the saddle and letting the machine tilt away from him gazed judiciously at the engine. 'Chain's flapping a bit,' he said. He had to say something, thought David.

'Oh,' said the young man, eager to get away, 'anybody can tighten that for you. I'll get it fixed—'

Bonar stroked the tank lovingly. 'No, no,' he said. 'It's a deal. Here—seven quid.' He took a fold of notes from his pocket and handed it to the young man.

There was a disturbance in the McFall doorway. A square, red-faced woman had appeared drying her hands on her apron. David heard Bonar moan softly under his breath. When her hands were dry she addressed Bonar's father. 'Well, Mr Rocky-feller, could you not come down from the clouds for a minute to save your son throwing away his hard-earned ha'pence?'

Mr McFall made her a deprecating gesture, but she was already halfway into the crowd, dragging after her like a dinghy a small boy clutched to her skirts. The delighted onlookers closed in behind them.

'What hellery is going on here?' she demanded.

'Go away, Mammy,' said Bonar.

'He's bought a motor bike, Mammy!' shouted the small boy.

'Are you out of your mind, you eejit?' she cried making a dart at Bonar, who clung to the machine unable to escape.

The late owner decided it was time he was moving away. His first step caught Mrs McFall's eye.

'Hi, mister! Are you the man that sold that thing to this fella?'

The young man halted. 'Yes—he bought it from me.'

'How much?'

'Seven pounds.'

Mrs McFall's mouth fell open. She gazed wild-eyed at the crowd. 'In the name of all that's sacred and holy, did yez ever hear the like?' She rounded on Bonar. 'Have you paid for it yet?'

Bonar nodded. 'That's not dear—' he ventured.

Mrs McFall turned on the young man. 'Give him back his money,' she said, with a wide sweep of her arm. 'Give him back his money and think shame on a grown man like you selling a wee fella a motor bike!' Reluctantly the young man drew the money out of his pocket. 'Of course,' he hesitated, 'your son answered the advertisement. The deal was made—'

Mrs McFall took a step towards him. She's bluffing, thought David, and he watched the bluff working. The young man thrust the money into Bonar's hand and snatched the machine from him.

'G'wan now, mister,' she added triumphantly, 'take your ould gate away to hell outa this street!' To an ironic hoot from the onlookers he kicked the bike into life and went roaring up the street and out of sight.

As the crowd drifted away Bonar perched himself on the window-sill of his house and kicked his heels morosely against the bricks. David leaned against the wall in sympathetic silence. 'Was it burning a hole in your pocket, son?' said Mr McFall, peering at them with sly amusement from the doorway.

'Who told on me?' demanded Bonar.

His father's eyes opened wide. 'Told on you? Sure the whole neighbourhood *heard* you!'

'Who brought my mammy out?' David winced and thought the title more inappropriate than ever.

'You don't think it was me, do you? It was Maureen,' said Mr McFall, closing his mouth with a snap.

'I mighta known.' After a few more kicks at the wall Bonar added, 'This is Davie Minnis, Da. He works with me.'

'You'd better bring him in,' said Mr McFall.

Bonar stood up. 'Would you like to come in?'

He hesitated for a moment, recalling Mrs McFall. 'Well, I dunno—if you think it's all right—'

Bonar stared at him. 'All right? Of course it's all right! Come on.' Mr McFall stepped aside to let them pass and followed them down the hall.

The flat rays of the sun poured into the tiny whitewashed back-yard and bounced into the McFall kitchen, blinding him. A large and a small figure were silhouetted against the window. He heard voices greeting him and moved quickly out of the glare. Mrs McFall was gazing at him with polite curiosity through a bead screen that draped the entrance down to the scullery. The girl, Maureen, loading a tray of soiled dishes at the table, had her back to him. The larger figure at the window, a young man in his mid-twenties, was stooped to lace a pair of oxblood-red shoes. David observed with a small stir of surprise that he was smartly dressed with a knife edge to his trouser legs and twinkling cuff-links above his stretched wrists. Beside him, staring at David, was the small boy who had seen the rout of the motor bike vendor.

'This is Davie Minnis. He works with me in Hamiltons.' Bonar's voice was chill. He wasn't going to be the one to make peace. Mrs McFall seemed quite unaffected. With a smile that reminded David of her son she came up through the bead screen, looking softer, kinder, more voluminous, than she had seemed in the street. Perhaps she can draw herself in for battle, he thought.

'How are you, David? You'll have to excuse the table. They eat here just as they come in from their work. Sit down if you can find a seat in this madhouse. Get up you,' she gave the small boy a prod with her foot, 'and give the visitor a seat. That,' she added, 'is Bonar's father. You've met him. That's Arthur.' The well-dressed young man nodded his round, thin-haired head silently and went on lacing his shoe. 'This is Maureen.' The girl gave him the smile that pretty girls give to boys of nearly seventeen; suitable for the occasion but not to be counted on in the future. 'And this is Willie.' The small boy's wriggle and grin was a momentary interruption in his open-mouthed stare at the newcomer.

The introductions completed, Mrs McFall went back to the scullery. David waited until Mr McFall was seated at the fireplace before he took the chair vacated by Willie. Maureen followed her mother with the last of the soiled dishes. They've had sausages, he decided, but the odour of the McFall household was a confused one, a blend of food, blacklead, soap, and drying garments. Glancing up he saw that the clothes-line was laden with women's under things. From then on he kept his scrutiny at eye level.

At his elbow was a plywood shelf curved under the weight of books. It was the lowest an of uneven pattern of shelves that mounted to the ceiling, stretched over the mantelpiece, and down the other side to where old McFall sat cleaning his pipe. Every compartment bulged with volumes and papers, and the whole crazy contraption seemed likely, at any moment, to topple forward into the room knocking the occupants dead or senseless.

As his friend obviously intended to sulk for a bit, he screwed his head round to read some of the titles. Compared with Mr Rankin's they looked a dull lot; those on the shelf beside him bore such unappetizing titles as *The Mind in Chains*, *Anti-Duhring*, *Labour in Irish History*, *Fundamental Problems in Marxism* and a pile of dusty journals called *New Masses*. He pressed back a yawn and wished that the girl would come back or that somebody would say something. But Mr McFall seemed fully taken up with his pipe, Bonar sat glooming at the empty hearth and his brother Arthur was hurriedly transferring to his own pockets the contents from those of a jacket hanging behind the door.

Then Maureen came in and to his surprise began to set out milk, sugar and crockery on the table again. Bonar scowled at her unavailingly. Then, 'Thanks!' he said in a loud voice. She turned on him, her cheeks darkening and a spark in her eyes, and David, watching her, let his breath out softly in appreciation.

'Thanks for what? Saving you breaking your neck?'

'Thanks for interfering in my business!'

Mrs McFall raised her voice from the scullery. 'That's enough now, Bonar! You and a motor bike! Sometimes I think you're the daftest child God ever put legs in. Maureen did quite right coming to me. If ould Thinker's Library there hadn't had his head in the clouds as usual, he's the one that should've stopped you.'

From the other side of the fireplace Mr McFall shrugged his shoulders and gave a small gesture of forbearance. The bead curtain parted and Mrs McFall looked at David. 'Had you anything to do with it?' But she smiled as she said it.

'No.'

'I thought not. You look a sensible fella. Where did you get all that money, son?' David, too, listened eagerly for the answer.

'I saved it up.'

'Seven pounds?'

'Yes. My Christmas money was in it.'

'Saving all that time?' Mrs McFall clucked indulgently. 'Why don't you buy yourself an ordinary bike?'

'I don't want an ordinary bike!'

Mrs McFall's sympathy waned. She withdrew again to the scullery. 'Well, you're getting no motor bike,' she called. 'If you want to put your money to good use you can buy yourself a suit.'

At the look of outrage on Bonar's face David laughed and Mr McFall chuckled. Mr McFall had his pipe filled. He gave his attention to David. 'So you work with Bonar, eh?'

'Yes, Mr McFall.'

'You would find it difficult to save seven quid working there—'

'Right enough, it's not much we get—'

Arthur rose silently and left them. David heard him hunting for his coat in the hall, but none of his family seemed to pay him any attention.

'Mebbe,' said Mr McFall as he lit his pipe, 'they can't afford to give you any more. They say Mr Hamilton lives in very impoverished circumstances—'

David looked at Bonar. He should know the answer to that. He'd been there longer. But Bonar was gazing glumly at his father.

'I don't know,' he said slowly. 'I don't think so. He's got a big car. They say he's got a big house—'

Maureen rose quietly from her chair and slipped away to join her mother in the scullery.

'Aye,' said Mr McFall, caressing his nose with the warm bowl, 'but no big money for his workers, eh? Mebbe he can't manage both. Never the time and the place and the loved one all together, as the poet says.'

No one spoke. Mr McFall took a draw at his pipe and let a ball of smoke roll out.

'Though, mind you, the problem has been considered. There was a Russian called Plekhanov—'

'That's enough!' Mrs McFall, in the scullery, had been waiting her cue. 'No more of that! It's bad enough to talk that nonsense to your own children. Leave the young fella alone!'

There was a metallic thud as an ill-fitting lid was bashed on to a teapot. She appeared with a laden tray in her hands. 'You'll take a mouthful of tea, Davie?' The invitation sounded like a command. But he knew that he wasn't the cause of her irritation and accepted the cup politely.

The talk turned to the cases of books that loomed over everyone. He told them that he had read a lot of Rider Haggard's stories, and Mr McFall with a smile that showed he preferred to be tolerant in such a genial atmosphere raised his eyebrows and said, 'You have, eh?'

' 'Course I read other books from the library. But we've got all Haggard's books in our house. And Kipling's—with leather covers.' He looked at Mr McFall challengingly.

'I am myself,' said Mr McFall, 'engaged in some literary work.'

'Oh?' said David politely, conscious of the glance that passed between mother and daughter.

'Some people mightn't consider it creative, perhaps. More a job of compilation.' Mr McFall reached up into one of the bookshelves. 'Ever see one of these?' He held out a Thought-for-the-Day calendar.

'Oh, sure,' said David.

'Ever read some of the Thoughts? Here's one that's a grand poultice for an uneasy conscience: "No economic equality can survive the working of biological inequality." ' Mr McFall flicked on through the pages, stopped, and ran his eyes round the company. 'Here's another pearl: "Constantly choose rather to want less than to have more." That's warm comfort for a five-quid-a-week clerk to start the day with, isn't it?' He tossed the calendar back and smiled down ironically at David. 'Know what that stuff's intended to encourage? Quietism.'

'I wish it would smite you,' said Mrs McFall.

Mr McFall gave her a little wave of the hand without taking his attention from David. 'I've gathered a few Thoughts together. Not the usual bits from the soothsayers, but trumpet calls from the pages of Marx, Paine, Gorki, Voltaire, Shelley and other great liberators of the human spirit. I'll have them printed in cheap calendars for the homes of the workers and in desk diaries for progressive members of the middle class. I'm calling it the "Radical's Almanac". Instead of church festivals it'll have the important dates in the history of trade unionism. Instead of saints, the names of martyrs in the working-class movement.' He paused to take breath. 'Well, what d'you think of it?'

'Oh—great,' said David.

Mrs McFall shook her head as she looked at her husband. 'Isn't he a terror, Davie?' she said. 'If he had a big stick he could break eggs.' But he sensed that he would be ill-advised to laugh at Mr McFall. That might be Mrs McFall's prerogative. At that moment there was a warmth in her voice, almost a genial pride in the look that rested on her husband.

Bonar jumped to his feet. 'Come on!' he shouted. 'I'm going out for a breath of fresh air!'

'That's manners!' exclaimed Mrs McFall.

'It's time I was going anyway,' said David. 'Thanks for the tea.'

'You're welcome, son. Come on, you, Willie, you should've been in bed an hour ago.' And she led her youngest upstairs.

Mr McFall had a roll of *New Masses* in his hand. 'Take these. They're mebbe old, but what they have to say is never out of date.'

He looked with apprehension at the grisly cartoons of squat, silk-hatted, cigar-smoking men, their moneybag bellies branded with the dollar sign.

'Well . . . thanks . . . I'll let you have them back.'

'I'm finished long ago. You keep 'em.'

Not on your life, he thought. He could imagine his mother's face if she came on these monstrosities in his room.

Bonar was already in the hall. David bade goodnight to Mr

McFall and Maureen. 'I think I'll take a dander up the street with you,' said Mr McFall, skipping after him into the hall and snatching down his cap. He saw Maureen make a gesture after her father as though to call him back. Bonar, too, looked displeased as the man fell into step with them.

'Where are you going, Da?'

Mr McFall smiled blandly. 'Up the street, sonny boy. Charlie Rusk wants a hand to fill up a claim.'

He wasn't sure that he wanted to be seen walking with old McFall in his duncher cap. But it was Bonar who scowled and quickened his pace. Then as they passed Barney Harkin's pub at the head of the street Mr McFall bade them a brisk goodnight and dived into the side entrance.

He daren't look at Bonar. It was disgraceful that a fella's father should give him a red face like that, in front of his friend. But Bonar's colour wasn't even faintly heightened.

'That's him,' he said with a shrug, 'Minding everybody's business but his own.'

'In that place—Harkin's?'

' 'Sright. He helps all the men round here with their forms—dole claims or pensions or trade union things. He's a kinda . . . poor man's lawyer.' The phrase surprised and pleased Bonar, and he gazed across the busy main road with a gloomy satisfaction.

'And does he talk that socialist stuff to them? "As somebody-or-other says"—like that Russian fella. . . .'

'Ah, he's always saying things like that! But what can his mates do? They need his help. 'Course there are times, like the Twelfth of July, when he might talk out of turn. Then they follow him down to the door and Mammy has to go out and clear the street.'

David giggled involuntarily. 'I'm sure she's the one could do that—'

'Mebbe she couldn't! 'Course they're helpless against her. Everybody around here knows that she's a red-hot Orangewoman.' He gazed at David doubtfully. 'I suppose you think it's shocking to have a mother that goes into a crowd of fellas swinging a brush shaft?'

David gaped at his friend. 'Would she do that? I think she's terrific. I like her.'

'Ah, Mammy's all right.'

'And your sister,' David murmured.

'Maureen's all right, too.' They had reached the edge of the pavement. 'Cheerio, Davie. See you in the morning.'

'Eight-forty sharp at the corner of Colinvista?'

'Sharp. On foot. I could have taken you down on the pillion if they'd let me buy that stink-bike.'

'I can see now that your mother knew what she was doing.'

Bonar laughed and turned away with a wave of his hand.

As he walked down Colinvista Street he imagined how he would feel if his mother hadn't allowed him to buy something when he had saved for months to get the money. Not very nice, he thought . . . Full of a sense of injury. But old Boney didn't seem to have any ill-feelings against anybody. He compared the McFall home to his own. Of course his house was much better, but there was a warmth and life in Boney's home, a sense of fun, an interest in the outside world that was missing from his own. He supposed that almost anyone would be welcome at the McFalls'. He was troubled with the thought that he might sometime have to ask Boney to his house.

As he let himself into the dark hall he heard the faint rhythmic throb from the room upstairs. He hung up his coat and went into the empty kitchen to eat the supper of bread and milk that lay on the table.

7

By the end of the second month the job fitted him like an old suit; easy and not worth worrying about overmuch. He knew his way around the big warehouse and had a nodding acquaintance with nearly everybody. Lack of pocket-money was his big worry. Out of his weekly thirty shillings he gave his mother twenty-five. Five shillings didn't go far just in trams and things. It went nowhere when it came to taking out a girl or buying what a fellow wanted. A pair of socks swallowed it.

'Well,' said Fogarty, when they had concealed themselves in the stockroom one afternoon, 'why don't you make a bit o' money on the side?'

'How d'you do that?'

'Come over here.' Fogarty led him to the end of the room. He hunted for a moment behind a pile of coat-hangers and then drew out a pad of receipts. David noticed that the firm's name was printed in a different type from that on the receipts they used in the warehouse. 'Old stock,' said Fogarty. 'They changed their printers a coupla years ago, but I planked two or three pads before they were all destroyed.'

'And where does that get us?'

Fogarty tapped the pad with a smoke-stained finger. 'You know that you can buy stuff here wholesale, don't you?' David nodded. 'This is what you do. You get some patterns and you show them to your friends. Tell them you can get a suit-length or a pair of blankets or something wholesale. They always go for that. Then you buy the stuff here, tear up the old receipt, make them out a new one from this pad, sticking on a couple a bob a yard. Two bob a yard on a suit-length gives you over six bob in your pocket. You can make three bob on blankets.'

Fogarty looked up and saw David's sceptical smile. 'What's wrong with six bob?' he demanded. 'You're no millionaire, are you? Listen, if you buy a suit-length for yourself, you get it at *cost*. If you sell it to somebody outside you can make a quid. Twenty silver shillings in your pocket—that's money, isn't it?'

'Oh, sure. But I dunno anybody I could ask. Anyway, it's not worth it . . .'

'Make up your mind. Which is it?'

'It's because I dunno anybody.'

'What about your own family?'

He jumped as if he had been stung. 'Hell, I couldn't do that!'

'O.K.,' said Fogarty, hiding the receipts again. 'But remember that pad means money. So keep your mouth shut about it.'

Fogarty was right. They always did go for it if you told them it was wholesale. Even to buy the stuff in a wholesale house seemed to make a difference to the mothers with their kids and the wives with their husbands. And the letters of introduction that they brought always said 'put on the usual' or 'quote plus fifty' or, as in the case of Mr Shriberger's customers, 'add hundred per cent.' Yet, Mr Shriberger's customers always came back. Mr Shriberger didn't look like a bloodsucker. He was a small, shabby man with a foreign accent and a grizzled beard with holes worn in it. They had become great friends.

'Mr Shriberger, can I ask you a question?'

'If you want.'

'Most of the other tick agents stick on twenty-five or fifty per cent profit. How do one or two people like you get away with a hundred?'

Mr Shriberger leaned forward, his hand on his chest. 'I am a . . . stranger in this city. That is all right. It is a good place for strangers. You are so busy tormenting each other you do not trouble with strangers. But one has to be prudent. Smith can take Robinson to the police courts and make her pay up the full twenty-five, fifty, you understand? No one makes a remark. But how does it look when Robinson is taken before the court by a Shriberger? Who gets the sympathy when it is read in the newspapers? No, boychic, I ask a hundred per cent profit and give them the satisfaction of defrauding me of half of it.'

He glanced at Mr Shriberger condescendingly. It sounded like a pushover. If an old foreign Jew with a funny voice and grubby clothes could make money like that what could a bright local boy not do? Of course they said that to make a tick drapery agency work you had to be on your feet fourteen hours a day, but he pushed that thought away. Perhaps he could build up such a good paying connection around Colinvista Street that in a year or so he could slip from this job to a better one without changing step, as it were. For a whole hour that afternoon visions of sugar plums danced in his head.

8

'HIDING from the customers?' said Alec Roden, shooting his head round the side of the packing-room doorway. None of them moved from his easy seat on the bales. 'What customers?' asked Bonar. Nobody seemed to want trousers this afternoon. 'What are you doing up here, Connif?' Connif didn't answer. Nobody ever expected Connif to answer. He got up from the bale and moved to the door. 'You shouldn't be here,' said Roden. 'Amn't I going?' said Connif. Roden took a breath and started again. 'Get up on your feet, you two!' he shouted. They got up, grinning.

'Wait a minute, Connif.' Roden took a sheet of paper from his pocket. 'Haberdashers Alliance starts in a fortnight's time. We're entering a team. What about you, Connif?'

This'll take time, thought David. At first he thought that the blank, unlighted stare with which Connif met questions came from stupidity. Now he knew it came from suspicion. Connif suspected everybody, turned every remark over, no matter how simple, to see if there was a wasp under it.

'I'm not a great footballer,' said Connif after a pause.

'This isn't great football. You played goalie last year, didn't you?'

Connif nodded and moved towards the stairs. 'Well,' said Roden in an exasperated voice, 'will you play this season?'

Connif stared, nodded again, and left them.

'If he was even good!' said Roden, jabbing angrily at the list with a pencil. 'Now, Boney, you and me in the halves again. What about you, Minnis?'

'I played a bit at school.'

'He says he's good,' said Bonar simply.

'I couldn't ask for a better testimonial. Where did you play?'

'Centre-forward.'

'We've got a centre-forward.' Roden stepped back and looked

him up and down. 'We need an outside-right. You're light but you're fast.' David smiled. Roden wiped it off his face. 'Very fast—I've watched you getting out of the place at knocking-off time.'

When the assistant's delighted chuckle and the rattle of his feet down the stairs had died away David said bitterly, 'Ought to be on the stage, that fella.' But he didn't say it with any vehemence. He had a new worry on his mind. He remembered the small, dried boots hanging in the outside lavatory.

'Boney, does the firm supply the jerseys?'

'That's right—red and yella.'

'What about shorts?'

'I forget whether Alec dished shorts out last year. I've a pair at home anyway.'

David looked at him with distaste. A fella that could lay his hands on seven quid wouldn't worry about a pair of football shorts.

'And what about—boots?'

Bonar laughed. 'I can see Hamiltons buying us football boots! You bring your own.' He walked out of the packing-room. 'Come on, let's do something for our wages.'

David moved towards the head of the stairs. 'Be with you in a minute, Boney. I want to see Fogarty about a thing.'

It was easy enough to spread out the patterns on the table after tea and say 'D'you like any of those? I can get suit-lengths like that wholesale or blankets or made-up clothes—'

His mother laughed. 'Blankets? I've enough blankets to do me my lifetime.' She picked up one of the patterns, rubbed it between her fingers and looked at the label gummed to it. 'That's nice. Seventeen and six? Reasonable enough.'

'Would you . . .'

'What would we do with a length of cloth? If you could get me a suit for Freddie, now?'

He looked at his young brother and saw his eyes shining with expectancy at the thought of something new, even if it was only clothes. Gloomily he pushed the patterns away. 'Yes, I suppose I could.'

Her voice sharpened. 'Of course, if it's any trouble—'

'It's no trouble, if you give me his size. But the patterns . . . I thought, mebbe, you wouldn't want to miss the chance . . .'

'They'll always be there, won't they?' She picked up a pattern of grey worsted, drew out a thread and snapped it. 'It's good. But too dear for you, son.'

'I wasn't thinking of myself.'

'Maybe Mr Shrubsole might like to see them.'

Yes, indeed. Mr Shrubsole was fair game. He would have no regrets about making a bit of cash out of Mr Shrubsole.

'When will he be here next?'

'Tomorrow, I suppose. He usually calls on a Thursday.'

'Tell him he'll need three and a quarter yards.'

She laughed. 'You're becoming quite an expert!'

Smiling, he lowered his head and mumbled, 'He's about my size, isn't he?'

On Saturday morning she laid a twist of money beside his plate. 'Mr Shrubsole liked the grey. There's two pounds seventeen there. Make sure you bring him back a receipt.'

He laid his knife and fork side by side on his plate as she had taught him and rose eagerly. 'I'll do that.'

'And a size eleven readymade for Freddie in a grey herring-bone, not too dear—'

'I'll bring one on appro and he can try it on. 'Bye, now.'

He walked to work, the hand cupping the money buried deep in his pocket. Only about seven and a tanner of it was his, a quarter of what the boots cost. He stopped at Malcolmson's Emporium and looked at them again. A nice golden brown, strapped insteps, but still thirty shillings. He moved moodily to the pawn window. He knew that window well; a motionless avalanche of level-gauges, fishing-rods, razors, furs, radios and dingy jewellery. But the second-hand football boots hadn't been there before. 'Property of old international now retired. Scores goals by themselves. Size seven.' His size. 'Sacrifice fifteen shillings.' Nearer, oh much nearer, his price. He squinted through lassos of jade and opal, noting that the toes were bulbous and undinged, the heels clean, the instep leathers not too curled. With a quick glance round he hunkered down and screwed his neck to see the soles. Not a glint of a nail in the studs. There was the clatter of a bolt, and half of the shop door opened. He pushed the second half open in his haste and dived into one of the shabby confessionals. The man who had opened the door appeared on the other side of the counter.

'You're'n helluva hurry. Whata ye got?'

'Those soccer boots in the window—'

'Them yours?'

David giggled in surprise. 'They belonged to a—are they for sale?'

'That's the drift. Ya wanna buy? I thought ya wanna hawk. Come on outa that.' He walked away, beckoning David to an open counter. 'What's marked on them?'

'Fifteen shillings.'

'That's the price.'

He fissled in Mr Shrubsole's money. 'I was wondering if I could lay a deposit on them—half a crown?'

The man's face closed. 'No deposits here. Only clean sales.'

'Any chance of them being sold before I get back?'

'Going far?'

'I'll be up the road again about one.'

The man lost interest. He ran his duster under a travelling clock. 'Could be.'

'Will you give me time to think?'

The man waved his disengaged hand. 'It's a free country.'

He took out the money and stared at it. Fogarty said that you got a suit-length at cost if you said it was for yourself. He dragged fifteen shillings from Mr Shrubsole's money and slapped it on the counter.

Fogarty was exasperatingly busy that morning. He ran up and down the stairs half a dozen times before he caught him alone.

'I've sold a length of that, Tits. I want it at cost, for myself.'

Fogarty studied the pattern gloomily. 'They wouldn't believe you. It's too damn good for an apprentice.'

'It's got to be for myself! I need the money.'

'All right. I'll see if I can get the hold of Alfie Taggart. He might cut it off for me. Gimme the money.'

'And I want a suit out of your department for my young brother—'

'One thing at a time,' said Fogarty, walking away.

Ten minutes later he came sliding up the stairs, a plump, smooth parcel under his arm.

'I got it.'

'Tits, you're a hero!' He reached for the parcel. Tits drew it back. He stopped his excited dancing. 'What's up?'

'You're shy half a dollar.'

'I gave you all the money I had!'

'You're still shy half a dollar.'

'How did you pay for it then?'

'Outa my own pocket.' Fogarty held out his hand. 'I'll take it now.'

'I haven't got it.'

Fogarty smiled unpleasantly. 'When'll you have it—Monday?'

'Monday—mebbe.'

'I need it for Monday. You haven't a hope in hell, have you?'

'I'll do my best, Tits.'

'Not good enough. What about this suit for your brother?'

'I was going to get it out on approval.'

'If he keeps it when'll he pay up?'

'Ah, it's nothing to do with him. He's only a wee fella.'

'Well, when will whoever's paying for it make up their mind?'

'Over . . . the weekend.'

'Right. I'll give you a couple out on appro and I'll mark them up half a dollar each.'

'Tits, I couldn't do that!'

'What size?' said Fogarty.

'Size . . . eleven.'

Fogarty moved closer. 'Don't be a fool, Minnis, she's still getting it cheaper than she would in the shops.'

He didn't answer. Fogarty said, 'I'll make you out a new receipt for the cloth and parcel it up with the suits.'

Without looking up he mumbled, 'Thanks, Tits.'

Fogarty made a shapeless job of the parcel, and in the crowded homeward tram the football boots slithered about maddeningly on top of it. They slipped to the floor and as he groped for them with his foot he had a wild urge to kick them out into the street. To get them he had had to go into a pawn-shop, put himself in debt to Fogarty and now he was going home to cheat his mother and brother. He felt for them among the feet of the strap hangers and realized that someone on the opposite seat was leaning forward. 'S'all right,' he said abruptly, 'I've got them.' He looked up into the face of Maureen, Bonar's sister. 'Oh, hullo,' he said, flushing. She didn't return his smile. 'It hit me on the foot,' she said. He was about to speak again, but as the wall of raincoats closed impatiently between them he saw her straightening herself and turning her head away. At the Colinvista Street stop he craned his neck to see her but she was gazing out of the window.

Walking down the street he forgot about the boots. Did she give him the cold shoulder because she didn't like him or because he had been rude? She was very nice-looking. She was lovely. He wished he hadn't been so sharp, but just at that moment he had had a lot of trouble on his mind.

Freddie met him in the hall. 'What's that?' he cried, grabbing at the smaller parcel. David tumbled it beside the hallstand. 'Only an old pair of soccer boots. *There's* yours.'

As he ate his dinner his mother tried the suits on Freddie. She stepped back to see the effect.

'Well, what d'you think?' he asked, his mouth full of food. He had to know and it seemed easier this way, his voice half-hidden.

She patted a lapel. 'It fits him nicely. D'you like it, son?' Freddie stroked the jacket and smiled. Watching them, he wished the whole business over and done with quickly.

She lifted the docket and looked at it. 'The shops don't make as much profit as I thought.'

'They make enough, don't they?'

'It'll do. I'll give you the money on Monday. Say thanks to David, Freddie, for bringing you the suit.'

Upstairs in his room he tried on the boots. He flexed his toes and stamped lightly on the rug. With the laces tight below the arch and over the instep he felt as though his feet were sheathed in speed. He stroked them lovingly. He lay down on his bed and crossed his feet over the bottom rail so that he could see the boots reflected in the wardrobe mirror. Mebbe it was a damn mean way to get them but a fella had to live. That half-dollar would be made up to her, all right. He chuckled as he thought of the morning's adventures. He swung his feet over his head and caught the soles of the boots. They were as light as slippers. B'God he would be a streak in these things. He stared at the ceiling between his new boots. Did that girl ever go up to watch her brother play?

9

ALEC RODEN hurried through the warehouse distributing jerseys and shorts. He nodded apologetically to the charge-hands for he was doing it in the firm's time and that worried Alec. Upstairs he found David and Bonar with Fogarty. 'You're last,' he said and tossed them each a bundle.

David spread his shorts on a counter. 'How d'you know they'll fit?' he asked.

'Pull in your ass like this,' said Fogarty, sucking in his cheeks, 'and they'll fit you like a glove.'

'You can make anything sound *low*, can't you, Fogarty?' said Roden. 'Get away down to your department this minute!' As Fogarty vanished he added, 'I wish that fella wasn't on the side—'

Bonar jigged impatiently. 'Forget Fogarty. Are we all meeting somewhere or are we going straight to the Park?'

'Straight to the Park. Kick-off three o'clock. Be there at a quarter to.'

'I'll be there. Come on, Davie, there's the knocking-off bell.'

David pulled the string in the letter-box and let himself in.

'I hope my dinner's ready,' he sang out as he flung his coat onto a hook in the hall and tossed the football kit on the floor.

His mother, with a steaming cabbage dish in her hand, paused halfway between table and stove.

'Of course it's ready. What's your hurry?'

'I'm playing football.' He glanced at the clock. 'And I've to be at Ormeau Park about half-two.'

Freddie jumped. 'Can I go with you, David?'

'Let him go alone and break his shins if he wants to,' said his mother, setting down his dinner plate forcibly in front of him. Why hadn't he told her he was playing this afternoon? If he had even mentioned it at breakfast time. Grudgingly she admitted that boys did play football. But could *her* son afford to? It seemed, somehow, such a dangerous, unprofitable expenditure of energy. Surely there was some way in which he could spend Saturday afternoon with more concern for herself and the home?

She rebuked him when he pushed away his half-emptied plate. 'I can't eat a lot when I'm going to play a match,' he protested.

'Going to play football?' called Mr Rankin from the foot of the stairs. 'Is that what I heard, David?'

'Yes, up at the Park, Mr Rankin,' he said, pushing the jersey, shorts and boots into a gladstone bag.

'I might walk up and watch,' said Mr Rankin looking in.

'Freddie wants to come up too.'

'Then Freddie and I will take a walk up to the park.'

The playing fields stretched from the elevated central avenue with its flower beds and clumps of laurel across a plateau of grass and cinders to the river. Already thin lines of supporters were gathered round some of the pitches, their drab colouring broken by a confetti of bright jerseys as the players limbered up.

Bonar, Roden and half a dozen others were standing near a hut under some trees. In the hut a number of young men were changing into navy blue jerseys with white chevrons.

As he approached Roden waved at him angrily. 'Come on, Minnis, put an inch to your step! How many of us are there, now?' They all counted noisily, making mistakes, but in the end everyone agreed there were only nine.

'There's Joe Greer and that fella from the Silks!' someone called. Roden waved to the two distant figures. 'Come on!

Come on! Come on! You're late!' He turned on the others. 'Well, what are you waiting for? Get stripped! Get stripped! If we're not out on the ground at the whistle we'll lose the points without kicking a ball!'

Their opponents came clattering out of the hut. Wilson, an apprentice, stared at them. 'God,' he said, 'they'll ate us without salt!'

Roden's tousled head and indignant face shot up out of a red and yellow jersey. 'That's enough of that talk, Wilson. Away home if you don't want to play.' He looked at his team; from slim, sullen Minnis to Connif, his sharp shoulders lost in the folds of a soiled yellow sweater, he saw that to a lesser or greater extent they all agreed with Wilson. 'All right. Do your best, boys. Provincial Merchants are at the top of the table. It'll be no shame on us if they beat us. Come on now, there's the ref.'

The whistle shrilled. The game started. There were a few fumbled kicks, then the play moved into Hamiltons half of the field and settled there. The Provincial Merchants backs moved further up the field; the Provincial Merchants goalkeeper leaned against his posts and opened a conversation with a supporter.

It'll be a massacre, thought Mr Rankin, where he stood among the trees. There was a momentary relief; Merchants scored. The ball was centred again. For one flattering moment it was kicked into the Merchants' half. Then it was back again, bobbing round the Hamiltons goal where Roden sprinted, kicked, bellowed to his wavering defence. Beside him Bonar grimly kicked and miskicked, behind them Connif punched, booted and flung the ball away, or clutching it to his soiled sweater took the charge of men twice his weight and kept his reeling feet on the right side of the goal line. As David, solitary on the wing, watched with rising derision, Merchants scored again. This time it was the inside-left. As he trotted back his team mates embraced him in mock congratulation. A massacre of the innocents, said Mr Rankin to himself among the trees.

It was a miskick by Bonar that sent the ball skying across the field with such spin that it ricocheted off the boot of a Merchants defender. David killed the spin, brought the ball down, pounced on it. A tap of his foot and he took it curving outside the opposing half-back. Behind him, the Hamiltons forwards straggled up, drawn by his imperious left hand.

He heard young Wilson's shout as the back came racing down on him. 'Cross, Minnis, cross!' He crossed. Right over the penalty spot, not too high, not too fast, not dropped too far forward; hanging, as it were, in the air came the perfect pass. It was so cunningly chipped that young Wilson didn't have to check his pace as he drove at it on the half-volley. A vast driving kick that missed, missed so completely that the boy, as he fell, thought that he had dislocated his knee in that vast kick into nothingness.

The straggle of spectators clapped and jeered, the Merchants goalkeeper straightened up and tugged at his shorts. Mr Rankin echoed Freddie's indignation. It was a sitter, he agreed, a perfect sitter.

The ball was thrown in and driven head, heel and toe with scarcely a check towards Connif and past his clutching hands. By half-time David and his team mates were five goals down. Dispirited, they clustered together. Roden tore off a strip of orange rind with his teeth. 'Some of yous aren't putting your backs into it! Stick into them, boys,' he commanded. 'Show them they'll get nothing free from Hamiltons!'

As spectators, Mr Rankin and Freddie were realists. When the teams changed over they moved down towards Connif in goal. In less than a minute he was beaten for the sixth time. Roden was now feeding the ball continuously to the right wing. At last he got through. David lifted the pass on his instep, pushed it forward and went flighting up the field. A feint, a scything turn inside and the half-back was left as still as Lot's wife. He cut towards the goal in an arc and the Merchants full-back failed to anticipate any point in it. In the lull that his beautifully balanced run won for him he shot. The opposing goalkeeper jumped, felt the savage spin in his fingertips and threw the ball out despairingly. Breasting up between the backs came Alec, red-faced, mouth agape, fighting to the last ditch. With a barbarous kick he sent the ball rocketing through and far beyond the netless posts. Six goals to one.

The ball was centred and again the soft plonk arose as it was driven and angled through the defence. Mr Rankin shivered and drew his coat closer. He summed up in his eye the rabble of red and gold jerseys tumbling in the goalmouth and the lone figure on the wing waiting stubbornly for the pass that would come only by a fluke. Nothing but the best for our young friend, he thought. Yes, he said, it would be all right for Freddie to wait for his brother. As he left the pitch a greyness hung over the surface of the river and already in the east side of the city the lights of the small shops were springing up in constellations. The voices from the playing fields came to him faintly through the river haze.

10

On his way to the lavatories at the back of the warehouse a fellow in the Silks called 'Nice work, Minnis' to him. That was the sixth greeting he had had, two of them silent thumbs-up because the Chairman was somewhere in the offing. On Saturday Hamiltons had won their first game of the season and he had made two of their three goals.

Roden had been pretty nice about it, too. But not for long. Saturday was past, this was the start of another week, and so far as Alec was concerned that meant five and a half days work and no letting up. Alec hadn't been very pleased with his work recently. He had been pretty tart five minutes ago about an order forgotten on Saturday morning. Told him that if he didn't pull himself together he would have to speak to Mr Whaley. That frightened him, and now he was angry because he had been frightened. He had been in Alec's good books for the first two or three months. Then he had watched the assistant daily become more curt and unsmiling until now he pitched into him far more than he did into Boney or even Fogarty. Was Boney a better worker? Mebbe. But then there was nothing *to* Boney, no imagination, no personality, no looks. He was just the right man to work in a place like this. And Boney had been there when Alec ticked him off. That's why he had come down here.

Once the bolt was shot it was a good place in which to sulk or day dream or to be out of the boss's way for a while. The board walls were piebald where decades of apprentices had inscribed their erotic yearnings or their politico-theological convictions. Some had been scrubbed out by the cleaners, others scribbled over by straight-laced members of the staff. At eye level, from where he sat, was the most recent epithet about the Pope, only partly erased. 'Defaced by vandals,' complained Fogarty bitterly, who had spent considerable time incising it there.

He brooded over the raw scraped wood and the glittering patches of pencil lead. The words were as ugly as the fellas who put them there; a commonplace, stupid crowd content to clip off wee cloth patterns day in day out, or measure off material they could never afford to wear, or slap fifty per cent on a boy's suit and lie about it to the mother just to please some tick man. What a life! And some of them had been doing this for fifty years! Very likely these were the sort of people old McFall meant when he talked about the 'lumpen proletariat'. No wonder the pay's bad. It was the right price for the job. Here he was, over seventeen, and the cheap seats at the pictures was a thrill and a fish-and-chip supper a treat. And, oh, those long penniless Sunday walks along the Lagan towpath or up the Malone Road with Boney in pursuit of girls! The brazen impudence you had to have to walk beside a couple of silent girls a hundred yards or more, trying to think up a joke that would strike a spark from them. And even when you knew that your one would like to strike up, the other one would pluck at her coat, which is only what you might expect when your pal has a face and dumb tongue like Boney's. Well, all that nonsense and misery would stop. He had better things than that in him. From tomorrow he would start watching the Situations Vacant in the paper. By gor, he would grin yet in Roden's face. And he would . . . study. He recalled the textbooks and the papers of the correspondence course for which his mother had paid six pounds. He was pretty sure they were on top of her wardrobe. She had stopped complaining about it, so it was safe enough to start again without giving her the idea that she had talked him into it.

He would start tomorrow. No, tonight . . . this very evening. He had the same delicious choking sensation and the stumbling heart beat he always experienced when he made a new resolution.

There was a thunderous battering on the door.

'Minnis, are you there?'

'Yes—yes, Alec—'

'What are you doing, clocking in there all morning? Come outa there at once and get upstairs. There's a pile of work waiting on you!'

The outer door slammed. Alec hadn't even gone into the next closet. He must have come down all that distance specially for him. Roast him for a bullying sanctimonious boss's bumlicker. Right, Roden, you've hammered the last nail in my determination. With a scowl on his face he strode back through the warehouse. Passing the Woollens cash office he wondered how his grim expression looked to the new girl there.

He carried his scowl upstairs.

'Was Alec after you?' asked Bonar.

'You know he was.'

'The summer flannels have to be put away. He says you should've had them papered up weeks ago.'

'How was I to know? This is my first year here! And it'll be my last.'

Dumb as usual, Boney misunderstood him. 'Ach, don't be silly, Davie. It isn't as serious as all that. Alec's only shouting—'

He felt a momentary weakness of fear in his stomach. So it might have been as serious as that?

His scowl deepened. 'Don't be buck stupid. I didn't mean that at all. I've plans. Think I'm gonna spend the rest of my days in this dump?'

Bonar chuckled. 'Give us a hand with these flannels before you leave us.'

It was a crisp, pleasant evening so they decided to walk home. There was just enough dusk in the air to make them idly aware of the street lights. With only hunger drawing them homeward, they drifted along looking at the shop windows and the girls, silently comparing themselves to other fellows, pausing to admire the gloss of new cars, scoffing at hurrying, aloof, well-dressed men.

'Doing anything tonight?' said Bonar.

He considered carefully. 'Why, were you, ah—'

'We're having a bit of a special supper—a kinda party.'

'What are you having a party for?'

'Oh, nothing. We just have a party when we feel like it.'

A party just when they felt like it! It made a night's solitary work sound like a prison sentence. But he smiled and shrugged, knowing what was ahead of him. The books to be taken down and dusted, the lessons to be uncurled and put in order. 'Sorry, Boney, I'd like to, but I've a bit of work to do.'

'Shoulda told you sooner,' said Bonar.

He tried to remember what was in those papers. General Knowledge, English, Geography. A small foreboding tantalized him. Oh, there was Economics! Oh, gor, there was Maths! He could get them down and straightened out, maybe. But it would take him a whole free day just to remember how far he had got. That meant next Sunday, nearly a whole week wasted. Still, if he got them down after tea, that would be a start. No good rushing at the thing and then giving it up.

At the corner of Colinvista Street he said 'Supper? That would be about—?'

Bonar gazed at him. 'You mean you might be able to come?'

'Yes, yes.' He tried very hard to keep the irritation out of his voice. 'What time d'you mean by "supper"?'

'About nine.'

'Oh, that's different! I was thinking of tea time. Stupid of me. Could I come?'

'Sure you could come,' said Bonar, grinning with pleasure.

After tea he sat thinking about the textbooks upstairs. If they were still on top of the wardrobe they would probably be buried under a lot of other junk. Her room was just above where they were sitting and she would hear him fiddling about in the dark.

'Those books,' he said with an effort, 'the correspondence course books—' He saw the light spring in her eyes and raised his hand. 'Now, don't be starting! I only want to know if they're still up on the wardrobe. I want to have a look at them—'

She subsided, hurt. 'Yes,' she said, 'they're still there.'

He took them to his room and spread them out on the bed. It was a sickening task. He flicked listlessly through the fat blue book where the entrails of his language were laid out on pages as cold as the slabs in a morgue. He read his answers to the last Economics lesson and refused to believe that he had ever been in possession of those words and terms. But there they were in his own handwriting and it was frightening to see that he had got them all correct and won a neat little red-ink V.G. in the corner of the page. He stared with apathy at the benign countenance stamped on all the covers. 'Thank God,' he whispered, 'I don't have to be *your* son.'

'David, the table's cleared now,' she called. 'It's warm down here and we don't need to have two lights burning.'

The trap was closing. He went to the door. 'I'll be down in a minute. I'm going out soon.'

He sat down again and looked at the papers. It was going to take a shocking amount of labour to catch up on all this stuff. And just to get out of a woollen warehouse. What must the whole knowledge and learning of the outside world be like? It must be heavens high and oceans deep! Even when he had crammed this lot into his head he would still be no better than ten thousand other fellas. But he would be better than the Rodens and the Fogartys. And after all the things he had determined this morning it would be bad for him to give in first go. But there was no great rush. He had all the questions and answers there from the first lesson. Looking back now, from the security of his own room and with his warm tea in him, he could see that Boney was right. He had taken the thing too seriously. And right enough he had been slacking a bit. He would watch that. And, of course, he would start the course again. Too late now, with half the evening gone. It would take a whole day to get the papers straightened. That meant Sunday. Then two nights a week when he got into the swing of it and three coming up to the exam. There was something nice about being a student, like a University fella. It gave you a lift, gave tomorrow a different taste. He carefully parcelled the books together and put them on top of his wardrobe.

When she saw him putting on his raincoat she made no effort to hide her disappointment.

'I suppose it was too much to hope!' she cried in a harsh angry voice.

He smiled contemptuously. 'You could be wrong,' he said.

Silence didn't come down with darkness on Majestic Street. Doors opened and shut, flicking rhomboids of light onto the pavement. Women backed into the street still talking, laughing, waving down their neighbours' excuses and goodnights with understanding hands. Children squeaked round street lamps like bats. Men clustered at corners, matches flaring in their hands.

The roadway in front of number ninety-three was washed with light from the four windows of the house. The light in the hall was orange coloured. 'Because it's kinda cheery,' Mrs McFall had said. 'Because it's the only light you know,' said Mr McFall sardonically. It shone on his face through the wrinkled glass of the door, anointing him for the festivities. The holland blind of the front window was suffused with brightness and gaiety. He didn't know that it was going to be as big as this. He wished now that he had come earlier and that he had put on his good suit.

II

Mr Rankin and he paused to watch the chess players. The flat shafts of the sun pierced the naked trees above them but brought no warmth to the strays and wayfarers huddled round the board and its brooding contestants. Mr Rankin had waited after the match while David changed but they had spoken very little as they walked homeward. David had the impression that his companion had something to tell him but found great difficulty in putting it into words. This halt was only to delay their return home. David had no interest in chess and he felt only the faintest flicker of surprise that the opposing pieces were coloured white and red and not white and black as he had always supposed.

'I think I'll push on and get a bath, Mr Rankin ... I don't want to stiffen up,' he added with a smile.

Mr Rankin came to with a start. 'Wait, David. I'm sorry—'

At that moment one of the onlookers raised his head. 'Here's Cowld Pint in a helluva hurry,' he said.

'Bread and work for all,' said another looking in the same direction.

The man hurrying towards them, he saw with surprise and some embarrassment, was Mr McFall. Without noticing him the little man swept briskly into the crowd. 'Knew I would get you here, Joe,' he said to one of the players. 'Job for you at Forkhill Street.'

Joe's opponent looked up irritably. 'He's in a game, Cowld Pint!'

'Life is real, life is earnest,' said Mr McFall inexorably. 'Memorize your end game, Joe, and put away the baubles.' He turned to one of the other men. 'You, Sam. Gas opening at the corner of Bernard Place. Take over tonight. The yard's sent up lamps, brazier and the hut. Now don't hang around. The ganger'll be wanting you there before half-five.'

Joe and Sam hurried off. Joe's late opponent, still seated on the bench, sulkily tipped the pieces into their box. The idlers drifted away. He lifted his hand in a half-salute. 'Hello, Mr McFall.'

The little man approached them. 'Getting some exercise?' he said with a glance at the football bag in David's hand. 'How did the contest go?'

'First win for weeks. Ah . . . this is Mr Rankin . . . Mr McFall.'

They shook hands. 'You made short work of *that* contest, Mr McFall,' said Mr Rankin with a smile.

'Got to look after the public weal, Mr Rankin. A broken leg can cost the ratepayer money.'

'And it's your concern to set a guard on these places?'

'That's it.'

'I should have thought that they would keep a list of watchmen at the City Hall?'

'Oh, they do,' agreed Mr McFall. 'Names in a book. But where in this great city are the owners of those names?' Mr McFall paused, and considered them with a gentle smile. 'That's where I come in. I know where at any given hour they are to be found—at their devotions, in a bar, or in bed.'

'Indispensable!' exclaimed Mr Rankin without irony.

Mr McFall gave a deprecatory wave. 'Nobody is indispensable, Mr Rankin. Of some small use to the system. No more than that. And now—I've a couple of other jobs to attend to.' The little man saluted them and hurried away through the park gates.

Cowld Pint. Gor, what a name to earn! Not that he was surprised. Most times he went round to Majestic Street old McFall smelt and sounded a bit tiddly. And Boney had let slip once that most of the porter that slid down his father's throttle in Barney Harkin's was in the shape of fees for advice of various sorts. Mebbe even for getting the Joes and Sams a night's watching. Terrible to think that a girl like Maureen McFall had such a cod of a father. He found himself hoping desperately that she had never heard that nickname.

Mr Rankin overtook him. 'Odd job your friend has. I never thought before where those men who watch holes in the road come from.'

He increased his pace. 'I wouldn't call him a friend. It's his son . . . I know him a bit.'

Mr Rankin raised his eyebrows. 'A bit? Isn't that your chum McFall who works in Hamiltons?'

Right enough, if you added up all the times he might have

mentioned Boney's name it probably did come to more than a bit. 'That's right. That's him.'

'How's he getting on in Hamiltons?'

'Boney? Oh, he's all right.'

'Does his work satisfy Alec Roden?'

He looked sharply at the man beside him. 'Alec Roden? What's he got to do with it?'

'I ran into him yesterday. He, ah, mentioned your name . . .'

'Oh?'

'Yes, he wanted me to speak to you about a thing—your work.'

'My work? What's wrong with my work?'

Mr Rankin's voice was much firmer. 'He wanted me to pass on a word of advice—Mr Whaley doesn't think your work's good enough.'

'Well, why didn't Roden come to me?'

'He never mentioned it?' said Mr Rankin looking askance.

He flushed. 'He shoulda told me. He needn't go around telling everybody. He has his knife in me for something.'

They were separated for a moment by a heavy, waddling woman with a laden basket.

'I don't think so. As a matter-of-fact I got the impression that he's rather fond of you.' David felt called on to make a derisive noise.

'Anyway,' continued Mr Rankin, 'he didn't want to see anything happening. You know, maybe losing your job—'

He turned, open-mouthed. 'Is it as bad as that?'

The man gave an impatient gesture. 'What do you expect? It won't be as bad as that if you take a tuck in yourself.'

'O.K., Mr Rankin. I'll watch myself.'

'Good man!' Mr Rankin stopped. 'I'm going in here for my tobacco. If you're in a hurry you'd better go on.'

'I think I will. I've a sorta date with Boney. And—thanks, Mr Rankin.'

But he didn't go out after tea. He got down the bundle of books from the top of the wardrobe, sorted them out, and with a suffocating incomprehension glimpsed through one of the subjects at the end of the textbook. When he had finished he sat for almost an hour, his hands knotted together, staring in dumb misery at the litter of papers on his bed. Here was no way of escape. There was a tap on the door and his mother came in carrying his supper. She set down the tray softly, and looked at him with an anxious smile.

'I thought, maybe, if you were studying, you would like it brought up.'

'Thanks—thanks, mother. You shouldn't have troubled.'

'Goodnight, son.'

'Goodnight.'

As she went out he noticed loose threads on her dress and he knew that she had stopped her own work to bring up his food. As he thought of all that she didn't know, his eyes smarted momentarily, as if they would have shed tears but had forgotten how.

Facing Roden next morning was a bit of a problem. The assistant solved it by calling him into the stockroom shortly after work had started.

'Did you see Mr Rankin over the weekend?'

'Yes.'

'Did he tell you what I said?'

'He did.'

'Well, have you thought about it?'

The calmness of the questioning drove him from his curt antagonism. 'Why did you do it?' he burst out.

'I thought it was better than going to your mother.'

'Just as well you didn't—'

Calmly Roden pressed him for an admission. 'Well, have you thought it over?'

'There's not much to think over, is there?' His voice and his lowered eyes admitted defeat.

The assistant was magnanimous. 'It's a bad business, Davie, to loaf about. There are ten thousand outa-works walking the streets of this city. Hamiltons could get a dozen young fellas like you in an hour's time just by sticking a notice in the window. And the Chairman would do it. This is no philanthropic institution.'

'Huh! As if I don't know!' He wondered nostalgically what

old McFall's comment would be on this sample of class ruthlessness.

'Well, don't forget it so often. And, Davie, if there's an improvement in your work—in a bit sharper in the mornings, a bit more eager to serve customers, a bit less horse-play in the stockrooms—I won't be behind in telling Mr Whaley that you've caught yourself on.'

'All right, Alec, all right,' he mumbled. 'I'm not as bad as you're trying to make out—'

He knew he could never be what Alec Roden wanted him to be. He hadn't the 'stickatitness' of the others. Bonar's steady docility; the surprisingly adult decisions and attitudes that Fogarty could produce when required; the busy responsibility of Alec himself—these were beyond him and he wasn't particularly sorry about it. He had a greater future before him, he was certain of that. Meantime he had to be careful.

A day or so later the shabby figure of Mr Shriberger mounted the stairs. He approached with his shy ironic smile. 'Well, my friend, give me a boiler suit and three of your doncharees, all size six.'

As he folded and pounded the stiff brown fabric into a parcel, Mr Shriberger talked about the weather, the awful steepness of the stairs, the vagaries of his customers. He glanced round the department. 'Well, how do you like now being employed in this great emporium?'

'D'you call this a great emporium?'

'I'm joking, my friend.'

He moved closer to Mr Shriberger. There was a pleasant thrill in being traitorous about Hamiltons to a customer. 'I'm fed up with it—to the teeth.'

Mr Shriberger shrugged. 'You came here of your own free will. You stay of your own free will. It is good enough for you.'

'I want to get out of it.'

'How much?'

'A lot. But I've got to have another job to go to—'

'You see. You start making conditions. Life has a rude noise for the man who makes conditions.'

'Well, I hate the bloody place!'

'You spend energy using bad words. I understand it better when you keep it plain.'

'Sorry.'

'What have you done about getting out?'

'Well, I've tried to study.'

'I respect the student. I am not one myself. In my home in Zagreb on the morning of my seventeenth birthday I looked at myself in a looking-glass and I said, "Baruch Shriberger, I have satisfied myself that you are not a student. So you will put away the law books. Now, what of value can you find in your pockets?" '

'What d'you mean—looking in your pockets?'

'What I mean is this: consider very carefully what knowledge of life you have. What you know in life is your capital. You are a young, poor boy. Consider what you can do with your head. Consider what you can do with your hands.'

'Or my feet?'

Mr Shriberger smiled politely, intimating that he had withdrawn from the conversation.

'No, I mean it. I'm good at football.'

'I knew a professional footballer in Leeds.'

'Oh, what was his name?'

But Mr Shriberger had kept his skin intact for a thousand years by not remembering names. He lifted his parcel.

'Take a stocktaking of yourself. If you can find a small skill, take it out into the world. Do not think of anyone—'

'What if you've a mother?'

'If you love your family you can make it up to them. If you do not—what is lost?'

His mention of football hadn't been mere flippancy. Saturday afternoon held the one bright hour or so in a week of discontent at home and morose subordination at work. He was still the attacking force in the Hamiltons team, and Alec Roden directed the strategy so that the play ran to the outside-right. In the rudimentary tactics of the Haberdashers Alliance rival captains pointed him out as a man to watch. He had never tasted sweeter joy than on the afternoon when a senior assistant in Craig & McCrudden Limited asked him was he not Minnis, Hamiltons' outside-right. It was the first faint ripple to break the dull surface of his anonymity.

One Saturday afternoon in early December he was standing close to the referee when the official flourished his wrist, glanced at his watch, and brought the game to an end with a long blast of the whistle. As he left the pitch the referee fell into step beside him.

'That wasn't a bad game you played today, Minnis.'

'Thanks.'

'Eh—' the referee glanced around. 'There's a fella here would like to have a word with you.'

'What fella?' He stopped and looked at the man with the quick mistrust of a city boy. 'What does he want?'

'It's all above board. He's over there near the trees. He wants to talk football to you.'

David assured himself that Bonar and Roden and Eddie Glenn were still in sight. 'Some other time,' he said, quickening his step.

'Don't be in a hurry. This is business.'

'What's it to you? You're a ref.'

'Sure, sure! Keep it down. Not a word. I told these fellas to come along and watch you. I'm doing you a good turn,' he expostulated.

'Fellas?' said David suspiciously.

The referee signalled abruptly and two men in raincoats and caps came out of the shadow of the trees. The referee left David briskly and as he approached the men David heard him say, 'He's all yours. Don't forget it was me that put you on to him.' The men didn't answer. As they approached David the taller of the two spoke: 'Your name Minnis?'

'That's right. There's m'pals over there.'

'We won't keep you.' They didn't look at him with any marked interest, which, in a way, restored his confidence.

'The ref say anything to you?'

'Only that you wanted to talk to me.'

'That's right. That's the best way.'

'Like to have a rub down before we talk?' said the second man with a friendly smile.

'I'm all right, thanks—if it's not too long.'

'Won't be a minute,' said the tall man. 'My name's McClenaghan, manager of Glenbank Athletic. This is Mr Mort, the trainer. Heard of Glenbank?' He smiled. 'We were watching the match. Not bad.'

'As far as *you* were concerned,' added Mr Mort gloomily.

'We'll put our errand in a nutshell,' said Mr McClenaghan. 'What would you think about signing a form for Glenbank?'

'Well, I dunno . . . I never really thought that—'

'Understandable,' said Mr McClenaghan crisply. 'You've never been approached before?'

'No. Is there any money in it?'

The manner in which Mr Mort smiled at Mr McClenaghan showed that this was a not uncommon misapprehension.

'Money?' Mr Mort chuckled. 'Not yet, young fella. Just an amateur form—'

'Look, Minnis,' said Mr McClenaghan earnestly. 'It's all right and fine running rings round a pack o' hallions like that on a cinder pitch. Wait till you play in the class that gives you something to think about. Then we'll see what you're worth.'

'What age are you?' asked Mr Mort.

'Seventeen. Eighteen next April.'

Mr McClenaghan seemed to think this a tactless question. 'You've got to start at the bottom, you know,' he said.

David scowled. You always had to start at the bottom. Even in soccer.

'Meantime free togs and training. When we see what you can do, we'll talk turkey.'

It sounded fair enough. There must be money somewhere in this game.

'What d'you say, Minnis?'

'Well, all right, thanks. What do I do?'

'Come along about seven on Tuesday to Glenbank's ground. Ireton Terrace—'

'I know it.'

'Like one of us to speak to your father or somebody?'

'No—no thanks. I can handle it.'

'Well, you know. Better give us your address, anyway.'

Mr McClenaghan noted it down. 'Tuesday night and ask for me—Billy McClenaghan.'

Bonar, Roden, and Eddie Glenn had waited for him in the dropping darkness; not too close to catch a private conversation, near enough if anybody started any rough stuff. They watched him part with the men.

'Get a leg on, will you!' shouted Glenn. 'I'm dropping you all home in the car.'

He bundled on his jacket and grabbed his shoes and the rest of his clothes.

'Who were those two comics?' asked Glenn.

He saw that they had already guessed and felt suddenly shy. 'They said they were from Glenbank.'

'*Said* they were?'

'What was it, Davie boy, a form?' As Glenn switched on the car lights, David saw good old Boney's face. It glowed with excitement and pleasure.

'Yes. They—ah—they want me to sign a form.'

Bonar chortled in glee; Roden, his boots in his lap, sat staring silently through the windscreen. They drove to his house first. He clambered out, gave them an unsmiling goodnight and slammed the door.

'What's biting him?' said Bonar.

Glenn, conscious of the loyalty due from one senior employee to another, laughed self-consciously. 'Who, Alec? Oh, nothing. Sorry to lose you from the team, mebbe.'

'He's jealous,' said Bonar. Although David joined in the laughter he knew his friend was right. He got no satisfaction from it, only an uneasiness for the future.

Tea was almost finished when he said, 'Coupla men asked me to sign a form for Glenbank Athletic after the match today.' He acknowledged Freddie's excited shout with a wink and a smile and watched for his mother's response. She was dimly aware that it was something of importance but she didn't understand this bit of jargon from the world of her sons.

'Oh, is that so? Who would Glenbank Athletic be?'

'A football team, Mammy. They're in the Senior League. They're miles better than Hamiltons. They've pros playing for them.'

'Pros?'

'Professionals, Mammy.'

Mrs Minnis smiled uncomprehendingly. He wasn't surprised at that. He couldn't expect her to know anything about football. Yet, in a way, he felt disappointed. Even with Freddie's help it still left a lot to explain. He rumpled his brother's hair playfully.

She laid down her knife and fork and looked at him. A word of Freddie's stirred in her mind. 'Professional?' She sounded the word as if there was something faintly nasty about it. 'You mean—being paid to play football?'

'Yes, but not me.'

'Oh, I thought you meant—'

'Not right now. But they might, if I'm any good.'

'Oh, David, I don't know. I'm not awfully keen on you playing this football. You might get hurt or something—'

'*Oh*, mother, not at all.'

Her voice rose. 'And I don't like the idea of you playing for money, so I don't!'

'I didn't say I was playing for money!'

'Aren't you only after saying that they might if you were good enough?'

'Well, if they do pay me what's wrong with that?'

'I don't know anything about the type o' characters that hang around these football grounds but I'm sure they don't give away much for nothing. How could you give the time to play football for money and you with your own work to do?'

He had an answer ready for that. 'It wouldn't interfere with my work. I would be playing in my own spare time.' The truculence left his voice and he asked her with pointed sweetness: 'What would you say if I could earn more money at playing football than I could in Hamiltons?'

'That there's something wrong with a world that allows it. I wouldn't have it at all.'

'Why not?'

'Because God put us into this world to work. To do useful things with our hands. That's the rent we pay for living here and—'

'I might be able to pay it with my feet.' It won a giggle from Freddie, but it fell as flat with his mother as it had with old Shriberger.

'—we're made for better things than kicking a hollow ball. He who will not work neither shall he eat. What would the neighbours think, David, if they heard a son of mine was earning money at a football club? It shows you can't earn your money in an honest way.'

'Honest—honest?' He was on the edge of an outburst about Hamiltons and his work there. He brought his voice down as flat as his hand tapping the table. 'You know nothing about these things. There's not a fella in this street that wouldn't love to be a good footballer and get paid for it.' He brushed aside her gesture: 'You're always complaining about how little I bring in—and then when I get a chance to earn more, you try to stop me. Well, I'm telling you now, if this football crowd offer me money, I'm taking it. And I don't want to hear any more about it.' He held out his cup. 'I'll have some more tea if you don't mind.'

After he had gone out it wasn't so much his words as his manner she remembered, cool, final. He was his own boss now, it seemed. No more childish flares of temper. No more flouncing out of the house. At the table, she had seen for the first time, not petulance but dislike in her son's eyes. It was frightening and she had tried so hard. She began to weep, the tears dropping into the basin in which she was washing-up. Freddie, as he dried the dishes, watched her in helpless distress.

Part Two

I

THE news of his athletic achievement in no way endeared him to the Chairman or Mr Clarence. They had had feckless employees before but none so indiscreet as to get himself talked about for being good at something outside business hours. They could clearly see a divided interest here, and a divided interest was of no use to them. Not, of course, that they betrayed any awareness of so trivial an incident in the life of such an obscure individual. But a couple of weeks later when he presented himself for his second year's increment it was handed to him with such restrained warmth by Mr Clarence in the silent presence of the Chairman that between them they all but destroyed his ecstasy in his four-bob-a-week rise.

It was different in the departments. Most of his younger mates doled out their leisure, in varying degree, in the pursuit of girls, the studying of horses, the pictures and football. Football was a twelvemonth's passion. The summer twilight between the seasons was the time to argue about last winter's humiliations and next winter's half-back line. And here, working with them, picked from their own team, was a young fella who might yet run with their heroes. As Tits Fogarty said, it made you think twice about the Sunday papers.

Even Alec Roden stopped sulking and asked him to find out if Glenbank would let him play for Hamiltons in the Shield Competition in February.

It was even better in the McFall household. He glowed under their admiration. Arthur slapped him on the back. Bonar recalled goals that he had forgotten. Mrs McFall wanted to know what it was all about and her husband told her, conjecturing at the same time how soon David would be playing for his country. Maureen, coming home late from work asked why she was expected to join in the congratulations. Waving Bonar into silence her father explained again. 'Is that important?' she asked, and her father assured her it was.

David saw her looking at him thoughtfully. Their appraisal of each other turned to a smile until she jumped to her feet and went to fetch her supper from the oven.

A few evenings later, as he sat in the kitchen in Majestic Street, she said, 'Would you two like to buy tickets for a social?'

He looked at Bonar. 'Well,' he said, 'I dunno—' Then, boldly, 'Are you going?'

''Course she's going,' said her brother.

'How d'you know, clever?'

'Because you'd have a helluva nerve to try and sell us tickets if you weren't.'

'Language,' murmured Mrs McFall from behind her evening paper.

'Well, as a matter of fact, Sadie Monteith and I *are* going.'

'When is it?' he asked.

'And what's the damage?' asked Bonar.

'It's on Friday and the tickets are two shillings each.'

'Pay night,' nodded Bonar with satisfaction.

'I'm sure that never dawned on them,' said Mr McFall. 'Who's throwing the hooley?'

'Answer your da, love,' said Mrs McFall.

'It's the Women's League of Empire, mother.'

'Any of your dusky sisters be there?' asked Mr McFall.

'We're all white,' snapped his daughter.

'I'm sure you are,' chuckled the little man. ' "A monstrous regiment of women", as your man John Knox has it—'

'Try not to be an ould eejit all your life,' said Mrs McFall without any great conviction. 'Sounds nice,' she said to Bonar.

Bonar glanced at David and read the answer. 'Sure, we'll go.'

'I'll get your tickets tomorrow. Sadie and me'll see you there.'

Two bob for the ticket, he thought, as he crossed the main road, and two and six for incidentals. Say two half-crowns all told. He could manage that. He would have liked to pay for her ticket but he hadn't been asked. Then who was taking her? Turning his back on the busy pavement he stared into a shop window. A fella could be badly hurt here. He mustered his small experience weighing this likelihood against that. Surely she wouldn't be so cruel as to ask him and then turn up with somebody else? The solitary article in the window came into focus; a blue and white straw hat shaped like a chamber-pot above a dingy card marked 'chic'. He glanced quickly over his shoulder, and hurried away.

Next morning he reconnoitred without any great success. 'Are we supposed to be going with this Sadie Monteith and—and your Maureen?'

Bonar scratched his chin. 'We'll be in their crowd.'

'I know, but aren't you supposed to have a girl when you go to these things?'

'If you haven't, you grab one when you get there.'

And he didn't come any greater speed in Majestic Street on Friday night. Mr McFall analysed the news at the fireside. Mrs McFall could be heard washing Willie's ears in the scullery. Bonar brushed the jacket of his new purplish worsted under the kitchen light. He recognized it as the expensive range A1795SB. There was no sign of the girls. Glumly he watched Bonar's long body twisting under the shining Italian cloth of his waistcoat. Mrs McFall pushed a blubbering Willie ahead of her through the bead screen. She stopped and smiled in admiration.

'You're looking smart, Davie.'

'Thanks, Mrs McFall.'

'Look at that fella! He's been dickeying at himself since he had his tea. The girls are away an hour ago. 'Course, they're on the committee.'

He sounded her inflexion over in his ear. It wasn't an apology. It wasn't even an explanation. Bonar shrugged into his jacket. Mrs McFall laid a tighter grip on Willie. 'Bed for you, boy.'

Bonar gave a last twist of the comb to the lock over his uneven forehead and they went out to the hall. 'Enjoy yourselves!'

Mrs McFall's voice floated down the stairs. They chorused their thanks as they lifted down their coats.

When they arrived at the hall there were about a dozen young fellows already in the cloakroom, setting their ties and hankies at the mirror or watering their hair at the cracked hand basin. Those already acquainted exchanged a word or two, ignoring the others. But a curiosity, a stir of antagonism, affected them all, and in side glances they examined each other's features, colouring, height, tie, clothes.

A newcomer swept in hailing Bonar with a shout. Bonar introduced him as Jimmie Coburn. Coburn stripped off his mackintosh and crooked his finger, inviting them to come closer. He drew them down into the darkness between the coat racks. 'Here you are, fellas, one wee slug and that's that—' He held out a bottle of cheap sweet wine.

'Aw, for any sakes!' said Bonar. 'Can you not go anywhere without liquor, Jimmie?'

Coburn made a rude jocular noise and offered the bottle to David. He hesitated. If only he knew the fella better. Bonar, hands in pockets, strolled away. David smiled nervously and nodded to Coburn.

The brassy liquid flooded round the roots of his tongue. He coughed and swallowed and coughed again. Coburn took the bottle from him, wiped the neck with the heel of his hand and took a long suck at it. He dropped it back into the pocket of the mackintosh. 'Any time you want a slug you'll get it here—this fawn coat.'

David thanked him and followed Bonar. So that was what drink was like. In the few seconds going from the cloakroom to the hall he felt the liquor running down through him loosening the strings that bound his heart, his gestures, his courage.

The hall had been built in the tumultuous days of 1912 and its walls were laden with emblems and icons of royalty and loyalty. Monarchs and forgotten people of importance gazed through paper chains, serene in the knowledge that this impertinent frivolity would pass. On the chairs below them the girls lit the dun-coloured walls with their frocks and gaiety.

Scattered among them were a few men, husbands and affianced. The other males filled the doorway in a dark wedge, hands deep in pockets, eyes darting here and there, thin-soled shoes pawing the ground discreetly.

Bonar waited for him in the front of the cluster. 'Come on,' he said, 'there's Maureen and our crowd.' David felt a slight sinking of his courage. 'Right,' he said, 'on you go.'

There was a young man with Maureen and her friends, in his mid-twenties and well dressed. It was hard to say whether he was there because of Maureen or Sadie Monteith or one of the other girls. She introduced Bonar to the girls, some of whom he already knew, and to the young man, Bob Kane. Then she introduced David. It was all very decorous and thorough, no mumbled names, everyone waiting politely and self-consciously until the circle was completed. No excuse, he thought, for not knowing any of her friends, even the hard-looking ones. He couldn't decide whether to take heart at this or not.

On the platform, a pianist, a drummer and a sax player sprawled in their chairs. The pianist straightened up and clashed the keys of the piano as a man in a shiny dinner-jacket sprang onto the platform and ducked his head to the crowd. Everybody stopped talking and looked up at him. He had the stoop, the lifted eyebrow, the throw-away voice of a droll master of ceremonies.

'And now, ladies and gentlemen, good evening and welcome to yous one and all. You all know what you're here for—'

The phalanx in the doorway intimated by guffaws, scuffles and muted ribaldries that they knew what *they* were there for, all right. David felt the hair bristle on his neck. Unperturbed, the M.C. took them under his notice '—And that goes for the handsome upstanding young fellas to my right.' The respectable in the hall took their revenge in a sustained jeer of laughter.

'Come on on into the body of the hall, gentlemen. There are plenty of young ladies'll move up and make room for you. Come on now, yous are blocking the gangway and holding up the fun.' He gave a sweep of his arm and induced a marginal erosion as half a dozen youths peeled off the front of the crowd and shuffled towards empty chairs.

'Thank you, thank you, thank you! And now ladies and gentlemen so's we can all get acquainted—a quick step! A—one, a—two!' With a nod to the trio he sprang to the floor and the pianist bashed off on the jangling keys.

He collapsed in his chair. Dancing? He hadn't thought of that. Maureen and Bob Kane stood up, moved close together and spun away. And why shouldn't they? Hadn't he brought her there? He looked round for Bonar. He was on his feet, in Sadie Monteith's arms, stumbling into the circling crowd. You had to have a thick skin to get up and make a fool of yourself like that.

He sat crossing and uncrossing his legs, occasionally nodding and waving to imaginary acquaintances on the floor. Maureen passed, and smiled over her partner's shoulder. He gave her a friendly if nonchalant wave in reply. From the corner of his eye he saw her partner say something and Maureen throw back her head and laugh. What a prize eejit he must look sitting here.

A numbing realization crept over him. Half a dozen chairs away sat two or three girls with everything but a partner. It must be plain to everybody in the hall that he couldn't dance.

He braced himself to stand up and skirt the dancers on his way to the entrance. Bonar, glistening with sweat and laughter, stumbled past with a shout. He grinned back, and fixing the grin on his face pushed forward as though to some enviable assignation.

Safely in the crowd he turned and watched the dancers. Most of the youths around him sucked cigarettes. He wished he had a cigarette. But he wouldn't have smoked it. He had to look after his wind. There was hardly likely to be a footballer with his name on a form in this crowd of pathetic wallflowers. He moved further back. He would go and wash his hands. That would kill time anyway.

As he entered the cloakroom he saw Coburn and two other young fellows half-hidden among the coat racks.

'There you are,' shouted Coburn. 'Have a drink!' He thrust a bottle at David, a different bottle. David hesitated and looked at the others. They were well on their way.

'Go on, have a gargle,' said a short, thickset character with black nails and scarred fingers. 'All right with you, Victor?' Victor steadied his pale, thinly-haired face long enough to focus David and smiled amiably.

He took the bottle and put it to his mouth. It was the same liquor, heavy, sweet, aromatic. He smacked his lips as he handed the bottle back.

'Good, eh?' Coburn held the bottle up to the light. 'One go left for the four o' us.'

'We'll get another,' said the squat mechanic. 'How much was it, Victor?'

'Five bob a charger.' Victor steadied himself and computed further. 'That's one an' thrupence each,' he added, and leaned back with a delighted cluck.

'Bloody marvel, isn't he?' the mechanic appealed to Coburn.

'Bloody. Here's my one an' thrupence. Where's everybody's?'

David made to move away. 'I don't think I'll—'

'Aye, but you'll take a drink, I notice,' said the mechanic truculently.

'I'm in,' replied David shortly. He took the bottle and swallowed his mouthful. Then he gave it back with his share of the money to Coburn. There was a rattle of applause from the hall. 'I'm going back. The dancing's over.'

He mingled with the dancers as they drifted back to their seats. Bonar, with Sadie on his knee, looked up as he approached.

'Where have you been?'

He giggled. 'Out seeing a dog about a man.'

Bonar shrugged. 'You poor eejit,' he said in a low voice.

'Aw go to hell,' said David turning away. Maureen, he noticed, was sitting on Kane's knee.

The M.C. bounded onto the platform. The pianist struck a chord. 'Now,' said the M.C., 'we'll play something quieter . . . more restful . . .' He was a devil as he said it. He began to outline the theory of Postman's Knock. His explanation was drowned in a hurroo of impatient shouting. The crowd around the door scattered like locusts across the hall. Pretty girls were pulled from one clan to another. The M.C. pointed to the gallery stairs, the kitchen, the committee rooms. In bounds or out of bounds? No one knew. No one cared. For most of the youths there, a social was the only chance to hug and kiss a girl under a dry roof.

Maureen's party and a few camp-followers moved to a corner near the kitchen door. Some of the girls protested against playing such a childish game, but he observed that none of them refused the number whispered to her. Bob Kane flourished a silver-plated cigarette case. He refused politely. Bonar noticed the raised eyebrows, the half-smile.

'He doesn't smoke, Bob. He's a footballer. Signed a form for Glenbank.'

Bob closed his case. 'Oh,' he said. 'Pardon. I didn't know.'

David's annoyance with Bonar melted. 'S'all right. Got to keep in trim,' he said graciously. He ran his tongue round his mouth and felt somewhat ashamed.

He watched closely the pattern played out before him. Although the numbers appeared to be distributed at random, he saw that every girl got her chosen male into the dark for a few moments. If they overstayed a chorus of whistles and catcalls reached them through the closed door. Bob Kane rose at his number and went into the kitchen. When the girl who had called him came out, flushed and smirking, David waited taut with apprehension. A number was called. Maureen blushed, and rising amidst the laughter of the other girls walked to the door and opened it. In the brief glimpse into the darkness over her shoulder he saw the luminous arc traced by the man's cigarette as he took it eagerly from his lips. Maureen went in and closed the door behind her.

No one seemed to want to disturb them. He sat with his hands crushed between his knees wondering if Coburn was still in the cloakroom. There might be a drop left if he went back. The door opened and Bob Kane came out. He was smiling and combing his hair. David didn't give the big fellow a second glance. All his rancour was sharpened and aimed at the girl behind the door.

A number was called. Bonar nudged him. 'Well, what are you waiting for?' His friend laughed at his gaping mouth. 'Seventeen, isn't that your number?'

He closed the door behind him and stepped falteringly into the darkness. She was leaning against a table her face turned a little from him. Neither spoke. He stretched out and caught her elbows, timidly trying to draw her towards him. 'I—' she began, and stopped, sensing that a word might drive him away. She followed the timid urge of his hands and swayed towards him to be kissed. He held his mouth to hers for a long time, more through nervous anxiety than passion. With his eyes closed he assured himself that this was a kiss to be taken away and savoured.

At last she drew back. 'You've been drinking,' she said, but her voice was smiling in the darkness.

'A fella gave me one from a bottle. Tell me, how did you know my number?'

She thrust him away so violently that he stumbled. 'I didn't know your number!' she said hurrying towards the door.

'Wait—wait! I'm sorry. I didn't mean—' He held out his hands tentatively and in the dim light of the window she guessed rather than saw the wonder and unbelief in his eyes. She forgave him quickly, resting her hands lightly on his shoulders as they kissed. 'Now,' she said, pushing him away, 'I'll have to go. They'll be talking.'

'Who'll be talking—Bob?'

She laughed softly. 'Don't be silly—Bob's nothing to me.' Then she was gone.

As he walked home only a few upper windows, subdued in the moonlight, shone in the silent tunnel of Colinvista Street. To-night Maureen McFall had actually allowed him to kiss her; had come into his arms to be kissed a second time. As he thought of it a great wave of ecstasy surged through him. He plucked off his hat and threw it high in the moonlit air. He caught it and set it soberly on his head. Tonight, also, he had tasted liquor for the first time. He blew into his cupped hands and wondered if his breath still smelled.

2

FREDDIE and he were kicking a tennis ball on the vacant lot at the end of the street when Mr Rankin joined them. Freddie looked forward to this brief outing every Saturday before lunch. Not that he had the makings of a footballer; too heavy on his heels, too ponderous about the stern. A swimmer, perhaps. The last time David had been coaxed to take him to the public baths he had noticed how the kid was beginning to pull his chunky body through the water with a touch of style. Much better than he had ever managed. He was teasing Freddie by keeping the ball just out of his reach, juggling it from toe to knee, when Mr Rankin came round the corner. The man watched for a moment, laughing. 'Come on, greedy, let it out!' he called. David brought the ball down, and kicked it towards him. For a few minutes the three of them, laughing and shouting, chased the ball over the bumpy waste.

Mr Rankin pulled up. 'Musn't keep your mother waiting. Time we were getting back, boys.' He gave Freddie a little push. 'On you go. Tell her we'll be up by the time she has lunch on the table.'

Obediently Freddie trotted away, but Mr Rankin, to David's mild surprise, seemed in no hurry. They had taken a few steps up the street when Mr Rankin suddenly turned and said, 'David, I'm leaving Colinvista Street.'

He stopped and stared at the man. 'Leaving . . . but I thought you couldn't . . .' He flushed and looked away.

'David—' When he looked up Mr Rankin was smiling a little bitterly. 'You've heard my story?'

'. . . A fella in work knows you.'

'Ah,' Mr Rankin moved on again. 'I'll never be able to repay your mother and her friends for what they've done for me. Mr Shrubsole . . . the Sintons . . . the people in the Hall. They probably saved my life. But now they want me to join them without any reservations. To accept their beliefs completely . . . their idea of God. I can't. And I can't disbelieve in Him.' The man gestured agitatedly. 'At times I'm torn in two!' He looked sharply at David. 'This is a dangerous way for me to talk to you.'

He shrugged slightly. It wasn't dangerous. Odd, maybe. About that sort of thing he didn't worry overmuch. An indifference, like a thick cuticle, was growing over that problem. 'Ah, that's all right, Mr Rankin. Couldn't you sort of . . . go along with them?'

Mr Rankin paused as if even yet he considered that possible. 'No, it doesn't work. They *know* . . . Anyway,' he said more briskly, 'I can't spend the rest of my life in hiding. I've been in harbour. I'm strong enough to venture out again.'

'That's great,' said David mechanically. The prospect of what this meant to the household was rapidly shaping in his mind.

'I've told your mother it's because of business reasons. I don't want to distress her. But I'm telling you the real reason. I couldn't go away without telling somebody the facts.'

They were at the door. He closed his eyes recalling what the man had just said. 'Oh, sure, Mr Rankin. Thanks. I'm sorry you're going. You'll come and see us sometimes?'

'I should think so!' declared Mr Rankin stoutly.

After lunch David flung himself on his bed and stared glumly at the ceiling. Why couldn't that sanctimonious mob have left the man alone! Now, without Rankin's money coming in, his mother would want every farthing he earned. And just when he had got himself a lovely girl.

They had seen each other several times since the night he had kissed her. But it had always been in her house and the kitchen seemed always full of people. Then they had met by accident in Ormeau Road and hurried towards each other, shyly but eagerly. 'Yes,' she said, 'I'd like to go out with you, David. But it can't be until some evening next week.' She saw his face shadow. 'I'm working every night. We're stocktaking.'

'Oh, I see. Well, couldn't I come and meet you?'

She smiled at his eagerness. 'It wouldn't be any good. We're never out till after ten. I come home with Sadie and another girl.'

'They work you hard enough,' he said scowling.

'Oh, it's all right. We get paid overtime.'

'I only get tea money.' He bit his lip at this childish irrelevance, but she nodded understandingly.

'I know. Bonar gets the same.'

He hastened to make up for his blunder. 'Well, that's great—I mean, coming out with me.'

When they parted he was so angry with himself he momentarily forgot her answer and his good fortune. Putting on a poor mouth before the girl. Almost crying poverty at your first date! Well, if it wasn't true I wouldn't have said it, he pleaded. Damn everybody, why have I no money? He walked down Colinvista Street, his shoulders slumped. There was no way out. Last night Mr Sinton had read from the paper that there were thirty thousand unemployed in the city alone. 'You're lucky you're in a job,' his mother had said with that look that made him knot his fingers in rage.

She had told Harry Peebles and the Sintons about Mr Emmet up the street. . . . He had a good business of his own once. Now he goes down to the shipyard every morning at five o'clock to fill in the two hours between the night-watchman going off and the workmen arriving. And he does the thirty-hour relief stretch on Saturdays and Sundays, sleeping in a dirty old hut. He's lucky to find any work to do in the shipyard, opined Mr Sinton. Grass growing on the slips, said Harry Peebles. Can't get money out of them shipyard homes these days, said Mrs Sinton. . . . 'And when he goes down there,' continued Mrs Minnis, 'the poor man puts on his hard hat and his gloves and his raincoat just like the old days. He's so ashamed of the neighbours knowing where he's working. Mrs Emmet tells me she's afraid for his mind at times.'

Although he had recognized the sympathy in her voice he had drawn his face into a ferocious sneer to remark that any man who thought his neighbours got up at five o'clock in the morning to see him go to work was out of his mind already. But Harry Peebles was before him with the opinion that men were making an awful mess of the world. After that it hadn't seemed worth while going on about Mr Emmet.

With his head pillowed on his arms he thought of Mr Rankin's departure, of Mr Emmet putting on his gloves and hard hat to watch over picks and shovels and steam-rollers, of his boredom and discontent in Hamiltons. Mebbe old Peebles wasn't so far off the mark after all. Then he recalled how Maureen had looked up into his face as if she had been waiting for him to ask her. Yes, that was good all right. That made you want to get out and fight. He got up and shook himself. He would take a walk over to Glenbank. Perhaps McClenaghan or Mort might have found a game for him at long last.

3

THERE was a cluster of assistants and apprentices reading the notice beside the time-clock. He scribbled his name opposite 9.02 a.m. and peered over their shoulders. It was typed on the firm's letterhead and signed by the Chairman:

> It has been brought to the notice of the Directors that efforts are being made to organize the employees of this and similar firms as members of a Trade Union. The Directors wish to remind you that the wages paid by Hamiltons, Ltd., are as liberal as those obtaining elsewhere and they are of the opinion that Trade Union activity in this firm is unnecessary. The Management is anxious that no loyal employee should suffer hardship by allowing himself to be misled by promises which cannot possibly be fulfilled in the present conditions of the Trade. The Directors therefore must request all persons in their employment not to support or attend any meetings organized for Trade Union purposes unless specifically authorized to do so by the Management.

'They could have put it in half a dozen words,' said Adam

Ramsay, the packer. 'Join a union and you're out on your backside.'

'Well said, Ramsay!' exclaimed Gallagher, the Woollens buyer, rubbing his hands vigorously. 'Take a note of that, you young bucks. Now, come on, come on, there's customers waiting!' And he shepherded his staff before him to the other end of the warehouse.

Ramsay watched him go with a hooded smile then he turned back to the notice. 'Well, what d'you think of that lot, Davie?'

'It was coming, wasn't it?'

Ramsay considered him for a moment. 'Yes, I s'pose it was. See anything quare about it?'

'No.'

Ramsay traced the words with a calloused finger. 'It's the directors that remind us about our liberal wages but it's a different bunch, the management, that threaten us with the sack—'

He was nettled by Ramsay's presumption in putting himself and his like on the same level as the salesmen. 'Well, of course, I don't know how it'll affect the messengers and you fellas in the packing room, but *I* don't see any threat in it.'

'You don't?'

'No.' He stabbed the notice in irritated retaliation. 'And you don't even read it right! They say here that they're giving us wages as liberal as any other wholesale house—'

'Liberal compared to what?' Ramsay's tongue peeped from the corner of his mouth. David viewed him with distaste.

'You're a dangerous man, Ramsay,' he said, backing up the stairs.

He had been showing off to Ramsay when he pretended to know about the imminence of the warning. But not entirely. There had been some whispering in the warehouse. And he knew where that sort of talk led to. It was impossible to listen to old McFall blethering night after night about class conflict and trade unionism without becoming a bit shaky on things that had seemed straight-forward and unchangeable.

Not that the talk had ever amounted to much more than a

whisper here or a joke there. 'D'you hear the union's gonna put an extra ten bob in our envelopes?' Or, 'We're gonna march to the Customs House Steps with a flute band and yardsticks at the slope to demand a quid.' He couldn't remember who had said those things. Probably he had repeated some of them himself. It was just joking. None of the salesmen would touch a trade union with a barge pole. But he was glad about the notice. It broke up the morning's work a bit.

'Where have you been?' demanded Roden, at the top of the stairs.

'Sorry, Alec. I was reading the notice.'

'Don't tell me it takes you half an hour to read a couple of dozen words. If you were that keen there was one up here. Now go on up to your department and see if you can do anything to help McFall.'

The assistant had raised his voice so that Mr Whaley could overhear. He saw the buyer look at them through the glass partition, shrug his shoulders, and bend over his work again. As he climbed the stairs to the Trousers he glanced sullenly through the banisters. A copy of the notice was pinned to Mr Whaley's door. It's people like Roden, he thought, that turn fellas like me into trade unionists.

Fogarty was making up an order. 'Hear you had difficulty reading the big words in the notice, Minnis?'

'Ah, it was Roden shouting . . .' As he hung up his coat he said, 'Whose time are you supposed to read the thing in, anyway?'

'You didn't have to read it all. There were only six words that meant anything to you or anybody else—"in the present conditions of the Trade".'

'What d'you mean?'

'The trade's in a bad way, Minnis. Every big, cheap ready-made firm that opens in this city drives another nail into the coffin. There are merchant tailors sitting up in wee backstairs rooms that'll never mark another suit-length with french chalk. They're living on repairs and alterations.'

'So it doesn't matter about trade unions?'

'Trade unions are all right for them that have that sort of mind.' He tapped his double-breasted waistcoat. 'Me, I run my own union. I'm the president, seketary, treasurer and fully paid-up number one member of the Fogarty Solo Benefit Society. And the membership's *permanently* closed, Minnis boy. Now, get outa my road. You're keeping me back.' And Fogarty went clattering down the stairs.

'Did you read the notice?' he asked Bonar as he strolled towards him.

'I did.'

'What d'you make of it?'

'Nothing. I don't know what it means. I never heard of any meetings.'

'Ah, you don't understand—'

'Mebbe not. You can explain to me after. We've a gross of tweed knickers to get parcelled up by half-ten. Come on.'

4

He was to meet her at the corner of Majestic Street. It had been her suggestion and he had agreed willingly. He wouldn't have minded meeting her mother or even her brother Arthur at the house. But the thought of meeting Bonar when he called for her filled him with misgiving. They had talked too much about girls in the past. He couldn't start explaining that this time it was different. Then shortly after five o'clock Bonar came swinging round the banister-head.

'You and our Maureen going out tonight?'

'That's right.'

'Don't be waiting for me at half-five. I won't be walking up. '

'No?' He looked at his friend apprehensively.

'Whaley's just after telling me he wants me to work in. I'll go round to Joe Snax for a cuppa something.'

'Sure.'

'Hope you see a decent picture.'

Of course he should have known it would be like that. Good old Boney hadn't enough imagination to be embarrassed.

At the kitchen door he called 'Hello, I'm home!' went straight upstairs, washed his face, put on a clean collar, changed into his other suit. He had discovered that this saved a lot of preliminary explanation at the tea table.

As he ate his meal he knew his mother was looking intently at his appearance but he refused to raise his eyes. At last she said, 'Are you going out tonight?'

'That's right,' he replied with a bright, quick smile.

'It must be special.'

'Very,' and he smothered her mounting annoyance by adding, 'I'm going round to the McFalls.' He failed to mollify her.

'Do they never get tired of you?'

But he wasn't going to fight tonight. He reassured Freddie with a grin. He dived for the hall, grabbed his raincoat and let himself out. Rain had fallen and the pavements glinted like chrysoberyl under the lamps.

On his way to Majestic Street he bought a packet of chocolates and then wasn't sure what to do with them. It was pansy-looking to carry them in his hand and he was afraid that if he put them in his pocket they would melt. He took off his raincoat, shoved the box into the pocket, and slung the coat over his arm.

She was passing under the distant lamp at the bend in the street when he picked her out from among the shadowy figures hurrying home. A tightness grew around his heart as he watched her disappear in the intervening darkness and emerge again, her head-scarf and mackintosh glowing momentarily in each pavilion of lamplight. Her light, unhesitating footfall grew out of the murmur of the streets. He could imagine the delicate rise of her instep, the line of her ankle. To his young man's ear, listening in the darkness, her step betrayed her shapeliness.

She smiled, opening her eyes wide in amused surprise. 'It's raining,' she said. 'Didn't you know?'

'Oh,' he said, 'I never thought.' He struggled into his coat gazing at her until she smiled again and lowered her head.

There was a queue at the parterre entrance to the cinema, but the steps leading to the balcony were empty. He sighed in relief. Expense or no expense one problem had been solved for him.

'We mightn't have to stand long,' said Maureen.

'Stand?' He was so surprised that his astonishment was only partly simulated. 'But there's no queue.' And he indicated the balcony stairs.

'We don't need to go to the balcony, David. Downstairs is all right.'

He smiled at her, enamoured, and taking her firmly by the arm led her up to the balcony. They crept down the stepped aisle, fumbled their way into seats, and raised expectant faces. On the screen a man and woman flung themselves into each other's arms and clung together until they were submerged in a lightning and thunder of gauze drops, credits, and distorted orchestral sound.

'Pity,' said Maureen.

'Don't worry,' he said. 'They'll be back. It took them an hour'n a half to get there.' He laid the chocolates in her lap as the house lights came on. She smiled and wrinkled her nose in reproof. 'You shouldn't've, David.' She removed the cellophane discreetly, a shade too discreetly, perhaps. He hoped people could see the bright box on her knee.

When he innocently took the chocolate she offered she leaned her head very close to his and said, 'Should footballers eat chocolates?' He almost choked with delight. It was the most intimate thing she had ever said to him.

They watched the leaf-flat figures on the screen. Once or twice as he started to move with the story he came back with a start of realization as to where he was and whom he was with. As he dipped into the chocolates, very occasionally he stole a glance at her profile. Without taking her eyes from the screen she smiled, aware of his admiration. He laid the back of his hand against her wrist. She didn't draw away. Turning his hand he slid it into hers. She didn't repulse him. Her smooth, cool, slender fingers opened to knit lightly with his. Even when they ate a chocolate they used their free hands, clumsily, turning to laugh secretively and silently into each other's eyes.

The seats around them emptied in singles and pairs. The Union Jack fluttered behind the monarch's head. They unclasped hands, sighed, shook out their creased coats and stumbled up the aisle.

There were no shadowy corners at the top of Majestic Street. Even the fanlight above Haskin's side door was bright although it was long after closing time. And he wanted to kiss Maureen. He wanted to kiss her for his own joy and because a kiss was merited. It was the custom. She knew that and allowed him to draw her into his arms where darkness hung between the lamps. Fleetingly, she pressed her lips to his in response.

'Thanks for the picture and everything, David.'

'It was great. Will you come out again?'

'Yes, all right.'

They walked a few paces. She said, 'You needn't come any further. I'm nearly home.'

'Sometime soon—next week?'

'If you like.'

They stopped under a lamp, their eyes searching each other's face with tender curiosity.

'I must go now.'

Footsteps quickened behind David.

'Hiya! Just getting home?' It was Bonar. He was grinning to show how pleased he was to meet two people he liked on his way home.

He's decent, thought David with an inexplicable pang. Good all through. Nobody or nothing could make him do a bad thing.

'Where did you go?'

'The Imperial.'

'Any use?'

'Not bad. Henrik Fleming was in it. About a quarrel in one of those countries where they get gold—you know, kinda Indians—'

He heard the laughter in her voice. 'About a vendetta in Mexico.'

'That's it.'

Suddenly she was shy. 'Well, good-night, David. I'll tell Mother you're coming, Bonar.'

'Right after you,' called her brother. David watched her go, marvelling because she knew not to throw him a sly, secretive, parting smile. Everything she did was perfect.

'There's gonna be trouble in the place tomorrow—'

He brought his attention back to Bonar. 'Place—what happened?'

'Between half-five and when we got back to the stocktaking at six somebody had hung cards about a trade union meeting over the boss's notices.'

'Is that nonsense still going on?'

'Looks like it. We'll know all about it if we're in early in the morning. See you at the corner of Colinvista at quarter-to-nine?'

'See you there. 'Bye, Boney.'

Pity Boney had to be such a simple soul. But it had been a great night. He was proud of it. He seemed almost to have grown into a man in one evening. As he walked home he turned the coins in his pocket exploring idly with his nail for any left with milled edges.

The cards advertising the meeting were still there at 9.25 a.m. Mr Gallagher, who made the discovery, had left them hanging for the Chairman to see. This impressed everybody even more than the audacity of the person who had put them up. They might examine them for fingerprints. The Chairman arrived at 9.30 and the cards disappeared from the walls like snow off a ditch.

Mr Clarence called an inquiry immediately. Upstairs, Bonar, Connif, Fogarty and David peered over the rail of the well to watch the buyers and charge-hands tramp on each other's heels into the ground floor office. Mr Clarence did most of the talking. Occasionally he referred to Mr Ankatell, the secretary, standing demurely in the background. The Chairman, a shrunken, bearded figure, sat tapping the arms of the swivel chair, his eyes feeling over the worried, intent faces. The spokesman for the senior employees was Mr. Gallagher. They could see his head jerk in response to Mr Clarence or Mr Ankatell and on the one occasion that the Chairman asked a question. His cheek, ear and neck were crimson. The rest stood around filled with an impotent eagerness to say the right thing. The Chairman waved Mr

Clarence aside. He leant forward and spoke slowly and emphatically to the herd of men. When he had finished he spun his chair round to the desk. Mr Clarence nodded and the department heads streamed out like men sent on an errand.

'Scatter, boys,' said Fogarty. 'The bloodhounds is out!' He went skipping down the stairs with Connif.

'What d'you think will happen now?' asked David.

Bonar drew up his shoulders. 'Look for the fella that hung up the cards.'

'Could they prosecute him?'

'Why, what crime has he done?'

'They could sack him.'

'They could.'

That was enough. Throughout the warehouse the juniors kept their heads down and worked silently and urgently. Everybody knew, even the most shallow-brained assistant in the Mantles, even David, that there were thirty thousand workless in the city. It was the grey cloud behind their lives. Get thrown out into that aimless tide of men, women, boys and girls flooding every day to the Labour Exchange and seeping back to parks, cheap cinema seats, reading rooms and street corners, and God knows where you might be carried.

The investigation went on throughout the day without disturbing the work of the warehouse. Just a nod from a senior and 'The boss wants to see you in his office.' Alec Roden came bounding up the stairs and paused on the top step. He looked over David's head and seeing Bonar crooked his finger. 'You're to go on down to Mr Clarence.'

Without speaking, Bonar dragged on his jacket and hurried past them.

'Are they going to send for me?'

'Why, what have you done?'

'Nothing, Alec.'

'That's what I was thinking,' said Alec humorously and followed Bonar.

He went back to the rail not certain whether to be relieved or disappointed. Apparently they didn't think it worth while to ask him questions. It might have done them good to hear the protestations of one junior but loyal employee. Downstairs, Bonar tapped at the door and was called in. The Chairman didn't look up from the list on the desk. Mr Clarence asked a couple of questions, nodded, and Bonar was out again. He met him at the top of the stairs.

'All right?' he whispered.

Bonar went back to the counter he had been working on before he answered. 'In a kinda way.'

It was an unsatisfactory answer but he had a more pressing curiosity to satisfy. 'Why did they send for you?'

'Because I was here last night.'

His vanity was soothed. 'I forgot about that, Boney. What did they ask you?'

'They wanted to know did I see anybody interfering with the notices.'

'But you didn't?'

'That's what I said.'

He helped Bonar lift down a pile of tweeds. 'What d'you mean "in a kind of way"?'

'They asked me had I read what was on the trade union card. When I said I had, I saw the Chairman putting a tick against my name . . .'

'Well, what's wrong with that?'

'I knew then that whoever they're hunting has something to do with me.'

'Speak for yourself. The fellas here wouldn't be caught dead in a trade union. We all come from decent homes, Boney.'

'Aw, I don't give a damn about trade unions, either! It was the way the old fella gave a flick of the wrist as he marked my name. He was trying to frighten me.'

'Oh, you're a marked man,' he jeered.

Bonar laughed. 'Now you're trying it. Don't worry. I'll keep my nose clean till it's all over.'

It was over at five minutes past three. '*They've caught him!*' cried Fogarty skipping into the department. They crowded to the well and looked down. Mr Clarence and Ankatell were soldiering Adam Ramsay from the office. The packer looked no hero now as they urged him with discreet little pushes of their shoulders through the gaping customers. His face was white and stricken as he tried to expostulate with the two men who hurried him forward. He was unable to get his words out but his hands were eloquent to the watchers on the third floor. On one outstretched hand they saw the leather pad that saved his palm from the packing-needle.

So that's what happens to them when they run across the boss, David concluded. Recalling his last encounter with Ramsay, he felt a twinge of gratification. He turned with a smile to Bonar, then remained silent. He looked at Connif. Both were intent on the scene below. Something in their faces told him that what he was about to say wouldn't be well received. He looked beyond Connif to Fogarty sprawled on a counter at the rail. Fogarty, the wag, met his eye, glanced unresponsively at the tempting quirk of a smile he allowed to play at the corner of his mouth, and looked over the rail again. It seemed they didn't think Ramsay good value for a laugh.

Fogarty swung his feet to the ground and dusted the marks of his heels from the counter. 'I would have throwed the sawdust on the blood if they'd asked me nice,' he said. Bonar didn't turn round. Although the ground floor had returned to its normal comings and goings of customers and assistants, he still hung meditatively over the rail.

'Look at that would you,' he said.

They saw that the Chairman, his head resting in his hand, was still studying Mr Ankatell's list, sliding the blunt end of a pencil up and down the column of names.

5

As he told Bonar, his first evening at Glenbank Athletic's ground started with a cold look and ended with a cold shower. When he entered the ground Mr Mort and Mr McClenaghan were

outside the dressing-rooms door talking with a stout middle-aged man in a crombie and grey homburg. Two minutes passed before Mr McClenaghan recognized the newcomer, excused himself to the well-dressed character and came across. Over the manager's shoulder he saw the stout man examining him with an unsmiling gaze. His voice was loud and curt. 'Who's that?' he demanded.
'A fella called Minnis we picked up in the Park,' said Mort.

He was so angry that he barely answered the manager as he followed him to the office. His annoyance cooled as Mr McClenaghan laid a form before him on the table, and explained that this was a gentleman's agreement between them and no more. But as the manager put the paper into a file he added, 'It'll be a different matter, Minnis, if you make the grade here and like the club. Then we'll get down to some serious signing. Fair enough?'

'Yes, Mr McClenaghan.'

'You're in luck tonight. We've enough gathered together for a trial. So get turned out. Fred Mort, the man you met in the Park, is the trainer. I'll send him down to look after you. Good luck, Minnis.'

Fred Mort came down to look after him. After his reception at the gate he wasn't so ready to be charming to everybody. But he thought he could like Mort, especially when the trainer explained the stout man in the homburg. 'That's Dr George Boustead, a director, *the* director. Dr Boustead takes himself very seriously, so don't you make the mistake of not taking Dr Boustead the same way. Always listen to what he wants you to do out there. Say "Yes, Dr Boustead, I'll remember that," and then forget it as soon as you can if you don't want to rupture your bloody self. Them boots fit?'

Dr Boustead eyed him from head to foot as he trotted past but he had no instructions to give. You'll remember me again, thought David. But when he got onto the pitch he found himself pushed into the half-back line. His performance that evening didn't give Dr Boustead or anyone else cause to remember him.

For almost a month after that he trotted obediently round the track, practised flying starts, dribbled a ball in and out through a fence of stakes. He could have had more football with Hamiltons in the Haberdashers Alliance. It was all very well talking about starting at the bottom but he had to make money at this game sometime. And Mr Rankin's departure from Colinvista Street had brought that time much closer. Once again his mother was spending long evenings at the sewing-machine.

One evening he was changing beside Charlie Lennox. Everybody said Lennox had a big future as a goalkeeper. Earlier in the year he had been given a game in the Reserves, and then, apparently, everybody had forgotten about him.

'Charlie,' said David combing his hair after pulling on a sweater. 'Isn't it about time one or two of us were getting a move on at this game? Any use in speaking to McClenaghan?'

Charlie tightened a lace, stood up, and walked around the dressing-room, working his feet into his boots. The studs made the rhythmic rocking noise on the wooden floor that David loved. The tall, stringy lad paused beside David. 'There's only two things that'll remind Billy that you and me exist and that's Boustead or bad luck.'

'Bad luck?'

'—For somebody else.'

David shrugged peevishly. 'S'far as I'm concerned they mean the same thing.'

'Give you a tip,' said Lennox, resting his hand on the doorpost. 'Don't get sour. Keen as mustard—that's the idea. It doesn't get you anywhere but they like it. Are you coming out?'

'Aye, as a non-playing spectator,' he said gloomily.

But that evening Dr Boustead and bad-luck-for-somebody-else were conspiring for him. There was another trial game. The sides were made up from the third string, a handful of the Reserves and two or three fresh hopefuls. At a word from Dr Boustead, Fred Mort trotted on to the pitch. 'Hold it,' said Mort. 'They want to try Garland at centre-forward.' David leaned against the barrier to watch. Dr Boustead, McClenaghan and two other club officials were behind him. He watched the bewildered Garland being pushed forward. 'And now what?' shouted Mort. Dr Boustead stroked his chin broodingly. 'Push

Red-head into centre-half and young Caruth drops back to right-half.'

'Ah, for God's sake, Doctor!' muttered McClenaghan, and David at the barrier shared his derision.

'It'll work, Billy, it'll work,' said the doctor soothingly.

'And what about Collins?' shouted Mort indicating the discarded and disconsolate centre-forward.

'Bring him off.'

'That leaves you an outside-right short,' said McClenaghan acidly.

'It does, Billy, it does,' agreed Dr Boustead. 'And what are all these other characters that you and Mort have hanging around here—ludo players?'

He gripped the barrier in front of him. His desire to draw their attention was almost overwhelming, but his fear of a rebuff was stronger. He widened his shoulder blades to catch McClenaghan's eye. The silence was too long. He must be sorting out and selecting a player from the bunch on the running-track at the end of the ground. He heard Boustead say: 'Is there anybody you other fellows would like to see given a run?' Then McClenaghan called: 'Hi, you, Minnis! You're a wing, aren't you? Well, away and get that sweater off and—'

'Sure,' he said 'sure,' and raced for the dressing-rooms. As he hurried back he heard Dr Boustead say irritably, 'Who *is* that red-headed character, Billy?'

The game had started before he got on to the pitch. He fell into his natural position at outside-right. The ball ran sweetly for him and he made better use of it that evening. As they trooped off at the final whistle McClenaghan captured the ball and called him over. The manager tapped the ball to his feet. 'Let me see you working that for a bit,' he said. McClenaghan watched him as he took the ball round and round. 'Come here,' he said at last. 'You're using both feet?'

'Yes, Mr McClenaghan.'

'Bring it up the field again and watch me taking it off you.'

Three times McClenaghan robbed him of the ball.

'Now,' he said, 'drop the left toe, right toe and back again touch. Which is your good foot?'

He considered. 'Both, I think.'

'Is that so?' The manager gave a hoarse crow of amusement and David flushed.

'Which is your *best* foot?'

'The right, I s'pose.'

'Bring it up on the right, then.'

He dribbled the ball up to McClenaghan, tried to take it past him, and lost it. But at the second attempt he turned in towards McClenaghan's right drawing his opponent with him, swung back, and pushed the ball past with his own right foot. He was a good five yards away before the manager turned to call him back.

'That's it!' he said. 'It's still rough, but work on it. Remember your right's your natural foot. You're fast, Minnis, but you'll be faster. Now, away and change. Fred Mort should have a message for you.'

Fred Mort met him outside the dressing-rooms. He had the smile of a man who had been taken, momentarily, into the confidence of his betters and meant to make the most of it. 'Well, young Minnis—eh?' He caught him by the shoulder and shook him gently backwards and forwards. Politely David endured it for a moment then shrank away until he was free. 'Did I do all right, Mr Mort?'

Mr Mort laughed. 'You can guess for yourself when I tell you the news. I've got you a rig to play for the Reserves against Moycross on Saturday. Seniors are away at Derry, so you'll be here. Good luck!' He slapped him on the back, opened the door, and pushed him into the dressing-room.

He towelled himself jubilantly in a vapour laden with the smells that hot water draws from soap, tiles, zinc and fatigued muscles. Around him the naked bodies of the players glimmered and receded. Collins, already clothed, thrust his hostile face through the mist.

'Heard you had a bit o' luck, Minnis?'

'Well, yes . . . you could call it that . . .'

'How many matches have you played since you came up here?'

'Two—counting tonight.' His volatile irritability rose. 'Why?'

'And you on the Reserves already? It's great to have friends in court.'

He was about to protest when Lennox flicked him with a towel. The goalkeeper shook his head and pursed his lips. Silence. He didn't have to explain himself to people like Collins any more.

Discovering a pleasure in reticence he told no one about his success. Maureen would be pleased without quite understanding, Freddie shrilly excited, his mother unsympathetic. He let the days pass without telling Bonar.

But as he watched his friend's silly preoccupation with the dismissed man, Ramsay, he drew him back with news of his success. He had Bonar's interest immediately. The expression on his face showed that he most certainly realized the full weight and significance of the news. 'You forgot to tell me *that*! Don't tell me it slipped your mind?'

'Well, no . . . I didn't want to sound like bumming . . . there was a bit of luck in it . . .' He mumbled into silence before Bonar's delighted grin.

'Wait till I tell Roden!'

'No, no!' He was urgent now. 'It mightn't come off. There *was* a bit of luck in it. But you'll come up on Saturday and watch me, won't you?'

'You bet!' said Bonar heartily.

After a time nobody mentioned Adam Ramsay or trade unionism again. If any of the employees felt that they had suffered a setback it wasn't apparent. Nor did the management signal a victory. Mr Clarence, it was well known, had nothing in principle against trade unions. The important thing, as Mr Whaley pointed out referring to a memo in his hand, was that all the facts were in the possession of the directors, and they added up to the unavoidable conclusion that in the present state of business there was no room for trade union activity in Hamiltons. Downstairs, Mr Gallagher conveyed the same opinion to his underlings in fewer but more colourful words.

6

'You didn't tell me that you'd got a move up in the football team.'

'Move up—?' For a moment he thought of making fun of her small inaccuracy. Then in the reflection from the water he saw the shade of reproach on her face. He shook himself boyishly. 'I should've. But I didn't want to bore you. I didn't think you'd be interested.'

'Oh?' She swayed away from him in the dusk, her footsteps suddenly lost in the grass between the river and the path.

'Really, it doesn't matter anything to me.' The distance between them was wider than at any moment since he had first kissed her. He smiled gently at her unreasonableness, but in the darkness only sound or touch communicated.

'Anyway, who told you?' He halted for her answer. Below them a water-hen fissled in the reeds and launched a ripple that shook the stars burning on the surface of the water.

'Bonar.'

'Honestly, I didn't think you'd be interested. It isn't a move up in the team. I've been given a place in the Reserves. That's a team—'

'D'you think I don't know the difference between Firsts and Seconds and things? Don't I play hockey?'

'Dammit, I never thought of that! Of course you'd know. I'm sorry, I was dumb.' He slipped his hand under her arm.

'I'll be knocking at your door the day they stick me on the Senior side!' She tightened her arm on his hand, surprising him that she saw so much in his playful promise. He fell silent for a time.

They walked round one last curve of the towpath. The dark, lovely river slid past to its defilement under the sullen bridges of the city. In the blacker darkness of the alders he took her in his arms. Beneath her coat he felt the softness of her body, different from any other softness. They had almost quarrelled. They kissed in passionate innocence, forgiving and forgiven. He tried to draw her closer into himself but the hand on his shoulder, which he thought rested there by chance, resisted gently.

'One kiss?' he said drawing back aggrieved. 'Are they rationed?'

'No, only rare.' She kissed him, her mouth still shaped in laughter. Then she drew him onto the path. With their arms round each other they travelled slowly back towards the overhanging glow that washed the stars from the sky.

He sat on the edge of his bed tossing a coin from one hand to the other. Going with a girl was a serious thing. You had to give attention to what she thought. It wasn't nearly as simple as he had been led to believe. Oh, well, he thought, I suppose you learn how to do it as you grow into a man. The prospect, he realized with apprehension, gave him little pleasure. He put it out of his mind and fell asleep.

At noon on Saturday Bonar rubbed a peephole through the dust on one of the department windows and squinted at the sky above the opposite rooftops. 'It's gonna keep dry,' he announced. 'That's what a winger needs, dry turf.' He turned to his friend. 'If you make the grade, you'll mebbe win an Irish cap some day, Davie boy. Did you ever think of that?'

'Aw, Boney, away and have your head felt!' But he was pleased, though he wished his friend would make a little more of the first steps to fame. Today's match for instance.

'Must be great to be picked to do something for Ireland,' said Bonar dreamily. 'Like, I don't mean Ireland as *Ireland*. That's political. I mean to be picked outa two or three million people because you're good at something. Must be great.'

'Must be. You won't be late?'

'Catch me! I'll be at our corner two sharp.'

He felt queasy in the tram that took them to Glenbank. For the first time he realized clearly how much luck there had been in his selection for the Reserves. No one had thought him a world-beater after his first trial match. If Boustead hadn't started acting the big football brain he mightn't have got a second chance. They should've given him more time, shown him more tricks. Here he was, pitchforked in against Moycross, a side that hadn't been out of the top three in the Intermediate League for the past five years. He stared out of the window observing absently that the pavements were still slate-dry under the hurrying feet. That was something, anyway.

'How're you feeling?' asked Bonar at his shoulder.

'Rotten.'

'You'll be O.K.'

Inside the ground Bonar slapped him on the shoulder. 'I'll go and lose myself. Besta luck. I'll be watching you.'

He had been looking forward to an encouraging word from Fred Mort. The trainer wasn't in the dressing-rooms. 'Fred and Mr Warnock the chairman are away with the Seniors to Derry,' explained Garland, the centre-forward. 'Billy Thompson's in charge. He's been looking for you.'

Thompson, the assistant trainer, hurried in from the bath rooms. 'Hullo, Minnis. Nearly sending a search party out for you. Well, don't stand around, boy. Get stripped. Anything you want, gimme a shout.'

As his head came out of the collar of the red and black hooped shirt he saw Dr Boustead come in followed by Billy McClenaghan and a director in a bright Harris overcoat. The Doctor looked them over, and nodded to the captain, Brian Campbell.

'Nothing much to say to the boys, Brian. No reason why you shouldn't give Moycross a hot afternoon. Garland, don't forget you're up forward, now. Keep up there no matter what happens. This is more'n just another match for you. What else?' He looked around. 'You're Minnis?'

'Yes . . . Dr Boustead.'

'I'll take a load off your mind, Minnis. We're not expecting a lot. So don't start working the ball in by yourself. They say you're fast. Let's see it, *with the ball*. Just keep squaring it across to Messrs Garland, Douthart and Company Limited.' Those facing the doctor smiled, the others stared at the back of his head. 'There's the ref tooting on his flute. Off you go.'

As they started to move out to a rumble of studded feet Billy McClenaghan pushed his way vigorously through them. He spoke to Campbell and to Pony Douthart the inside-left. Then he turned back and faced David.

'Minnis, remember the advice Fred Mort gave you before the trial game?'

'Fred Mort . . .? No, I . . .'

'D'you remember what he told you to do when you were on the field!'

'Oh, that . . . yes, I remember.'

'Well, do it.'

'Sure, Mr McClenaghan.'

McClenaghan didn't return his smile. Behind them Dr Boustead watched them both.

As he trotted after the other players he shook his arms down to the tips of his fingers and threw out his legs loosely in front of him. It was hard not to get all tightened up inside when the manager thought it worth while to give him the tip that Garland wasn't the only player being watched. He ran his hands down his flanks. He had never worn a football rig like this. The shirt fitted, the shorts held him firmly across his lean, concave belly. Ever since his schooldays he had always travelled to a football match in his clumsiest shoes and thickest socks. When he had dropped them off and laced up his football boots his feet felt light and winged. It was a private ritual. He had never told anybody about it.

Two Glenbank excursion trains had pulled out for Derry earlier in the day, but there was still a dusting of supporters along the rail on the unreserved banking, and the lower tiers of the big stand were filled.

The captains met in the centre of the pitch. The falling coin twinkled in the air. The referee stared down at it and threw the ball to Garland of Glenbank. Brian Campbell trotted back to his position at left-half.

Not the first kick of the match, prayed David, with Dr Boustead and that lot staring down the back of my neck. The whistle sounded and the Glenbank outsides were streaming up the field, glancing over their shoulders, their speed checked by a taut string of expectancy. He lost sight of the ball and stretched his neck to glimpse it, his forward momentum whittled down to short dancing steps. Garland had turned it back to Campbell. The captain steadied the ball, moved aside from an aggressive shoulder and foot, glanced up to check his strategy and pushed the ball through and forward to Pony Douthart. Douthart picked it up as neatly as a greyhound lifting a rabbit. He had won three Scottish caps, and even now, a lean man in his late thirties, he was an organism of explosive shots and subtle glances. Away on the right wing, David gulped with fear. Something unexpected now, a cross-field shot from the veteran might reveal his clumsy feet, his inexperience. Douthart dragged the ball away from a half-back and passed it out to the left. It was misdirected and fell behind Peden at outside-left. David let a long breath escape. There's more than one of us can make mistakes, he thought.

The game hung at mid-field and then moved up into the Glenbank half. The Moycross half-backs, fast, aggressive, punched and rattled the opposing forwards. Douthart, for all his guile, was too slow, and Garland trotted ineffectively up and down, drawn by the tide of the play. Mulhern, David's inside man, bored his way through on one occasion and fed the ball out to his partner. David heard the cry from the stand, 'Right, Minnis, up and over! *Minnis!*' As he turned into his stride the ball and his feet were plucked from under him and he struck the turf on shoulder and cheek. The Glenbank men flung their arms wide demanding a free kick. The Moycross player who had robbed him was urging the ball deep into the Glenbank defence trailed by a deaf and blind referee. And through the shouts and counter-shouts David heard a cackle of laughter from the banking. There was a coppery taste of blood in his mouth. He wiped away the mud so harshly that his face burned.

In the Glenbank goal Lennox was brought to his knees as he pounced on a rocketing ball. He flung it away and it was sliced into touch. The attack swept back again and David saw Lennox arch his body and rise like a bird to palm a shot over the bar.

The corner kick curving inward again drew him high above the heads of defenders and attackers. He pulled the ball down and flung it in a great arc upfield. David raced forward, judging the dropping ball by watching the eyes of the opposing half-back. In a dart of acceleration he arrived with the ball, hooked it off his opponent's toe, feinted to go inward, moved in the opposite direction out and around, and pushed a long shot into the centre. Garland was up to trap the pass, balance himself, and shoot high and swirling for the angle of the posts. The Moycross goalkeeper leapt, grasped, dragged the ball down and booted it up the field. There had been poise, speed, precision in the duel. For a moment the game had come alight. A volley of handclaps greeted the cross, the shot, the save.

'Well, Doc, what d'you think of that?'

Dr Boustead shrugged in indifference and glanced at McClenaghan who was leaning forward eagerly. 'What's the name of the Moycross keeper, Billy?'

The manager scowled and sat back. 'Kid called Agnew. We're not interested. We're coming down with goalies.'

'Sure, Billy. I just asked.' Dr Boustead winked at his fellow-director.

The astute Campbell had noted Mulhern's break-through and the new winger's run. On the few occasions that the harassed Glenbank halves got the ball they now switched the flow of passes from Douthart and Peden to the right wing. The change in tactics stretched the opposing defence a little, gave them less time to think.

Mulhern thrust the ball far into the corner, too far, it seemed, to defence and spectators. A loping full-back felt his shoulder brushed by a flying red-and-black-hooped figure. Derision rose and died along the banking. That speed merchant *might* make it. As he fell he chipped it back off the dead-ball line into the penalty area. Pony Douthart trapped it under the flying body of the keeper and touched it into the floor of the goal. As the applause dropped to excited chatter the whistle sounded for half-time.

'Come on and have a drink, boys,' said Dr Boustead. Followed by the others he scrambled down into the gangway that led to the boardroom. The bottle and jug and glasses were set out on the table beside a portable radio. 'Let's hear the worst, Blackie,' said the doctor. The director in the bright tweed turned the knob. A voice, riding on a surf of many voices, rushed into the grille of the set . . .

' . . . back to Kilpatrick and out. Throw-in to Glenbank. Crilly to take it. Seven, no, six minutes to go to half-time and Glenbank down three goals to a Derry side that seems to be increasing the pressure all the time. Crilly out to Baillie, Baillie across to—oh, beautifully placed—Baillie to—'

The doctor leaned over and switched off. 'Three-nil! Six won't save them. Well, Billy, what d'you think of Garland?'

McClenaghan raised his glass and stared at it. 'Could do worse, Doc,' he said judiciously.

The doctor jerked his thumb at the radio. 'A hell of a lot worse, it seems. What d'you think, Blackie?'

'He would help. But we want more. We want a new forward line. What about Mulhern, too?'

Dr Boustead threw out his hand irritably. Apparently he had thought of that, too. 'One thing at a time. I asked you about Garland.'

'All right by me,' said Blackie, and busied himself slapping water into another whiskey.

'I'll mention it to Harry Warnock when he gets home from Derry tonight,' said the doctor, staring truculently at his companions in case one of them had the same idea.

'What about young Minnis, Doc?' said McClenaghan.

'Well, what about him, Billy. He has a pair of feet. All right. Has he any head?'

'I thought you'd seen enough to judge,' said McClenaghan mutinously.

'All I've seen so far was him landing on the back of it.'

This remark squeezed an incredulous grunt from Blackie. He caught the doctor's eye and said, 'If you want a word with the boys you'll have to hurry.'

David sat easing the laces of his boots and adjusting his

guards, Brian Campbell spoke to him. 'Sticking it all right, Davie?'

'Yes, thanks.'

'Think you could do it again?'

He ran his hand down his muddy thigh. 'Hope I won't have to,' he said ruefully.

Pony Douthard shuffled towards him through the players and ruffled his hair. An irritating trick but he accepted it as an accolade. 'Give us another, Davie,' said the old international. He grinned, and then watched Douthart as he chatted with other members of the team. He observed the long muscles under the mottled skin, the little web of wrinkles at the eyes. He looked what he was, a man who worked to keep in condition for physical effort that was growing too much for him. As he relaced his boot he wondered idly what was the answer to that problem. Become a team manager? Own a pub? Ah well, that problem was still light-years away.

Dr Boustead and Billy McClenaghan came in. Blackie stood in the doorway hugging the portable. The doctor looked about him. 'Everybody happy?'

Everybody said they were happy.

'Well, so are we. Heard what's happening to the Seniors?'

They said they had.

'Well, you boys can take a bit of the bad look off that story. Turn us in another half like the first.'

'Brian,' said the manager, 'keep swinging it out to *both* wings. It looks like paying.' He turned and followed the doctor and Blackie out of the dressing-room.

'Now, there's a profound thought,' said Bap Peden.

Campbell chuckled. 'With the doc's big lugs cocked in the doorway it's profounder than you think, Bap.' He raised his voice. 'Come on, lads, time we were upstairs.'

Moycross started boisterously as if they meant to sweep their opponents from the field. But they found themselves against an eager and stubborn defence. Campbell, with McClenaghan's eye on him, exhorted his backs to make intelligent use of their clearances. Fifteen minutes after the restart Kinnear pushed a pass through to Douthart. The forward jinked his way deep into the Moycross defence and parted with the ball to Peden who carried it a little farther and crossed it back over the penalty area. The speed deceived Garland but Mulhern was up to trap the ball and backheel it to Kinnear. The centre-half aimed his body for a long swing out to David, and as the defence tacked to the left, checked and rolled the ball once more in front of Garland's toe. There was the thump of leather striking leather. The Moycross keeper, spread-eagled on his belly, twisted his head to watch the ball drop from the back of the net.

'Gor,' said Blackie, turning from the tale of disaster that chattered from the portable on his knee. 'This looks like a football match. We ought to have our heads examined sending that other bunch to Derry.'

'We know what we're doing,' said Dr Boustead coldly. 'Don't you strain yourself watching one thing and listening to something else—Garland, me boy!' and he rubbed his hands ecstatically.

The Glenbank forwards, jubilant, skipped back for the restart. All but Pony Douthart. The inside-left shuffled along behind them, doubling himself over his folded hands, then straightening up to blow out a great breath. Campbell trotted towards him full of a captain's concern. The older man waved him away. 'It's nothing. Just my insides.'

The Moycross centre-forward sidled the ball to his inside-left. Mulhern moved back. The ball was forced across to the Moycross right-half. Douthart went after it, captured it, and stumbled to a standstill. The defence hesitated, then the right-half recovered and made a tentative rush. Douthart, falling stiffly, collapsed into his arms.

With head down and small bag swinging, Billy Thompson came scuttling from the shadow of the big stand. Douthart lay on his back, his mouth open, his eyes rolled up in his head like veined marbles. David was frightened. This might mean death. Thompson massaged the stricken man's chest and face. Pony's mouth closed, his eyes slid back into his face. A deeper tinge crept round his cheekbones. The trainer gave him a whiff of ammonia.

Douthart grimaced and struggled into a sitting position. 'All right, Pony?' asked Thompson.

'All right?' asked the referee.

Douthart looked up at him blankly. 'Give him a hand off,' said the referee. David, who was nearest, drew an arm of the sick man over his shoulder. Now that the possibility of death had receded he felt a thrill. A sense of his importance came welling back. He was helping off an international, a member of his own side. As he parted with Pony to Billy Thompson and a hanger-on he saw McClenaghan sidling hurriedly along the front tier towards the dressing-rooms.

The Glenbank forward line was reshaped and the game started again. A few aimless kicks and the ball spun into touch on David's wing. The linesman's flag flicked up smartly. After playing in the type of football where there was no linesman, or, at best, a boy in bicycle clips waving a grubby hanky, such organization pleased him. Almost more than playing before paying spectators it made the game a serious matter worth a footballer's best. This afternoon it helped to keep alive the vehement desire to see his opponents humbled that had been aroused when he had been knocked over so unceremoniously earlier in the game.

He knew now that he had the beating of the opposing half-back and full-back. Doing his own fetching and carrying with skill he fastened on the ball deep in the Glenbank half. He risked some intricate footwork in a run along the line. In his twinkling passage he beat one man more than was absolutely necessary. But it came off. Even before the pattern of his foray was apparent he heard the growing murmur of approval that greeted his sharp turn and sudden dangerous angle of flight towards the goal. He caught Garland in the corner of his eye moving up for the pass. Straightening out he shot for goal. There was no pith behind the drive. The Moycross keeper safely basketed the shot in his hands and chest.

As the ball winged over his head upfield he knew he should have passed to Garland. In the stand Dr Boustead was luridly expressing the same opinion. Brian Campbell trotted across. 'Nice to watch, Davie, but too much of the crochet-work.

Garland was standing clear.' As he spoke the final whistle sounded.

They were floundering out of the showers when the manager came in followed by Dr Boustead and Blackie. The three of them had the look of men who had switched off a heated argument on the other side of the door.

'Heard what happened to the Seniors?' said the doctor. 'Duffed seven–two. Makes it look like a cripples' outing.'

In the doorway, Blackie still cradled his portable. 'But not you boys!' he called over the murmur. 'You boys put a bit of jam on Glenbank's bread. Nice to watch. How's Douthart?'

'All right, Mr Blackie,' said Billy Thompson. 'Just a passing twinge.'

Dr Boustead grunted. 'Old age's no passing twinge, is it, Pony?'

Douthart, sitting with his legs up on a bench, grinned palely.

The doctor looked around the dressing-room. 'You,' he pointed at David, 'come here.' With a gold-ringed knuckle he tapped him playfully on the cheek. 'I'm cross with you. You didn't do what you were told—'

McClenaghan insinuated himself. 'Ah, now, Doc, he made a goal for Pony—'

'All right he made a goal. If he had pushed that last one across he could have made it two. If you throw away chances like that, young man, you won't make a goal—or anything else.'

He had thought over that tap on the cheek with the gold ring and decided he didn't like it. Unsmiling, he watched the doctor leave the dressing-room. Then he remembered about Bonar waiting outside and hurried into his clothes. As he pulled on a shoe he felt something hard under his foot. He withdrew the impediment. It was a pound note wrapped around ten shillings in silver.

He sidled over to Pony Douthart. 'Look what I found. Where did it come from?'

The man glanced at his cupped hand. 'I wouldna worry overmuch about where it come from. Stick it in your pooch and forget about it. Or can a young buck like you forget thirty bob?'

He laughed as he thrust the money deep into his pocket.

'Not on your life, Pony, but I get the idea.' He grabbed his raincoat, then hesitated. 'Are you all right?'

'I'm all right. Billy Mac's taking me home in his car.' He looked David over appraisingly. 'You've the right idea, laddie. Look after yourself.'

In the twenty minutes that had passed since the final whistle Bonar's excitement had cooled somewhat, but he threw his arm around David's shoulders when his friend appeared.

'It was class stuff, Davie—real class!' He looked at him with admiration and affection. 'You have it in you, boy. There's not a doubt!'

'Thanks, Boney—thanks. 'Course the ball ran my way—'

'Ah, how are ye? You had to hunt for it!' With their hands on each other's shoulders they left the ground and walked to the tram stop.

From a window-seat he looked down on the hungry, homing crowds and listened absently as Bonar recalled incidents in the game, the pattern of the play, crises that David's speed had brought about in the Moycross defence. Bonar was a discriminating spectator and if David had listened intently he might have built up a complete picture of the match. But he was fingering the thirty shillings in his pocket, uncertain whether he should tell Bonar about it. He felt that his mother should be the first to know what had happened to him this afternoon, and, after her, Maureen. He let the money slip to the bottom of his pocket.

A crowd of youths with football gear in bags and parcels were waiting at the stop on the Albert Bridge. As the tram approached they shouted and waved to their team mates streaming round the corner from Ravenhill Road. Bonar leaned across David and looked down. 'Been up playing at the Park.' The footballers came clattering up the stairs. Bonar watched them as they threw themselves noisily into their seats. David turned away to look down at the light-flecked river running in full tide under the bridge.

'Seems years ago since you played up there, doesn't it?' said Bonar.

Yes, he agreed, it did. To him it seemed part of a past as

misty as the pitches along the embankment. 'How are Hamiltons doing?' he asked.

Bonar looked at him and laughed. 'You'd think you didn't work there! No better'n usual—three from the bottom. They miss you.'

'Ach, I was only one man . . .'

'There's another reason,' said Boney.

'Oh?' He turned sharply from the window. 'What's that?'

'Some of the fellas chucked it in after the firm slapped down on the trade union organizing—'

'For God's sake, Boney!' His voice was sharp with exasperation. 'What's that got to do with a game of football!'

'Some of the fellas say they're not gonna support anything to do with the firm outside working hours—'

'If I remember rightly, the firm had very little to do with the team.'

'It carries the firm's name.'

He grunted in derision and peered out of the window. 'What's holding up this tram?'

'Mebbe they're changing conductors.' Bonar sat silent for a moment, then, 'There's a union recruiting meeting on Friday night. I'm going.'

'Why?'

'It's a question of solidarity—'

' "Solidarity"? When your father talks like that you laugh at him!'

'That's right. He only talks. I *do*. Well, what do you say—are you going?'

'I am not. Why should I?'

' 'Cos I'm going.'

He closed his lips swiftly on the retort he was about to make, turned and looked at his friend. Bonar met his gaze steadily, calmly. There was to be no further appeal to his loyalty. He wriggled angrily in his seat. 'We'll never get home at this rate!' They watched the mild horse-play among the lads in the front seats.

'Well, Davie, what about it?'

'I think you're daft!'

'But you'll go to the meeting?'

He stared sullenly before him. 'O.K.—I'll go.'

Bonar punched him softly on the arm. Downstairs, the new conductor sprang lightly on to the platform, shook his money-bag, grinned genially at the angry faces peering at him from the lower compartment and pinged the motorman's bell.

7

'You mean they've real baths in a football field?' She leaned on the table looking down at him with incredulous amusement.

'Not in the field, mother, in the dressing-rooms under the big stand. There's a boardroom and an office and all.'

She picked up some soiled dishes and turned away with a chuckle. Notwithstanding Freddie's eager and exhaustive explanations, her elder son's move from one football team to another had meant nothing to her. But now that he had arrived home soaped and combed instead of tousled and muddy, it dawned on her that this new place where he kicked a football was much more important and better got-up than she would have thought possible.

She poured a fresh cup of tea and sat down. 'And where does the money come from for all these faldilals?'

'From the crowds that come to see us playing football.' He glanced sidelong to see how she took the identification of himself with this dubious affair.

'And the footballers get money, too,' said Freddie impatiently. 'Sure, I told you that about a billion times.'

'Don't be rude,' she said.

It was his chance. He took the pound note from his pocket and spread it on the table before her.

'What's this?'

'A pound note.'

'I can see that. Where did it come from?'

'I got it playing football.'

With her eyes fixed on the money she drew her hands away from it until they hung loosely from the wrists in mid-air. He felt his anger rise at the theatrical posture.

'It's for you,' he said harshly.

The irritation in his voice warned her. She picked up the note, finding it hard to smile in thanks, for the first sign of his temper unfailingly roused her own. 'I don't know, David. It seems an awful lot . . .'

'Ah, don't worry. There's plenty more where that came from.'

'Gee!' shouted Freddie. 'You're a pro!'

She stood up, the hand clutching the note under her apron. 'I hope not,' she said. 'I hope you haven't done anything so silly or sinful.'

'And what would you call silly or sinful?'

'Selling yourself to these football people. I've told you what I think about them—'

'You know nothing about them, Mother.'

'I know they're a class of men that squander all their days kicking a ball or tempting others to do it. Do they think the world can afford the burden of men that just live to sport themselves?'

'There's nothing wrong with them—'

'Where were they reared? Did they never hear it said that in the sweat of thy face shalt thou eat bread? Don't they know the words of St Paul "Study to show thyself approved unto God, a workman that needeth not be ashamed—" '

'Ach, that stuff—'

'You've no room to sneer at the wisdom that guided your father and men better than you'll ever be—' By comparing him with his father she knew she was reviving a gibe that had dropped from their disputes. He whitened and got up from his chair.

'How could you ever know what I'll be?'

'I can only judge on what I see now!'

'If I took from now to Doomsday to explain to you what I hope to be you still wouldn't understand.'

'You tell me nothing! I don't know how much money you get at your work—'

'You ought to—you get most of it!'

'I don't know how you're spending your time at nights. Are you running after girls?'

' 'Course you don't know if I've got a girl. Say I had, would you ever ask me to bring her here? You don't know anything about my life. All that worries you is you don't know how much I'm getting—'

'Is it too much to ask you to pay something towards the up-keep of this house?'

'What do I care about this cursed house!'

'David—!'

'I spend my life skulking about without a penny in my pocket. I've nothing, nothing, nothing!' He struck the table with his fist, and Freddie burst into tears. Silenced, they looked at the child. The malignity and passion of their dispute had carried them far beyond its source.

'Don't fight,' the boy whimpered, 'don't fight. I don't like it—'

It was impossible now for him to spend the evening at home. Even in his own room he would hear the small preparations his brother made on his way to bed. Usually, he fooled about with the kid in the bathroom or talked over the day's school and street adventures until she came up to send one to bed and the other downstairs. Now he would have to sit in a guilty silence behind a closed door. Without speaking he hurried from the house.

At nine o'clock he was to meet Maureen at the railway station as she came up from a hockey game with some country crowd. That left two hours to kill. He wandered listlessly from one small shop window to the next, his mother's face growing between him and every tawdry object. Curtains of light dropping from street standards and swinging car lamps flooded and melted on the precipitous, broken horizon around him. In all this tumble of facades and gables, these offices, houses, factories, churches, halls, cinemas, not one person to whom he could turn. Among his friends, not one to whom he could go and talk about his own unhappiness, the unhappiness in his home. He wondered where Mr Rankin was at this very minute. He could have talked it over with Mr Rankin. He took his hands from his pockets and quickened his step.

At the City Hall he bought an *Ireland's Saturday Night* and glimpsed through the football results. 'Glenbank swamped at Derry,' he read. He shook out the page with a chuckle. Hold on, he said, just hold on, I'm coming! He hunted among the junior reports. Ah, there it was! 'Moycross surprised . . . former Scottish international carried off . . . Gorman . . . Lennox . . . for this the Reserves have to thank their right wing of Mulhern a forceful inside and Minnis a newcomer.' He read the last sentence three times. Shove that in your stethoscope and smoke it, me bould Dr Boustead! He folded the paper, slapped it delightedly against his knee and put it in his pocket.

He drifted with the evening crowds along Donegall Place, down Castle Lane, across Cornmarket. Between a windowful of yellow shoes and a delicatessen display he stopped to read the menu outside a cafe. Already, in his small experience of eating out at other places, he knew that the portions were usually meagre, tepid, and not very well cooked. But a line of print at the bottom of the card caught his eye. 'This café is open on Sundays.' The Glenbank money burned in his pocket. He decided that he would take Maureen to tea in a restaurant when they met tomorrow. He looked at one of the many clocks that stared down impassively on the babbling streets and hurried away.

The long train, trailing darkness from the fields it had crossed, slid into the station. There was a scattered volley of carriage doors closing, an outpouring of scarfed and muffled passengers. Two or three of her companions were carried off by young men who had been waiting at the ticket barrier. He shouldn't have been lurking in the background. As he hurried forward he saw her pause and look around for him, inattentive to the farewells of her friends. The smile that dawned on her face told him that she too had hurried the train to its destination. He took the hockey bag into his care, as he had seen the others do, slid his fingers under her arm, and they strolled out to the street, pretending an unawareness of everyone else in the crowded draughty station.

She told him about the game, the massive tea that the home side had given them in the old country hotel, the steamy railway carriages. He was gratified when she remembered to ask him about the football match. He showed her the newspaper report. Seeing his name in print impressed her more than he had hoped. At the corner of Majestic Street he asked her to have tea downtown when they met the following afternoon.

She looked at him in surprise. 'On Sunday? Everywhere's shut up—'

'Oh, no, it's not. I know a place.'

'But won't it cost a lot of money?'

'It's a celebration. I've got my name in the paper, haven't I?'

'All right—a celebration! Thanks, David.'

The living-room would be empty when he got home. Freddie would be in bed, his mother in her workroom. Since Mr Rankin's departure she had spent more and more of her evenings there. As he let himself cautiously into the house he heard the throb of the sewing-machine. He went into the scullery and buttered himself a round of bread to take to his room. At the top of the first flight of stairs he saw the pencil of light under her door. He paused for a moment and then crept up to the next flight. Freddie's door was open. He looked in, and the boy stirred in bed. The floor was checkered with light from the street lamp outside.

'Are you never sleeping yet?'

'No.' The boy's voice was sulky.

He sat down on the bed. 'That was a row you made after tea!' There was no reply. 'Frightened me.' The shadowy head stirred on the pillow. 'Did it?'

'Almost out of my pants.'

As he had hoped he coaxed a giggle from the boy in bed.

'Going to Sunday School in the morning?'

' 'A course I am!'

'Sssh! Like me to walk down with you?'

Freddie sat up. 'Would you—would you walk down with me, David?'

'Sure. Freddie, that pound note wasn't all the money I got at the football match.'

There was a pause. 'Wasn't it?' The face was turned into the pillow again.

'No, look.' He took out a half-crown and dipped his hand until the light shone on the coin. 'Know what that is?'

'It's a half-dollar.'

'That's right. Take it. It's for you.'

Freddie, his wide eyes fixed on his brother's face, fumbled for the coin. 'For me?' he whispered.

'That's right. But not a word.'

The boy flung the fist grasping the coin round his brother's neck. He pressed his lips to his cheek. 'Thanks, Davie!' he said.

He felt his throat fill. Gently he disengaged himself. 'Right. G'night, old son,' he whispered, and tiptoed from the room.

8

SEVERAL times during the midday meal their eyes met, but there was no hostility in her look, only a quiet thoughtfulness that stilled his restlessness. As the meal ended he said, 'I won't be in to tea.'

'Oh?' She paused. 'What time are you going out at?'

'About three.'

'But you'll get something to eat?'

'Oh, sure. I'll be all right.'

He softened when he saw that she wanted to say more and didn't quite know how to put it.

'You wouldn't like to bring your friend—your friends here for tea? You could have it in the front room—'

'No, thank you, mother.' He looked up with a smile. 'It's kinda fixed.'

He was about to say that he had a girl; she was about to say that he was always welcome to bring his friend to the house . . . the front room was vacant now. Neither spoke. She took the soiled dishes to the scullery. He went upstairs to lie on his bed and read the paper until it was time to go out.

They decided on a walk in the Botanic Gardens before going downtown. The sun dropping behind the Castlereagh Hills glittered on the pastel coats of the women, the starched collars of the respectable young men, the diamanté ornament in Maureen's fur collar. There was a tingle in the air that pierced their hands and turned their laughter to smoke. At the entrance to the new rose garden he caught her hand and they fled under the rustic arches, past the children and the dogs, past the gaping park attendant fumbling in his memory for a by-law that restrained young men and pretty girls from running in the winter sunlight, past the rude young men hooting at them from the shelter by the bandstand.

They halted at the top of a flight of shallow steps, breathless with laughter. 'You're mad!' she said. She had drawn her collar around her glowing face. 'You're lovely!' he said, and leaning forward kissed her quickly on the lips. Aware of a dozen eyes staring reproachfully at their youth and gaiety they linked arms and hurried from the Gardens.

The menu, he knew, should be proffered first to Maureen. He drew it from among the sauce bottles and handed it to her. She waved aside his tentative suggestions of the dishes at the top of the list, steaks, pork chops, even the fish. At the two-shillings section she said, 'This is us!' and chose sardines on toast.

'Surely you could go in for something fancier than that?' he expostulated.

'I love sardines,' she assured him. 'But you have something else—'

'No, we'll keep it simple.' He glanced at the brush-haired waiter leaning against the wall. 'That fella looks easily confused.'

They were silent as the waiter arranged the table, leaned forward to exchange guarded remarks when he left with the order, fell silent again as he ambled up with the bread, the butter, the hot dishes, the coffee. At last they were left alone.

He happened to look at her as she lifted the pot to pour the coffee. To his surprise she was blushing and when she handed him his cup, her eyes, soft and shy, avoided his. He tried to recall, unavailingly, what he might have said to affect her so much. After a few moments he gave up the effort.

They drank their coffee slowly, drawing for entertainment on the small incidents of the past week or confiding in each other the problems and perplexities that might be expected in the next week. Their conversation was made up of trivialities. To talk together, intimately and without interruption, over a table that was theirs for an hour, that was the satisfying and delightful thing. He didn't say anything about the dispute he had had with his mother. Somehow, a quarrel at home was much too big a thing to impose, as yet, on their relationship.

At times they fell silent and watched the family groups come and go, the solitary men munching gloomily through their food, the couples that perplexed Maureen by having nothing to say to each other. As each customer got up from the table David watched intently to see what the waiter picked up and slipped into his shiny waistcoat pocket.

The empty cups grew cold in their fingers. He flipped sixpence under his saucer, helped Maureen with her coat, caught the waiter's eye and called for the bill. The evening air in the streets was cool and fresh and they walked home to prolong their enjoyment in being together. I don't want to hurry through these moments, he thought. I'm with my girl and I'm not anxious and uncertain about how I feel towards her. I was a success yesterday. My mother is more or less happy again. Tomorrow would probably bring the usual amount of trouble at Hamiltons. But at this moment, he reminded himself, smiling to her in response, I am happy.

9

YESTERDAY evening, as they parted at the corner, Bonar had said: 'See you here at twenty to nine tomorra morning? We'll walk down together.' He had agreed. But, somehow, he just couldn't get out of the house this morning. Couldn't find the tie he wanted, couldn't get the mud off his heels, couldn't be expected to bolt his breakfast just to walk down with Boney McFall. Not that he minded walking down alone. Ever since Saturday he hadn't felt the need of Boney so much. Things had changed. For one thing, he had lifted himself out of a rut by his football laces. Those were Boney's own words. Fair's fair. Bonar Law McFall got an awful lot of joy out of other people's good luck. He never salted his praise with malice, even if, at times, that square, shining face of his made him look a bit of an eejit. But he was ruthless in his interpretation of what it meant to be friends. And this morning he knew that Boney had wanted to blether to him about the daft trade union meeting. So he didn't mind walking down alone. In fact, he liked it better that way.

The streets looked as drab as they did on any other winter morning. He knew at what corners the wind from the snow-covered hills swirled and plucked and where it thrust as inexorably as a shaft of cold metal, and he clutched his hat and poised his body accordingly. Most mornings this journey from home to work was like exercise in a prison yard. He had got that idea from old McFall. A row with Roden and next morning he would glance up between the tall linen-houses noting with gloomy relish the little tent of blue (or grey) that wage-slaves call the sky. But since Saturday all that nonsense was past. When he stepped out of the house now in the mornings he was a footballer good enough to get his name in the papers. The unsmiling faces intent on beating the first stroke of the hour failed to depress him. As he slid and side-stepped through the crowd he pushed his hat over one ear and looked the pretty girls straight in the eye. He was no small apples, now.

Upstairs, Roden watched his leisurely arrival with growing irritation. When David had clocked in, the assistant leaned over the rail and in a voice that brought all work within earshot to a temporary halt urged him to put an inch to his stride.

'You're late!'

'Only three minutes, Alec—'

'That's still late. Everybody's looking for you. Mr Whaley had to send McFall out round the warehouses. Now, get down to the packing room and see if you can find a skep of Bedford cords that should've arrived. Go on, there's half a dozen orders waiting.'

'Let me get my coat off—'

'And don't spend half the day combing your hair.' Roden waited expectantly for the insolent retort and when it didn't come grunted and went clattering down the stairs.

He laid out the contents of the skep in neat piles and watched them being up-ended by Mr Whaley, Roden, Fogarty, even by Connif, as they hunted through them for sizes. But he didn't mind. He was much more concerned with Bonar's whereabouts. Perhaps the errand that his friend had been sent might keep him out among the warehouses all day. Then, tomorrow, when they met, he could plead that he didn't know where the meeting was to have been held.

But Bonar was back after lunch. David heard his voice in Mr Whaley's office then his foot on the stair. He eyed him reproachfully as he swung round the banister-head.

'What happened to you? I was there before the quarter-to. Couldn't you have waited on me?'

Bonar stared at him open-mouthed, then his face cleared. 'Oh, that! Ah, forget it—' He glanced around to make sure they were alone. 'About the meeting. It's at eight in the Spinners Hall in Serbia Street. O.K?'

'Oh, sure.' He made one final effort to extricate himself. 'Look, Boney, I'm with you all the way in this—but what use can I be? I know nothing about trade unions—'

'Don't worry, Davie boy. You'll hear all about it tonight. All we want is just for you to fill a chair. Solidarity, d'you see?'

He sighed inwardly. 'Yeh. Who else is going?'

Bonar eyed him, and then smiled. 'Davie, I'm the only one that knows *you're* going. If you're there you'll see who turns up. Fair enough?'

'Oh—sure. I only asked.'

'You can find your own way to the hall. I've to go there early to put handbills on the seats.'

It was too much. He beat his clenched fists against his forehead. 'Jasus, Boney, not *handbills*!' And Bonar laughed uproariously and slapped him on the shoulder. Then he sobered. 'Not a squeak out of you, Davie boy. Come on, let's get these cords priced and packed away.'

While he had the warm, stolid personality of his friend beside him the meeting seemed to promise, at worst, just another dull evening. It was pay-day, he would have a few shillings in his pocket, they could have gone to the pictures. But he had a date tomorrow night with Maureen. And another game for the Reserves. If it gave old Boney any joy he supposed he could stand one night's boredom.

About four o'clock Bonar was called downstairs by Mr Whaley. He had to go round the warehouses again. 'You'd better push on and finish the job yourself. I mightn't get back before closing time. Be seeing you.'

It was when Bonar had gone that David began to feel uneasy. He couldn't understand why. He knew he was being silly. He had anticipated every eventuality of the evening. You go to the meeting and you sit at the back. All right. You're as bored as hell but Solidarity's your middle name. You've done your bit. And you don't go back again, ever, even if he goes down on his knees. That's all. But if that's all why won't Boney say who else is going? His uneasiness turned to fear and a growing anger. Jumping up, he strode to the window and stood chewing his pencil. Why pick on me? Does he think I'm gonna get all sweaty and mebbe throw away my job fighting the bosses for another couple of bob a week? With contempt he looked at the neat, brushed pillars of tweed, serge, cord, mole, flannel. Shoddy sacks for fat guts piled from floor to ceiling, window to wall. Dumb dead walls. Slowly he drew the pencil from his lips. Come to think of it, why does McFall knowing what he does know think that my future lies in this dump? Why does he pick on me!

He sped across the department and down the stairs. Roden wasn't in sight. Connif, just finished with a customer, was refolding raincoats. At the far end of the counter, Tits Fogarty, gabbling away, was rattling a soft small boy into a stiff tweed suit, anxiously watched by a woman and three other boys of various sizes who were temporarily encased in the same material.

'Connif—' He paused. 'Connif, are you seeing Boney McFall tonight?' Feeling he was being imprudent and yet unable to resist showing that he too might be recognized by the initiated, he added, ' 'Course, don't answer if you don't want to . . .'

Connif didn't. Nothing for five seconds but that hard expressionless stare that might or might not be stupidity. David bit his lip. 'Aw, go to hell,' he muttered. As he moved away he felt the other's stare between his shoulder blades.

Fogarty leaned against the counter and watched appreciatively while the woman grasped a fistful of the new tweed jacket and shook the small boy unmercifully. She raised a harassed face. 'Like, I know he's got to get three years out of it, but . . .'

'Missis,' said Fogarty confidently, 'that suit may look big on him at the moment but when it gets the heat of his body it'll settle down on him like a glove, at the same time allowing ample room for the development of his sturdy young limbs in the years to come.'

'And you said it was good stuff,' the woman reminded him suspiciously.

Fogarty gave her a patient smile. 'Missis, them suits are all wool but the buttons.' He looked round, and with an exaggerated gesture recognized David. 'Ah, boy! Mr Whaley send you along to clear up?' He waved a hand at the tumbled heap of jackets, vests and shorts behind him. 'You can start on that lot right away.'

David leaned across the counter. 'Tits—' he whispered desperately.

'All right,' said the woman with dragging reluctance, 'I'll take that one, too.'

The four small boys, shot out of their jackets by Fogarty as neatly as if he were shelling peas, struggled back into their old garments with tearful joy. Fogarty gathered the purchases under his arm and prepared to move away.

'Tits—'

Fogarty stopped and gave him an ear. 'Well?'

'I'd like to see you for a minute.'

'Well, take a good look at me and then bugger off. I'm busy.'

'Aw, Tits—'

'What is it? Is it important?'

'Yes.'

Fogarty looked at him suspiciously. 'All right. Clear the place up a bit and I'll be back when I get rid of this litter.'

As he languidly assembled a suit or two he began to regret his panic and flight. Connif had given him the brush-off. All he could expect from Fogarty was a lot of old man's talk about looking after Number One. That he had thought of discussing Bonar with them filled him now with a sense of shame. He tiptoed down the long floor and took the stairs two at a time, hoping that Fogarty, who was loading the woman with a great cushion of a parcel, had forgotten him. But as he got down beside his unfinished work he heard the familiar tap of the patent-leather shoes.

'I see you near killed yourself clearing away for me.'

'I couldn't stay out of my department any longer, Tits.'

'And what was so important to bring you out of it, a coupla minutes ago?'

He scratched intently at a stain on his cuff. 'Aw, it was nothing—really—'

'You mean I came trailing up here for nothing?'

'Sorry, Tits.'

'You're a hell of a wag. I've a good mind to give you a toe in the backside.'

David rose lightly from his knees. 'And who's stopping you?' But Fogarty had discovered that there was no profit in trying to rough-house young Minnis. He was hard to catch and harder to hold. He framed a silent obscenity with his lips and trotted away. David chuckled. He felt he had struck a blow already for loyalty, for solidarity.

The mood stayed with him all the way home. He was almost looking forward to eight o'clock and the Spinners Hall. Not that he gave a damn about the meeting but it would be interesting to hear how they were going to make types like the Chairman jump through a hoop. And it would show Bonar how wrong he had been to doubt him.

The door of his house lay open. That was unusual. He called, 'Hullo, there!' but there was no reply. At this time of the evening his mother should be in the kitchen making the tea. Freddie should be at the table scampering through his homework before his books were pushed aside by the tea things. The kitchen and the living-room were empty. He felt the kettle. It was warm but the gas had been turned off. He shouted up the stairs. No reply. 'Like the bleeding Marie Celeste,' he muttered, beginning to feel uneasy. He pulled the front door open again and dodged a poke on the nose from Mrs Moore of No. 9 who was staring down the street while she fumbled for the knocker. She peered at him in the gloom.

'Davie, is that you? Your ma's away down to poor Mrs Emmet's—'

'What's she doing there?'

'It's terrible, Davie. Mr Emmet drowned himself in the river. Your ma's away down to see if there's anything she can do. Like, the Emmets are Church of Ireland, but when anything happens everybody sends—'

'Yes, Mrs Moore.'

'Would you like to come into our house and have a cuppa tea till she gets back?'

'No, thanks, Mrs Moore. Where's Freddie?'

'He followed your ma.'

A handful of people had collected across the street from the

Emmets' door. They drifted up and down the pavement as if to exonerate themselves from the charge of gathering there out of heartless curiosity. Two of them crossed the roadway and without pausing returned to the others. Gloating over the drops of river water on the pavement, he decided. 'Well, thanks again, Mrs Moore,' he said, and went indoors.

He turned on all the ground floor lights and put a match to the gas under the kettle. Freddie's books were scattered over the table. He pushed them aside and started to lay the three places. But he didn't know whether she was going to give them a knife-and-fork tea or maybe cheese and jam . . . Somehow, he didn't care about tea, now. That grey, dumb river must be icy tonight. He dropped the handful of cutlery on the table, and sat down at the fire.

. . . A dark thin-faced man who walked very quickly . . . raised that bowler hat of his right off his head when he met a woman, didn't just flick the brim like the other men . . . and he spoke nicely . . . the old ones said he gave the street a bit of tone . . . like the class of people who lived here before the Kaiser War . . . that is, when you heard his voice . . . mebbe that shyness and quick walk was a sign of being a bit cracked . . . wonder what the three kids'll do . . . the verdict was always of 'unsound mind' . . . wonder what would happen if one of them came back and told the coroner he was a liar . . . like a Marx Brothers film or something . . . the oldest one is going to be a lovely looking bit in a year or two . . . she'll have to go out and find a job . . . in this case the verdict would be dead right. You didn't knock yourself off just because you were out of work . . . things couldn't get as tough as that . . .?

His mother came in followed by Freddie. She was flushed and a little breathless. 'I'm sorry, son. I'm sure you're starving—'

'Ah, that's all right.' He followed her into the kitchen. 'I didn't know what we were going to have or I mighta had something started.'

She turned, smiling in protest against the small distress of her breathlessness. 'It won't take me a minute.'

'You shouldn't take so much out of yourself, mother.'

Peeling bacon slices apart she said, 'You heard?'

'Yes, Old Moore's Almanack said he drowned himself. Is that true?'

'I'm afraid so, David. Mrs Emmet sent up for me, of course.'

Of course. Mrs Shrubsole or no Mrs Shrubsole, *she* was still the pastor's wife to Colinvista Street. 'Is he . . . down there now?'

'Oh, no, the police have inquiries to make.'

'He's in the morgue,' said Freddie.

She thrust some plates into the boy's hand. 'And you take up the salt and pepper, David.'

As Freddie arranged the plates he looked up wide-eyed at his brother and whispered, 'He wus floating upside-down.'

In a spasm of frightened anger David drew back his hand to hit him. 'Shut up! It's not funny!'

Freddie's lip dropped. 'I didn't say it was funny, Mammy!' he shouted, protesting.

She looked through the doorway at them, her hand to her head. 'I know, son, but don't talk about it. D'you think we could have a little quiet? I don't feel very grand.'

They ate in silence for a time, then he said, 'Have you to go down again?'

'No, Mrs Emmet's mother had arrived before I came away. And we sent a wire to his brother in Ballinasloe. Where's that?'

'Dunno. Somewhere in the south.'

'Yes, he had that sort of voice.'

'What d'you think they'll do now?'

She drew her shoulders up in mournful speculation. 'Dear knows. The girl'll have to look for a job. Maybe Mrs Emmet could get some making-up work from the factory.'

Circumspectly he said, 'Poor man . . .'

'I'm thinking of his family. It was a terrible thing . . . doing that . . . losing hope.'

'Mebbe he wasn't to blame. They say people who do that aren't right—I mean aren't right in the head.'

'He was his ordinary self when he left home last night. It wasn't that.' She moved her hands as if to allay any further questioning.

'Well, what was it?'

'God knows what else was on the poor creature's mind, but—this morning—he was told that they wouldn't want him after the end of the week.'

'How d'you know that?'

'A timekeeper who lives up the road brought his pay envelope home. I answered the door. He told me that they had warned Mr Emmet last night that his job was going to someone else. A man who had worked in the drawing-office. They said he needed it more.'

He laughed shortly. 'They'll be down on their knees tonight thanking God they'll never be asked to prove it.'

'David . . .' But she didn't sound really angry.

'And then what?'

'They didn't have anything else for him.' After a time she continued. 'The timekeeper was a good man. He told me that they'd docked Mr Emmet a night's lying-money because he wasn't on the job at half-five this evening. We opened the envelope and made it up between us. Four and sixpence each. Imagine five of them living on fifty-four shillings. Just one pay coming into that house. Fifty-four shillings with growing children to feed.'

Under the small sounds of the room he became aware of the murmurs of the city; tens of thousands of urgent voices and hurrying footsteps, the roar and whine of cars rushing out to the suburbs, the crash and flicker of trams and buses, a great tide of sound flowing between the façades of banks and warehouses, shops and government buildings, hotels and theatres. Civility, discipline, co-operation between men, all these were necessary if this great machine was to work. No one was left to die in the streets, no one could starve in the midst of all this busyness.

'All right, he lost his job. But he didn't need to do this. They wouldn't have starved to death. There must be some kind of assistance—'

'Maybe that's what he was afraid of. To some people there are worse things than starving.'

'Such as?'

'Losing their pride, David.'

The clock struck seven. He pushed back his chair.

'Are you going out?'

'I've a kinda date with Bonar McFall. Can I give a hand with the dishes?'

'No, thanks, they're nothing. Freddie, get the table cleared down and then get your homework finished.'

He went upstairs and lay on his bed until he was chilled. The clock downstairs struck the half-hour. Time he was getting ready if he was going to this meeting. He stood before the mirror sawing his tie back and forth under his collar. One pay coming into the house. Why, since Mr Rankin had gone it was just the same in this house! And his weekly pay wasn't as big as what Mr Emmet had been getting. His mother must horse away at those blouses and things harder than he had thought. And with that came the realization of how little he knew about where the money came from to run their home. Even the price of his own clothes was a half-hearted compromise between the few shillings he had saved and what she in the end had to give him.

Of course it was different for Bonar McFall. There were four pays coming into his house. McFall could afford to think of buying motor bikes and playing about with his job. And the jobs of his mates. He had been changing his tie to go to the meeting. He tore it from his neck and threw it away. To hell with the meeting. To hell with McFall. That fella didn't care what danger he put his friends in.

He sat in the cold room until he heard the clock strike eight. Freddie went past to bed and he answered his brother's good-night through the closed door. He heard the sewing-machine start in the room below. She looked up in surprise as he opened the door. 'I thought you were going out?'

'Changed my mind. Ah—any use me going down to the Emmets'? Could I do anything?'

She shook her head. 'I wouldn't think so. When I left the neighbours had started to run in and out. To tell you the truth, David, there was very little to do.'

'Oh.' He drew back almost closing the door. Then he suddenly reappeared. 'Well, is there a job you want done? Anything.'

Foot impatient on the treadle she chuckled in perplexity. 'Well, I can't think—any job? Yes, would you clean Freddie's shoes? They're in an awful pickle.'

Grateful, he hurried away. The shoes were soaked with street mud now drying grey. It would be almost impossible to get a shine back on them. But he was in no hurry. He had all the evening before him.

10

'I KNOW,' said Bonar. 'Sure, I saw it in the paper.' From the beginning he had kept his face averted from his friend's candid gaze.

'Well, I was in the *middle* of that, Boney. When Mrs Emmet sent up for my old woman I had to stand by. As it worked out,' he added with disarming frankness, 'I didn't actually have to do any jobs for the Emmets, but how was I to know that? You can see the position I was in?'

Bonar nodded. 'Oh, sure, Davie, I can see that. It was tough on the Emmets.'

'You don't know half of it. Three kids in the family.' He studied the comings and goings of the foreshortened figures in the Mantles. 'Was your—was the meeting any good?'

The other shrugged. 'It coulda been better. There's too much talking from the platform. Some of the weaker brethren are getting windy.' He looked up, and laughed angrily. 'Better organize the dozen of us that want to go ahead instead of waiting for the cold-feet brigade to make up their mind. *We'll* do the organizing! Sergeants of industry, as Marx said, only this time the other way round.'

Gor, he's beginning to *look* like his old man. He moved away a step. 'Come on, Boney,' he said, 'This is a half-day and I want to get out sharp at one.'

As they dragged down a tangled pile of hopsacks, Roden's head rose from the well of the stairs.

'McFall—is Bonar McFall there?'

David saw a garment slither from the hard, white hand.

'Here, Alec.'

'Mr Clarence wants to see you in his office.'

'Me?' Roden was already dropping down the stairs. 'Alec—me?'

The voice came drifting back. 'Yes. Mr Clarence wants to see you immediately.'

Bonar pushed his hands down his trouser legs. 'Be seeing you.'

'Sure, Boney.'

He waited for a moment then slipped across to the well and peered down through the floriated iron. Mr Ankatell fiddled at the boss's desk with a handful of insurance cards. Mr Clarence rocked gently toe to heel in the middle of the little office, hands loosely clasped behind him, head tilted to gaze at the fragment of sky above the street. A Man of Good Intentions, wounded. But resolved to demonstrate to those he had summoned that disloyalty, too, earned its full rate. They came trailing forward from different parts of the warehouse. David's face went slack as he recognized them. Young Wilson, Curdy from the Silks, Greer the packer, Connif. They waited for Bonar to take the lead. The door closed behind them. He stepped quietly back to his work. If he learnt the end of the story now, he doubted his ability to muster enough amazement, enough anger, when it was most needed.

But Bonar made no demands on him. Grinning thinly, he walked past him and lifted down his raincoat. He couldn't make it clearer that I'm outside this, thought David. Bonar struggled into his coat. 'S'pose you've guessed?' he said.

David looked at him angrily. 'Why the hell should I have to guess? Or is this a secret, too?'

He was pleased to see that he had silenced the other for a moment. 'No, no secret, Davie boy. I can now reveal to you the names of the five employees set out on their backsides by Mr Clarence Hamilton. Greer—'

'Being funny doesn't suit you, Boney. I know about Greer. I watched you going in . . . Connif, too.'

'That's right, Connif, too.'

'Well, what happened?'

Bonar drew an insurance card from his pocket and fanned himself mockingly. 'Stamped right up to date. Ready and all.'

'Acting tough doesn't suit you either.'

Bonar's shoulders sagged. He thrust the cards back into his pocket. 'I know. I feel more like being sick.' He thought for a moment. 'All the same it's kind of—exciting, Davie.'

'Yeh. What are you gonna do now?'

'Right now, d'you mean?'

'Well . . . yes.'

'I'm gonna say cheero to Mr Whaley. The only white man in the place. Then I'm going home.' He stopped. 'No I'm not. I'm going round to Joe Snax for a cuppa tea.' He hesitated. 'What time will you be out at, Davie?'

'This is Saturday, Mr McFall. We close here at one o'clock.' They smiled at each other and David grasped his friend by the elbows. 'Boney, what'll I do in this dump, alone?'

'You'll get company, Davie.'

They heard Alec Roden on the stairs. Bonar thrust his hands and wrists deep into his pockets and turned away. The assistant came round the banister-head, his face hangdog with concern.

'I just heard, Boney. I needn't say I'm terribly sorry.'

'Thanks, Alec. I know how you feel.'

Roden raised his hand, and let it fall to his side. 'If there's ever anything . . .'

'I couldn't think what it would be, Alec. But thanks all the same.' Unsmiling, he turned to David. 'See you at Joe's?'

'Sure—sure, Boney.'

They saw him pause and give a quick, flickering glance around the department before he plunged down the stairs.

There was silence between the two he had left. Then Roden, speaking over his shoulder, said, 'Did you want to go with him to Joe's?'

'I wouldn't mind, Alec.'

'All right. Tidy up here first. Go out by the packing-room. If anybody says anything, you're doing a message for me.' He was so surprised that the assistant had gone before he could thank him.

As he pushed odds and ends out of sight he realized with a sense of shame that he felt neither anger nor sorrow about what had happened to his friend—All I could think about was myself. How dull it'll be up here with some kid apprentice. He plucked his coat irritably from the hook—It's because my mind hasn't fully grasped the fact yet that Boney's gone. There's nothing wrong with me. I can be as sympathetic as anybody.

In the packing room, Mr Gallagher was talking to Tommy Kirk, the head packer. '. . . Well, whoever reported them did a damn good day's work. That's what I say . . .' As he slipped past he heard Tommy's reply: 'I've lost two good boys, Mr Gallagher. For my own peace o' mind, I hope I never find out who the informer was . . .'

II

THE defence took the blame for the rout at Derry. On the following Saturday Kinnear was lifted into the senior side to block the broad highway to the Glenbank goal travelled by so many opposing centre-forwards. But he was an attacking player and too often his long searching passes were lost or trodden on by the Glenbank line. Two weeks later, Dr Boustead's white-haired boy, Garland, went up; a month after that Sam Mulhern, the inside-right.

He took the news about Kinnear and Garland without too much suffering, but not Mulhern's elevation. Not that he was sore about a man getting a chance. But Mulhern and he had worked the right wing like a machine. And that machine had carried the Reserves up to third place in the league table. If Mulhern looked good it was largely because of the man outside him. He could recall, like scraps of film, the many times they had worked the ball up and in.

As he dressed after training he said to Bap Peden, 'See the teams on the board?'

'Sure,' Peden smiled. 'See your man Mulhern's gone up.'

'Can you tell me why?'

'He's good.'

He swallowed. 'And what about me?'

'You're good, too, Minnis.' Peden stared at him, his small ginger-cat face impassive. 'Come to that, what about me?'

He struggled to prevent a laugh breaking through his chagrin. 'You're a marvel! But, Bap, why did they break us up?'

'Elliot's off form. They drop him for Mulhern. But Gill's still a good outside-right. Mebbe no better than you but he's the man in possession. So he stays till you play him out of his place. Make sense?'

'Kind of. But it's not good tactics—'

'Mebbe not. Fellas always wave their arms and talk about what's good for the team when they really mean what's good for themselves. Don't be in a hurry. I'm not in a hurry. Come on, I'll give you a lift home.'

He felt grown up as they walked to the car. 'You're a hard man, Bap,' he said.

'I'm not,' said Peden. 'That's my trouble. I'm too damn brittle.'

That wasn't what he had meant but he let it pass. Peden *was* brittle. He was too easily lifted off his feet. Hardly a game passed that he didn't need a touch of the sponge. Sitting in the car David tensed and eased his thigh muscles, feeling them under the cloth of his trousers. He wasn't soft. He, too, could wait. For a while, anyway.

'What would happen, Bap, if you got crocked and didn't make the Seniors?'

'I would be disappointed, of course. But not heartbroken. I've my job. That goes on, soccer or no soccer. It has to. I'm gonna build it up into something. Gonna get married. What about you?'

'Me? Oh, sure. Who isn't?'

Peden took his eye off the road for a second. 'What about bringing her along for a run when the good weather comes? Maureen and me would be delighted.'

'Is your girl's name Maureen? So's mine!'

'Well!' They laughed, pleased with the growth of the acquaintanceship. As Peden leaned forward to change gear, he noted with approval the cut of his roll lapel.

'I like football all right, Davie, but you've got to look ahead. You can't go on for ever. Remember Pony Douthart?'

Yes, he remembered.

'You've got to think ahead. That's what I meant when I asked you about yourself.'

'Oh, I thought you meant girls.'

'Those too.'

As he walked down Colinvista Street he thought of Peden's admonition to look ahead and sniggered to himself. He looked ahead to finding those welcome shillings hidden in his shoe or his jacket pocket every Saturday afternoon. In Hamiltons he would do exactly the same things tomorrow as he had yesterday. Nothing had changed. Even the first-year kid who had come into the Trousers went about his work in a dull, conscientious way that reminded him of Bonar. And the new apprentice who had replaced Connif was there not because he was eager to devote his life to the woollen trade, but because he was a Catholic—a tactical necessity from the management's point of view—and knew it. Already he was behaving to everybody with the wary hostility of his predecessor.

12

THEIR affair progressed smoothly, and, to David's satisfaction, without undue haste. Before they parted they always arranged the time and place of their next date. His appearances in the McFall kitchen became infrequent. He thought this a prudent arrangement. Sitting around in a girl's house most nights was too sudden a development in an intimacy that should be given time to grow. Not that there was any doubt about their feelings for each other. But as he very well knew there was nothing in life that could be relied upon completely. Least of all one's self.

Bonar's dismissal from Hamiltons upset this convenient state of affairs. When they had been working side by side, day in day out, it had been easy to make plans, to improvise an evening's fun. He had parted with Bonar on Saturday, shortly after they left Joe Snax's coffee bar. By Tuesday, he realized with annoyance that he hadn't seen his friend since and knew nothing of his whereabouts. Perhaps it was too much to expect Bonar would meet him coming out of Hamiltons. It was *he* who would have to make the effort if their comradeship was to continue. That evening he went round to the house in Majestic Street. Maureen, he knew, was out with Sadie Monteith.

Bonar was poking idly at the fire. He didn't stir from his chair but his grin was friendly enough. Mr McFall sat on the other side of the fireplace skimming the evening paper. He lowered it cautiously to glance at the visitor. With a qualm David recognized the signs. The old boy was in the dog-house again. He was sorry now that he hadn't arranged to meet Bonar outside. He looked at the two men seated at the fireplace. The young one drifting onto the dole. The old one after a day in pubs and parks fiddling jobs for other wrecks. Cowld Pint. He hoped with all the fervour of which he was capable that the women of the house didn't know about that name.

The talk turned to Mr Emmet's suicide. His body, it seemed, had been taken out of the river opposite the end of Majestic Street. Mr McFall's paper slipped lower and lower. He wanted into the talk. When he heard that Mr Emmet had been employed as a night-watchman he was unable to resist a professional comment. In his opinion the unfortunate man had had little chance of making good.

'In these times with so many folk out of work,' said Mrs McFall, eyeing her husband sternly, 'a man has to be ready to put his hand to anything.'

But Mr McFall wasn't prepared, as yet, to address her directly. 'He was a classy sort of fella, wasn't he—seen better days?'

David agreed that that was very likely.

'It never works,' said Mr McFall decisively. 'Never works. As a dacent Frenchman Léon Blum once said: "For a worker to rise to a bourgeois is a miracle; for a bourgeois to sink to manual labour is a tragedy." And remember, Davie boy,' said Mr McFall with an involuntary drunken jerk of the head, 'that a helluva lot of bourgeoisie had to drown themselves before Monsieur Blum was able to arrive at that conclusion.'

Mrs McFall snatched the poker from the lax hand of her son and stirred the sullen coals. Her husband, in happy possession of the floor once again, blethered on. He motioned to Bonar who sat dreaming at the awakened blaze. '. . . And there's another. Look at him. Just because he stood up for his rights. Look well at him—a hapless victim of the class struggle—'

'Ah, quit your damn tomfoolery!' cried Mrs McFall. 'Is he gonna sit on his backside there showing his independence for the rest of his life? If you were any sort of a father you would be trying to get the poor child a job!'

The poor child looked up and David didn't care for the sardonic smile in his eyes.

'Is that all?' said Mr McFall fishing up the paper from beside his chair. 'Let's have a look at the labour market.' He ran his finger down the Wanted list. ' "Refrigerating Engineer"—no? "Seven Christian Girls to learn Wallpaper Sales"—I think not. Ah, here we are! "Sturdy Protestant boy to sell soda farls. Must be able to ride bicycle—" '

'Aw, Mr McFall . . .' expostulated David, laughing. But Mr McFall pressed on relentlessly. 'Now what does "sturdy" mean in the first bit? Does it refer to the strength of the applicant's Lutheran principles or the strength of his arms? His arms I would say, eh? Your soda bread man is always a realist. Yes, I think you'll pass there. You're sturdy enough—'

He knew that there was a raw edge to this clowning. But he couldn't resist it. 'What about the bicycle-riding?' he threw in. For a moment the little man was disconcerted. He hadn't counted on an appreciative listener in his audience. He pretended to weigh the question judiciously. 'A justifiable demand, I think. A fair enough expectation in this era of technical progress. But—' he examined the others with eyes narrowed in drunken slyness '—what about "Protestant"? What about that, eh?'

Outraged, Mrs McFall was driven from her silence. 'Protestant? Of course your child's a Protestant!'

Mr McFall leaned back with a smile. 'Oh, yes, he's a *protestant*, all right—about wages and working conditions. And look where it's put him. *Them* sort of Protestants are very unfashionable nowadays in certain circles not unknown to the ladies of this house.'

His wife beat the paper out of his grasp with the flat of her hand. The impact, like a pistol shot, silenced everyone. She stood in the middle of the floor crumpling her apron in one hand. Tears gathered in her eyes. As David looked away she rushed from the kitchen and they heard her blundering up the stairs. There was silence for a moment, and then Mr McFall looked across at his son with a timorous smile. 'Mebbe I joked too much. But she didn't see the Marxist inference underneath. Like, she doesn't understand me . . .'

Bonar examined his father dispassionately. When he spoke his voice was quiet, almost with a touch of amusement. 'She understands you only too well, Da. It's you that's out in the dark. This was a time to be serious and you missed it, old fella.'

Mr McFall rubbed his hand across his face. 'I'll make it up to her,' he mumbled.

'That's the style, Da.' Bonar clapped the man's drooping shoulder, stretched himself, and stood up. 'Fancy a dander, Davie?'

He followed his friend out of the house. As they walked up the street he glanced out of the corner of his eye with a shade of envy. Old Boney had grown into a man in a day or two. Gor, the way he had talked down to his father. Clapped him on the shoulder! And apparently not a hair out of him after a scene like that. And those tears in Mrs McFall's eyes. As if a curtain had been twitched, he saw for a moment his own mother's irksome love. He wished he could think of something to say. Something that would show Boney he understood.

'How are the fellas down below?' said Bonar.

'The—ah—you mean Tits and that lot?'

'S'right.'

'Same as you left them.' He punched his friend playfully in the side. 'Why didn't you come down and meet me after work, ye ould bugger ye?'

Bonar grinned obligingly. 'It wouldn't have suited me. I don't want to be seen hanging round Hamiltons or talking to any of the fellas—for a while yet.'

His hand slipped away from Bonar's shoulder. 'Why? . . . You mean you're still at that union organizing carry-on?'

His friend nodded.

'That seems to have become very important to you.'

'S'right.'

They arrived at the main road and stood for a moment at a loss.

'Fancy a feeda chips, Boney?'

'Sounds all right.'

As they turned into the supper saloon they were careful to avoid their elbows touching each other. He found himself wondering morosely what Bap Peden did with himself on his spare evenings.

13

THE football season came to an end without him getting a game for the Glenbank senior side. The little wads of cash dropped into his jacket pocket also came to an end. He looked forward impatiently to the last day of the third year of his apprenticeship and an additional twelve and sixpence in his weekly pay packet.

His mother also was filled with pleasant anticipation. Since his friend Bonar's dismissal she had congratulated him several times on his prudence in not getting mixed up with such folly. He grimaced in embarrassment. 'I keep on telling you it wasn't good sense on my part. If that thing hadn't happened to Mr Emmet I'd have been at the trade union meeting, too.' By now he almost believed that. But she would have none of it. It was just that he was upset at his friend's misfortune and felt that he had to affirm his loyalty. She could understand that. But it would be madness for anybody in his circumstances to do anything deliberately that would annoy his employer. 'Especially,' she concluded, 'as you'll soon be coming out of your third year. You hadn't forgotten?' She smiled as she said it.

How could he, with that calendar behind the kitchen door on which she crossed out each day? The marks had crept up and down the weeks and across the months until now they were within a few days of the date ringed in red ink.

'No, I hadn't forgotten.'

'You must feel proud . . .'

They had developed such an understanding of each other's looks and unfinished phrases that he was fully aware of everything she left unexpressed; the extra money, that it seemed certain now (if he was spared) that he was going to complete *this* apprenticeship, her pride in him as an almost full-blown journeyman, an adult. And always her ineluctable and infuriating need of his money.

'Oh, sure, I'm glad all right.'

He didn't tell her that he'd very little to be proud of. They hadn't gone so far as to make the new boy his equal, but they hadn't vested him with authority over the new boy. And he had an uneasy feeling that the new boy was tumbling to it. In the old days when Alec Roden was out Mr Whaley came upstairs to discuss matters of Trousers policy with Boney. Now he waited impatiently for Alec's return. None of the bosses slighted him, but none favoured him with the man-to-man jokes they shared with, say, Fogarty. None of those little condescensions that would have fallen on his aggrieved spirit like water on parched soil. They tolerated him, perhaps shook their heads despondently when he was out of sight. Nice enough fella, good footballer they say, pity his heart's not in his work. No, he hadn't much to be glad about.

On Friday, ten minutes before the pay bells buzzed in the departments, the Chairman sent for him. As he entered the office the old man stared at him over gold rims and drew a thin file onto his morocco-leather blotter. 'Ah, Minnis. I have to have a word with you. Know what day this is?'

'Yessir. The end of my third year . . .'

The Chairman opened the file. 'I've been looking over your record with us here.' The words were like a thin blade prising him away from the happy limpet family that clung to the rock of Hamiltons. The Chairman studied him. 'Tell me, Minnis, do you think this is the work you're best suited for, eh?'

'I dunno, sir. I don't have much experience of other jobs.' And then hopefully, dutifully, 'I like the work.'

The Chairman wasn't to be deluded. He tapped the file. 'It doesn't say that here. What it says here doesn't make very encouraging reading. I don't see much of a future for you in the trade, Minnis . . .' He paused and David's heartbeat waited for him. 'I'm afraid a man who wants to make a success of this business has to show more initiative, more *go*, than you've shown.' He studied David's face again, more than willing to be fair, to take cognizance of any points in favour of the condemned. He shook his head slowly. 'You seem to be more interested in skylarking than attending to your work.'

'I'm sorry, sir,' he mumbled, choking. 'I didn't think I was doing badly—'

'You are.' The Chairman leaned back in his soft, grey, voluminous suit. Even in his distraction David recognized with sensuous pleasure the quality of the cloth. 'Your mother's a widow, isn't she, and you're the elder of two boys?'

His sight blurred suddenly in facile tears and hatred because of them. 'Yessir.'

The Chairman stroked his beard. 'We're prepared to keep you on for a while, Minnis, but I can't promise you more money. Meantime, I think you had better look out for something else.' He prodded a pay envelope across the desk. 'That's yours,' he said. David pocketed it, and hesitated. The old man poised the file over the out-tray and cocked his head interrogatively. 'That's all, Minnis,' he said.

As he feared, his mother had made a feast night of it. The living-room fire burned cleanly above shining tiles, Freddie's exercise books were tidied away, there was a baker's cake on the table. Warm plates were being shuffled in the kitchen. She put her head out and smiled. 'Hullo there, just in time!' she called. Freddie whooped and clapped his hands. He laughed in response, waved his hand, even managed a little step dance. Then he went out to hang up his coat. He leaned his head against the painted wall. The very most I can squeeze for her is an extra five bob. He closed his eyes when he remembered what that left in his pocket for the week.

It was a grand tea. 'Look!' said Freddie pointing to his plate. 'Sure,' he said. 'Steak. Terrific.' He turned and laid his hand on her arm. She leaned towards him. Their heads were close together. He touched her cheek with his lips. 'Thanks,' he said. They bent over their plates. Thank God for Freddie's bright chatter.

It was a real tightener of a tea. Between the steak and the cake was pears, jelly and real cream. After the cake, biscuits. 'I've got to keep in trim!' he protested. 'Surely you can find a corner for a fig roll?' 'Oh, all right, but I'll be puffing like a grampus after it.'

'What is a grampus?' asked Freddie.

'I don't know. David?'

'Nor me.'

'I tell you what, you go and get the Lexicon and David will show you how to spell it while I clear down the table.'

'And then will you play, Mammy?'

'Of course.'

She had a flair for the game, seeing a coherence in the jumble much quicker than either of her sons. You had to be on your toes to win even one game against her. As the rounds went on she became a shade more impatient with Freddie's slowness. 'Yes, you've got one!' she'd say, leaning over to look at his hand, or, when he tumbled out a three-letter effort, scoffing, 'What a B-for-Baby word!' She'll spoil it, he thought. Freddie began to yawn and sulk. It was too much like old school. She eased up, trying to recapture the early fun. He made little jokes to keep Freddie with them. But the boy was determined to punish her. He wanted his nightly apple. He wanted to go to bed.

In the few minutes that she was upstairs tucking-in Freddie he rehearsed his story. It sounded appallingly thin. She would never believe it.

'We'll have a mouthful of tea first,' she said when she came back, 'then you can tell me how you got on.'

'Aw, mother, there's nothing to tell. I'm only going into my last year. I hope you don't think they've made me manager or something?' he said as he sugared the cups.

'I hope you got what was your due, son.' He was silent.

She sat down beside him at the hearth kilting her skirts decorously to warm her shins. 'Was Mr Hamilton nice—which one was it?'

'The old one. He was all right. Not terribly excited about the future.' He turned to her with candour. 'Things are pretty dull in the trade, you know.' That was the first nail driven home.

They sipped their tea, urging each other on in the ensuing silence. 'But he did something?'

'Oh, yeh.' He drew the money from his pocket and laid it on the table, the two half-crowns on top of the two pound notes. Thank God the difference was two clean, round coins. She wouldn't have to search long to find out the answer. But she did. She pushed the cash aside and counted the notes. Fingered them again. She turned to him unbelievingly. 'This?' she said holding up the coins between finger and thumb.

'Yes.'

'But they gave you ten shillings at the end of your second year. Ah!' her mouth cracked in a smile, 'you're joking me!'

'No m'not.'

'But I can't believe it,' she whispered. 'Five measly shillings for a grown man going into his last year?' She stared at him, her face darkening. Suddenly she planked the money on his knee.

'You're not telling the truth. You got more'n that. You're keeping it back!'

He sprang up, the coins in his fist. 'I tell you I got no more!' He opened his hand. 'That's all I have to give you!'

'There's barely enough to clothe and feed you there. How am I going to keep this house going if you're not going to help?'

'I'm helping all I can. You got your share of my football money—'

She flared as if she were about to strike him. 'So you grudged me that!'

'No I didn't, Mother. But this is all I have to give you.'

She wrinkled her face in disgust. 'I don't want your mean money—'

'You'll take it!' He swung his hand and hurled the coins at her feet. As he dragged the door shut behind him he heard a coin chuckle along the tiled floor beneath the table.

There was no overt break between them. They only moved a shade farther apart. It became a little more difficult to overcome the reluctance to speak to each other with humour or affection.

As the evenings lengthened into summer he saw less of Bonar. They met when he took Maureen home, went for an occasional stroll, dropped into a fadgee's for ice-cream or chips. But the intimacy had gone. Neither found it necessary any more to top his friend's voice in excited agreement or contradiction. They didn't talk about the same things now, and, realizing this, each out of pride concealed any regret he may have felt for times past.

One Sunday afternoon Maureen invited him home to tea. He found the McFall family engaged in various literary activities. Mrs McFall was filling in a competition in *John Bull*; Bonar, with several of his father's books spread around him on the floor, was labouring in pursuit of a subject from volume to volume; Mr McFall was shuffling the contents of the 'Radical's Almanac' on the table; Arthur, blanketed in Sunday papers, was dozing on the sofa.

They were pleased to see him and made him welcome. Bonar would have put away the books, but David insisted that the work musn't be interrupted.

'Well—if you don't mind,' said his friend. 'I'm just looking up a reference I need for a meeting.'

'Ah . . .' He turned his attention quickly to Bonar's father. 'And how's the work going?'

Mr McFall reversed the position of two slips of paper. 'Grand, Davie boy. The magnum opus is nearing completion. By July I hope to be placing an order with the printers for the first twenty-five thousand.'

He had heard often enough that the Almanac was on its way to the printers. This was the first time the magnitude of the project had been mentioned. His eyes opened wide. 'Thousands? The *first* twenty-five . . .?'

'Ah, now, Davie, you're taking my father seriously,' said Arthur from the sofa.

'What surprises you, Davie boy?' queried Mr McFall paying no attention to his eldest son.

He blushed, but with Maureen's eye on him pressed on. 'Well, where are you going to find twenty-five thousand of the kind of people who would want to buy that type of thing?'

'What d'you mean by "kind of people"?'

He screwed his head to read the name again ' "Radicals".'

'Davie's right, Radicals are kinda bullfish, aren't they?' said Mrs McFall accusingly.

'I've told you before the word is "bolshevist". And they aren't the same.' The little man again gave his attention to David. 'How many people would you say you know?'

'Well, I couldn't give you a figure, but I know all the people in our street, and all the people that go to the Hall and the fellas at Glenbank.' He was on the point of adding 'and in Hamiltons', but thought better of it. 'Hundreds, mebbe.'

'Scarcely a cosmopolitan circle,' said Mr McFall. His smile conveyed more to David than his words.

'They're the sort of people you've got to sell your calendar to!' he declared hotly.

'Well said, Davie!' cried Mrs McFall, and Maureen and Arthur laughed.

Mr McFall leaned forward, the soul of patience. 'Davie boy, you wouldn't know. You can never be sure till the barricades are out. Just a minute—' He sifted through the litter of pencilled slips on the table until he found the one he sought. He held it up to the light. 'Tell me what you think of this: "The forces secretly arrayed against the present social order are pervasive and universal, in the air one breathed, in the ground one trod, in the hand of an acquaintance that one might touch or the eye of a stranger that might rest a moment on one's own".' Mr McFall replaced the slip, folded his arms and eyed David.

'It sounds kinda nice,' he admitted. 'Who wrote it?'

'An American, Henry James.'

'Is he a *New Masses* man?'

'No, Davie boy, you couldn't call him *that*. Anyway, he's dead years ago. But you get his point?'

'Oh, sure.'

Bonar looked up from his books. 'I know where there's some real live ones if you want to meet them. In the Spinners Hall—'

'You would have little to do going there, Davie,' said Mrs McFall.

'Aw, Boney, in this weather?' and he nodded at the flood of late sunlight on the whitewashed wall outside.

Bonar shrugged, and turned back to his books. 'Please yourself. I thought you were serious.'

'You might enjoy it, Davie,' said Mr McFall.

He turned his shoulder to Bonar. 'Why, what's it about, Mr McFall?'

Without raising his head Bonar answered, 'We're gonna talk about why Ulster workers have to emigrate to England and Scotland to get jobs.'

'And it's on Friday coming. One of your free evenings,' said Mr McFall delicately.

'How d'you know the boy's free?' demanded his wife.

'It's Maureen's Empire-building night. I know about these

things. I watch over the comings and goings of my offspring with a brooding eye,' the father concluded mildly.

'When you can see out of them,' said Mrs McFall rising. 'Get that table cleared till Maureen and me get the tea set.'

There was no reason why he shouldn't go to the Spinners Hall now that Bonar was safely out of Hamiltons. And he did feel guilty about that other time. He could slide easily enough into believing what was comforting to his conscience, but he could never quite fool himself about what had happened on the night Mr Emmet died. Here was a chance to get the score straight again with Bonar McFall. And he felt a jealous curiosity as to where his friend stood with these new acquaintances of his.

'Right,' he said, 'I'll go.'

Bonar looked up quickly. 'Good. We'll leave from here at half-seven, Friday.'

McFall was at his best when they left Majestic Street on Friday evening. He was sober. He didn't ask them to step aside at Harkin's pub. And to David's satisfaction he had left off his scarf and duncher for a hat and raincoat. In the tram he twitted him.

'Ah, don't worry, Davie boy. I don't have to dress proletarian. I *am* proletarian. You'll see some of the other sort at the Hall.'

'What other sort?'

'The ones that have been driven into our ranks by "moral conviction rather than economic pressure" as the saying goes—'

Bonar leaned forward. 'Don't bother to tell us who said it, Da.'

'Keep it for your Almanac,' added David.

'You're a couple of great wags,' said Mr McFall.

The Spinners Hall stood back from the street behind a wrenched and broken iron fence set in a low wall. Shouting children swung on the railings and tumbled on the strip of beaten earth between the wall and the building. As Mr McFall and David threaded their way through the hubbub they lost Bonar to a cluster of men and women in the entrance. Inside, a few early arrivals were scattered along the benches. The posters and proclamations of the two or three heterodox organizations that kept the building alive speckled the walls. The ceiling was high and stained. Dust, cobwebs and shadows rounded out the angularity of its corners. He viewed, with distaste, his surroundings and the shabby people communing with themselves. 'Who are those fellas?' he whispered.

Mr McFall cocked a knee, set his elbow on it and took his pipe from his lips. 'I see there's some very significant minds here tonight.'

Mistakenly, David carried on the facetious mood of the tram ride. 'They look a parcel of hooks to me.' He indicated a dusty looking individual two benches away. 'That fella hasn't had a hair-cut since he left gaol.'

' "Parcel of hooks"?' Mr McFall, shocked at this euhemerism, stared at him angrily, then doubting his own senses ran his eye round the hall again. What he saw reassured him. 'You may well say "gaol",' he declared reprovingly. 'That comrade did six months for printing an I.R.A. manifesto.' He jerked his thumb at a round-shouldered man whose scalp showed like a whip-lash through his hair. 'That 'un got his skull opened by the peelers in a Glasgow dock strike. And *that* old fella near the wall is a genuine Balkan anarchist—talked to Kalyaev and Savinkov in his day.' Mr McFall stretched his neck and lifted his voice, ' 'Evening, Baruch!' The man at the wall turned his head slowly revealing a mouth open in wary curiosity above a ragged beard. He clicked his head in response and turned quickly away. David goggled in astonishment. The anarchist was Mr Shriberger. 'I know that—' He stopped. The less said about whom you knew here the better.

But Mr McFall, smiling triumphantly, had heard nothing. 'You're looking at the real thing tonight, Davie boy. These fellas have seen history in the making and given it a shove when it was going too slow.' The little man's expression changed, and he threw one leg pettishly over the other. ' "Hooks", b'God!'

'Well, of course I didn't know, Mr McFall . . .' he mumbled. He sat silent, observing the yards of polished bench stretching between the figures scattered around them. 'Do they know each other?' he ventured.

'The comrades? 'Course they know each other!'

'Well, why don't they have a bit of a chat?'

Mr McFall had some small difficulty with his pipe. 'They—ah—disagree on a few basic principles.'

Men and women, young and old, neat and shabby, were drifting in, filling the gaps between the silent fundamentalists. A pretty woman in a head-scarf followed by her stout escort in tweeds carried her argument in a high, cultivated gabble down the hall and into the benches. When they were seated her companion leant his head attentively towards her, folded his arms, sucked his pipe, nodded understandingly as he let his thoughts wander off. A short, fat young man in a raincoat with burst armpits slipped into the seat beside David and sat nursing his duncher and rocking his feet impatiently.

'Are we supposed to be keeping this seat for Bonar, Mr McFall?'

'Not at all. Bonar'll be on the platform.'

He turned to watch the group coming in from the porch. Bonar was talking to a man and a girl. He leant back to see who they were. The man was Connif. The girl had Connif's dark hair and brows and she revealed how good-looking Connif might have been had his face been a different shape. Bonar found them seats and followed three men onto the platform where they shuffled self-consciously for a moment arranging themselves in chairs.

The man behind the table struck a push-bell and stood up. 'Comrades and friends, this meeting is called by the Unemployed Workers' Organization and other progressive bodies to consider the problem of Ulster men and women—'

'Irish men and women,' said a voice from the front. David judged it to be in the proximity of the man who had been jailed for printing the manifesto.

The chairman paused and allowed his glance to linger thoughtfully over the audience so that they should be quite clear as to who was wasting who's time. 'Comrade,' he said, 'this problem is above any petty partisanship.'

'That's what I mean,' said the voice, unabashed, 'so call us something we can all accept—Irish.'

The audience watched the man behind the table discarding the rest of his introductory remarks. 'I call therefore on Brother McKelvey to give us the trade union point of view.'

'On what?' prompted Brother McKelvey without leaving his chair. Reluctantly the chairman straightened up again: '—the trade union point of view on workers being forced across the water to seek employment.' With his backside poised over his chair he added, 'And I hope the meeting's time won't be wasted by comrades dragging in issues dead as Brian Boru.' He was seated and Brother McKelvey was on his feet before the patriot at the front could get his mouth open again.

Brother McKelvey dealt only in facts. He gave the number of unemployed on the books of his union, commented on the attitude of Ministry officials, described rooming conditions in Glasgow and Birmingham, calculated dispassionately how a worker might keep two homes on one pay packet. The companion of the woman in the head-scarf had a question about building an Irish fishing fleet in the Queen's Island shipyard. David liked his voice. Brother McKelvey seemed to think that the question was meant as a joke.

A labourer got up at the back of the hall and spoke briefly but with some bitterness about what had been promised him at the Labour Exchange and what he had found on a building-site in Scotland. The audience listened with apathetic interest. The fat fellow beside David nodded until his chin rested on his shirt front. Brother McKelvey sat down to a patter of handclaps.

Mr McFall shifted on the hard bench. With apprehension David raised his eyes to the platform. His skin prickled as he watched Bonar approach the table. After the first two or three phrases in that flat commonplace voice he closed his eyes. A murmur grew at the back of the hall. Bonar tried to top it, and failed. He looked flustered, silly. The murmur swelled, and splintered into laughter. Suddenly Mr McFall was on his feet facing the back of the hall. '*Shut your mouths!*' he shouted. In an instant they were the centre of circle within circle of staring faces. He lowered his head and gripped his hands between his knees. He shoulda known that something like this would happen. The chairman struggled to his feet. 'If the comrade would leave the control of this meeting to me—'

'Then why don't you control it?' shouted the labourer at the back. 'Give the young fella a chance!'

The chairman waved his hand reprovingly. 'That's enough, comrade . . .' With long pauses and a hunting for words Bonar again took up his argument. It appeared, to those who troubled to follow him, that he differed with Brother McKelvey on the question of the mobility of labour. For a moment he became eloquent. He struck the table and shouted, 'No man should have to leave these shores! A government owes its people a living!' David heard someone behind him rise to speak. He glanced back. A young man was on his feet looking quickly from side to side as though invoking support for what he was about to say. 'If that's the comrade's opinion will he give the meeting his views on the forced transfer of labour from the so-called people's democracy of Greater Livonia—'

David sat up. This was what was wanted. Marx Brothers stuff. He turned, ready to laugh at the next lunacy. The interrupter was being dragged violently back into his seat. There was a pause and then people were springing up all over the place, applauding, shouting angrily, appealing to the platform. With a shock David realized that no one thought the interruption funny. The woman in the head-scarf was glaring over his shoulder, her knuckles gleaming white on the rail of the bench. With his eyes fixed on Bonar the fat fellow was chanting and stamping his feet. Some of those around picked up his cry—*Answer! answer! answer!* Beside him David felt Mr McFall bounce about as he screamed at someone farther along the bench.

Everybody seemed to be shouting and waving their arms about except Mr Shriberger. His shoulders were hunched and every line of his curved back spoke disgust. Bonar thumped the table, the chairman pinged his bell. '*Agent provocateur!*' screamed the woman catching sight of the youth who had started all the trouble. 'Yah, coupla aborted Webbs!' came the reply. The man in the tweeds tried to get out, the woman clung to his arm imploringly, half of the people on the bench urged him on and the others told him to sit down and shut his big mouth.

Bonar lumbered from the platform and pushed his way through the hubbub towards Connif and the dark girl. The chairman abandoned his bell and sat, chin in hand, gazing mournfully at the gesticulating figures. Someone looked up, saw him, and laughed. Slowly the audience became aware that the speakers had retired, that the chairman admitted defeat. Noisy threatening groups dissolved, the clamour lessened, men and women slid into their seats again. The chairman's shoulders only sagged more despondently. The last murmurs died away until there was silence in the hall. To those sitting below him the chairman's unblinking stare became an accusation more than an admission of defeat. He rose mightily in David's estimation.

'Hi, what about the meeting?' someone called. It was taken up by a score of voices. David noted with indignation that the demand came from the same crowd that had shouted Bonar down. Nor did the coincidence escape the chairman. He leaned across the table. 'You're getting no meeting. You came here to wreck this one. You can go home now and tell the crowd that sent you that you did what you were told . . .' He slammed the bell savagely against the rising protest. 'Meeting suspended,' he shouted, and disappeared through a doorway beside the platform.

No one seemed eager to occupy the empty platform. Reluctantly the crowd began to shuffle towards the door. Mr McFall and David pressed forward to overtake Bonar. Suddenly they saw him rise above the heads of the crowd. 'Comrades,' he shouted, 'this meeting was—' He disappeared abruptly. David heard the father's frightened, angry voice: 'If anybody's giving our Bonar a hoagin'—' He grasped the small veined fist. 'Bonar's all right, Mr McFall.' He knew that he was all right. Among those he had seen pull Bonar down from the bench was the girl with the dark hair.

Old McFall, Mr Shriberger and two young men had crossed the street and gathered under the roseate sign of the Serbia Bar. As he joined them Mr Shriberger gave him a fleeting, furtive smile as if amused to see him there. He responded with an abrupt nod, and moved restlessly around the fringe of the group, impatient to get away. Bonar, Connif and the girl came out of the Hall. He had no desire to meet Connif again. 'I think I'll push on, Mr McFall . . .'

'Ah, not at all, Davie boy! We came together, didn't we? We'll go home together. Have you met the boys? Paddy . . . Brendan . . . Oh, you know Baruch Shriberger?' For a moment the little man seemed at a loss. 'Gotta wait for Bonar, anyway. But first I'm for a pint—' and he thrust open the doors of the pub. Paddy and Brendan followed him eagerly. Hesitating, David came face to face on the threshold with Shriberger. At such close proximity he saw that the Jew's expression was dry, speculative, and yet affectionate. Mr Shriberger gestured at the swinging doors. 'Why not, Dovid'll?' They went in together.

The frequenters of the Spinners Hall, it seemed, were well known here. The boss, polishing a glass behind the counter, nodded affably. A daft lot of characters, he agreed with the wife, but not to be sneezed at when it came to the custom of a back-street pub. And well behaved. They spent that much time arguing and drinking they had no breath left for singing and that kept the peelers away. 'And some good heads there. Educated men, if you cared to listen. I could go a bit of the way with some of those fellas,' he told the wife. So as Mr McFall led his friends into a snug the boss came round personally to take their order.

The air was full of the smells of cheap wines, greyhounds, porter, working clothes, whiskey, varnished timber. One sniff and Mr McFall was exhilarated. He ran a glowing eye round the snug table. 'Catholic, Jew and Protestant met in sociable intercourse. In our banausic society a refinement permitted only to minorities —the moneyed and the emancipated.' He waved a hand to the boss. 'Three pints, a black spool and a ball o' malt, Edmund, at your kind convenience.' The little man sobered. 'B'God, I'm glad that fella of mine didn't get bashed tonight!'

'Yah,' said Brendan examining his fist, 'and who would bash him? Sure there's nobody in that lot fit to punch his way out of a wet paper bag.'

That's not the point,' said Paddy. 'We mustn't have trouble at our meetings. We're only making bullets for our enemies to fire—'

'You're talking sense,' said Bonar entering the snug.

They greeted him. Brendan asked him what he would drink.

'Nothing. I don't drink.'

'A soft 'un?'

'All right, a soft 'un.'

When the drinks were served, the talk turned to the interrupted meeting.

'If they want to interfere with this damn place Liv-whatever-you-call-it, let them,' said Bonar. 'Let them amuse themselves at their own meeting.'

'Who are "they"?' asked Brendan.

Bonar shrugged. 'I only know the faces. The names change every night.'

'Livonia's important—' said Mr Shriberger.

'And our own people rotting in the streets!'

'Livonia could lead to war,' said Mr Shriberger.

'In such a struggle between capitalism and communism, Ireland would declare her neutrality,' said Brendan folding his arms.

Bonar stared at him in disgust, then turned again on Mr Shriberger. 'And what the hell makes you think the Livonians ever heard of Serbia Street, Belfast?'

'Or Belfast, come to that?' said Mr McFall.

'Ah, now,' said Brendan and Paddy.

David withdrew into a corner of the seat and watched them waving hands, making points, quoting authorities, contradicting each other. So this was the new excitement that Boney had found. He felt a gleeful satisfaction. He didn't mind being left out of this lot. Of course, so far as Boney was concerned, there was the girl with the dark hair. But you didn't have to get bored to hell just to see a girl occasionally. He examined his friend as he leaned across the table, a flush on his pale face, lank hair falling over his brow, a square finger stabbing the wood, and felt a chill shadow of doubt. Perhaps there were anonymous fools like McFall who did think they could change the world.

Mr McFall's eye was on him. He knew by that flickering glance that the old fellow sought some further distraction. A moment later he leaned over and whispered into David's ear, 'So you know Shriberger?'

' 'Course I do. He buys stuff in our place.'

Mr McFall clapped his hands softly. 'I never thought of that!' He leaned closer. 'Bet you there's something you don't know about him . . .?'

Not caring much for that portery breath playing on his cheek David drew back a little. 'Could be,' he said.

'Hi, Baruch!'

Arrested in his argument the Jew looked across at them, 'Yes?'

'Got your snapshot collection with you?'

It took a moment for Mr Shriberger to grasp the query. Then he shook his hand irritably to and fro. 'No, no, no, no . . .'

Paddy heaved himself forward. 'Aw, g'wan, Mr Shriberger—'

'It's for this fella. He's never seen it,' said Mr McFall.

Mr Shriberger sighed, looked quizzically at David, then slid his hand inside his jacket and brought out a flat package which he laid carefully on a dry patch of the table. 'You can do the talking,' he said to Mr McFall. 'I am tired.'

The package resembled a folded map. It was backed with some stout material, but had been opened and refolded so often that the hinges had a fragile lace-like consistency. Very carefully Mr McFall picked it open between finger and thumb and held it up.

Photographs in pairs filled the sheet. Below each group was a name, a description, an age. Each pair of photographs depicted the same man, full face and profile.

'See anybody you know among those artistic portraits?' said Mr McFall.

The faces stared up at David, disdainful, sullen, mocking. After a moment's scrutiny he drew back from their accumulative contempt and defiance.

'There!' said Mr McFall pointing.

He examined again the close-curled head, tilted defiantly,

the throat rising from the soiled prison jacket. He looked up in astonishment. 'It's Mr Shriberger!'

Mr Shriberger smiled gently.

'But what is it?'

Mr McFall traced some faded pencil marks on the back. ' "This file of proscribed aliens, outlawed politicals and terrorist agents was compiled for the use of police and immigration authorities at Atlantic ports in Europe" and the date—' he held the inscription up to the light—' "1898".'

'Gor,' said Paddy, gazing sympathetically at Mr Shriberger, 'those musta been terrible times—'

'No, Paddy boy, great times!' declared Mr McFall reprovingly. Bonar considered his father with tolerant amusement. 'Sorry your likeness isn't in that lot, Da?'

'I deeply regret it, my son. Deeply regret not being active in that period of history when "ecstasy" as Karl Marx put it "was the mood of the hour, and men and things seemed set in sparkling brilliants". We live in a drab age, Bonar boy.' Mr McFall took a long slug at his pint, folded his arms, and sighed.

David studied the photograph once more and then looked up at the original. 'And that was you?'

'Yes.'

'How did you get hold of this?'

'An immigration officer with the sense of the comic gave it to me.'

'But, wouldn't they . . . need it again?'

Mr Shriberger laughed silently. 'Don't fear. I am a respectable tax-payer for many years. The others? They are dead. Some in prisons, some on the gallows, some in the streets. This one will die in bed.'

David examined the faces again. 'Did you know any of them?'

'A few. You will see that I am much younger than most.' He laid his finger on the face of an Old Testament prophet. 'Geza . . . It is strange. He was a Livonian. But what he died for is not what they have there tonight.'

'And this one?'

'I did not know him.' Mr Shriberger took the sheet, and laid it along his forearm above the wet table. 'But this man. This was my . . . leader. An Italian silversmith. A man who understood everything but fear . . .'

From a photograph Mr Shriberger unwound a story of black bread and cold fearlessness and treachery and smoking oil lamps on tables and swift executions. As he talked David glimpsed a ceaseless conflict running beneath the great wars and intervening lulls of the history books. A struggle waged against protectors, princes, archdukes, archbishops, and dictators in countries with names that seemed to come from the pages of a stamp album. It was all so far away. But great to listen to. It made the night.

'Time, gentlemen,' called Edmund the boss, 'time, now, if you please.'

In Ormeau Road, on their way home, they parted with Mr McFall. He had a watchman to visit. They saw him scuttle down a side street until he disappeared in the murk. 'He's away to a booze club,' said Bonar. They walked on in silence for a time.

'Well, what did you think of it?'

'Ah, it was all right, Boney. Old Shriberger was a bit of an eye-opener.'

'Yes. Is that all?'

'I was sorry for you, of course.'

'Don't worry about me. I can look after myself. What about the rest of it?'

Bonar's curt insistence irked him. 'I thought it was a bore.' He paused, and then added, 'I suppose that makes me what you fellas call a "reactionary"?'

Bonar shrugged and smiled.

They didn't speak again until they came to Colinvista Street corner. This is where our roads part. Better get it over as soon as possible. He barely paused at the corner.

'Well, be seeing you, Boney.'

'Be seeing you, Davie.'

It was the first time in their acquaintanceship that they could say the next time we meet it will be by accident, the way strangers meet.

Part Three

I

THE good weather came and Peden didn't forget about the picnic. Ever since his friend had phoned him at Hamiltons David had looked forward to a day at Portrush with Maureen. But when Peden and his girl picked them up at the top of Majestic Street he was irked to find that it had already been decided that they were to go to Strangford Lough, from where, as far as he could remember, herrings or something came. What was wrong with Portrush full of other young, gay, brightly-dressed people? In the back seat of the car he muttered, 'Sure, Bap, I'm easy.' He shrugged, and felt the pressure of Maureen's shoulder restrain him. Mebbe she was right, as usual. The fella that owned the car always had the last say.

He ceased to sulk as they ran under the checkered shade of the suburban trees. He was a pavement-bound creature. At first the contour and colour of the hills and vales of Down was nothing more than a hundred, half-remembered rumours had led him to expect. But as this loveliness swooped and eddied on either hand, mile after mile, the chatter died in the car. 'Yes,' he breathed in response to Maureen. 'Yes, it's terrific.'

They crossed the heavy grey bridge over the bird-haunted Quoile, drove quickly through and beyond the dispirited town of Downpatrick to the Struell Wells. Bap brought a picnic basket from the boot of the car. They would eat, he said jokingly, in the Long Acre, the strip of grass that bordered the road. David watched while Bap's Maureen painstakingly garnished four plates with chicken, fragments of ham, tomato, lettuce, thin cucumber sandwiches. The young matron, rehearsing. As he watched he thought how comforting it was to be out with two people who were so much in one mind about the future.

After the dishes had been cleared and packed away the couples drifted apart. Maureen and he wandered down to the Wells, stared into the hurrying, bubbling water, and wondered at the people who lowered themselves into these shadowy troughs in the belief that they would be cured.

They climbed a stile and found a bay in the hedge filled with feathered quicken grass and shaded by a rowan tree. She lay drowsily in his embrace disarmed by the sun and his closeness. He ventured farther with his mouth and hands than he had ever dared before. After a time she asked him to be still, and they lay listening to the beating of their hearts, gradually aware of the insect sounds that ringed them round. When he raised his head her eyes were closed. A grain of grass seed clung to her flushed cheek. He brushed it tenderly away and she looked up at him. 'I love you, Maureen.'

'I love you.' Her answer was like a sigh.

'I want to marry you.'

She drew his head down, and kissed him.

They heard Peden's voice calling, thin, distant. She ran to the stile, waved and called back. 'Here we are. We're not far away!' As they hurried across the fields to the road they flicked grass from each other's clothes.

'Well, you two look pleased enough with yourselves!' said Bap over the driver's door. David hooked his thumbs in his belt, drew a great breath, looked around. Responsibility brings a cunning. 'Could you blame us? It's a wonderful day and a wonderful place.'

'It's all that. Hop in. We'll push on to Ardglass. Ever been there?'

No, they had never been there, they said, smiling into each other's eyes and holding hands on the hot leather of the seat.

'We might see the fishing boats, if we're lucky.'

But apart from a hulk and a couple of dinghies the port was empty. They walked down the long arm of the quay among the stacks of empty herring-boxes waiting the shoals and the Donegal fishergirls. The air was so still that the smoke from a village chimney rose as straight as a wand above the roofs. The white grin of the surf on the rocks opposite the quay surprised him. 'Oh, it's a hard old life,' said Bap Peden. He climbed the breast wall and looked over. The sun's glare blotted all character from the sea. But out there men were fishing. And he sold them another man's jacket and trousers, thirty-four waist, twenty-one inside leg. If they came throbbing round the horn of the quay would those oil-skinned men recognize him for what he was? He jumped down in sudden anger. 'Well, what d'you say, Bap? Will we have a dander through the place?'

'Sure,' said Bap. As they strolled back towards the village Peden pointed out the castles and fortified planters' houses that rose above the modest roofs. But David wasn't listening. Peden and his girl had been very decent taking them out and supplying the grub and everything. There was a pub above the harbour. Should he offer them a drink? Mebbe Peden didn't when he was driving? Mebbe he didn't at any time? Mebbe the girls would be annoyed? As they passed the pub he trailed behind. The door opened abruptly. Two men stumbled out half-carrying, half-dragging another. He shrank into a doorway. There was something familiar about the silly, lolling head. They tottered across the pavement to a car. The drunk man's hat fell off, and rolled to David's feet. He recognized it but made no effort to lift it. One of the men came back, snatched up the hat and jammed it on the drunk's head. They tried to force him into the back seat. Giggling, he raised his foot fantastically high and clawed at the burning roof. 'Aw, for Chrissake, Maurice!' one of the men said. The hand was torn from the roof. They bundled him in, and the car rolled away down the hill.

Hidden in the doorway he closed his eyes. If I had a father and saw that happen to him this is how I would feel. I musn't tell her when I get home. I musn't let it slip out.

The others were looking back. As he hurried to join them Peden said, 'Thought you were slipping in for a quick 'un!'

'No, no,' he mumbled, 'I thought just—would anybody like a cup of tea or something?'

They drove back slowly through the ripened sunlight content to speak only when the fancy moved them. He held Maureen's hand until she loosed her fingers from the heat of the clasp. That was something he had to learn. Not to feel offended when she did things like that. It was because she was sensible, matter-of-fact. It was the way she was made. The two people in front were chatting quietly, winning a chuckle from each other without trying too hard. Once he was properly engaged he would share that ease. He knew where there was a window full of engagement rings . . .

2

IT was Maureen who decided they should keep their engagement a secret. He demurred, but not vehemently. Being an engaged man on his wages wasn't even a bad joke. And he daren't think of the look on his mother's face if he told her about Maureen. The decision to keep their engagement a secret also got rid of the awkward question of raising the wind for a ring. He wondered if that was what Maureen had in mind. He didn't want to think about that either. It made him curl up inside in anger and embarrassment.

But in every other way they shaped their small resources to suit the new relationship. Sometimes she paid for her own seat in the pictures. When he protested she told him that the girls she worked with often did that when they got engaged. From now on their first loyalty was to be to each other, their leisure hours at each other's disposal. Not that she was available every evening and she made it clear that she didn't think much of girls who were. But now he always knew what she was doing; out with Sadie Monteith, helping her mother at home, working late, attending some hen party at the Women's League of Empire. Even there, she told him, you come into my mind. As he kissed her he assured her there could be no sterner test and wondered delightedly at her instinctive knowledge of what engaged people said to each other.

He didn't have much to give up; a very occasional night at

the Empire Theatre with Fogarty or some of the other fellows from Hamiltons, a swim at the baths, a read at a book, an evening spent round an old car at the end of the street. He didn't mix much with the locals from Colinvista Street but sometimes as the owner tinkered underneath he would lie over the bonnet discussing with them transmissions, bodywork, miles per gallon. For an hour or so everyone indulged in the pleasant illusion of being the owner of a car. Anyway, it killed a night. It had been different, of course, when he was knocking about with Boney. Then there had been no difficulty in filling a spare evening.

Maureen and he were taken up by Bap Peden. They shared in another picnic, and in the July holidays Peden's girl asked Maureen to help arrange a dance party for Bangor. That meant asking Sadie Monteith, and Sadie to his surprise and annoyance brought along Bob Kane, the fellow with the silver cigarette case. Kane had a car. 'Only fifty quid and look at the bald tires,' he said, kicking them. Everyone thought it very sporting of him to make little of his car like that. But David observed that he had dressed it up with a spotlight and all sorts of badges including some, David suspected, that he had no right to. He was big, blond, formidable in a pleasant way. Peden's girl said he was a very jolly fellow. No, not jolly, thought Peden, amiable. Always smiling. Only David noticed that the quiet, thoughtful smile was more often than not fixed on him, as if Kane knew something and was in no hurry to disclose it. Apart from that he had to admit that Kane behaved himself quite well. The big fellow danced with Sadie no more and no less than he danced with any other girl in the party. But David wasn't sorry when the dance was over. He would see to it that Kane didn't come out with the crowd again.

At the same time he felt ashamed of his dislike of Kane. It's lack of money, he decided. I can't be at ease with these people when I've got to count every shilling before I set out. I'm always pulling the devil by the tail. He had tried hard enough to make extra money. Sometimes it seemed to him that he would always lack the opportunity and the ability. His friends couldn't fail to see that he was a nondescript young man anchored to a poor job by fear and ignorance. His small successes had brought him nothing but a sense of shame. There had been the few shillings he made on the coat for old Mrs Moore, next door. And the pound on Harry Peebles' suit. At night, in bed, he prickled with sweat when he thought of the profit he had made out of a friend of his mother's. And when these sorry sums had melted he was no better off. The cost of living, he discovered, was cumulative.

With mounting impatience he awaited the passing of summer and the arrival of the football season. The evenings crept in, the tired lupin in Mrs Moore's yard seeded slowly up its length. Then one morning as he came downstairs Freddie was waving a letter. 'It's for you, Davie!' He tore it open. Training would start at Glenbank on the following Tuesday. As he left the house he thought he could smell the tang of autumn in the air.

3

RONNIE DUNLOP, Jack Taggart . . . Davie Minnis . . . Charlie Lennox . . . sure, I forgot you know Charlie . . . well, Sam McIlveen . . .' McClenaghan and Mort had been working hard during the summer. They had collected six of them, barely more than schoolboys. He saw with indifference their excitement and apprehension. The question was which one of them had that innate balance to overcome the apprehension, harness the excitement. He had looked forward to challenging those above him, he had never thought there might be a challenge pressing on his own heels.

'Right,' said Fred Mort, 'stick a pair of boots on, and out yous come.'

It was great to hear the drumming of studded feet, to feel again the laced tautness on his insteps. He paused for a moment to look up at the cavernous stand hanging over the pitch. You'll be kind to me, he prayed. Halfway up a stooped figure moved among the seats. He recognized the centre-forward who had been dropped from the Reserves in the previous season.

'I see Collins is still around, Fred.'

Mort didn't trouble to look up. 'Sure he is. He's not much of a footballer but he's handy round the place with a hammer and nails.'

He laughed, shaking his arms and fingers loose. Nobody was going to give him the hammer. 'Come on, Lennox,' he said, 'get in between the sticks till we see if we can get that belly of yours down.'

Mort waved a reproving finger. 'Hold it, lads. You'll do it my way.'

Mulhern and he renewed their partnership, bringing to it a year's weight, experience, guile. They played for the Reserves in an evening game, the first match for a Glenbank side in the new season. Before a small crowd the Reserves overran their opponents by six goals. David worked two of the goals for Mulhern, a third for McIlveen, the young centre-forward. Dr Boustead acknowledged his performance as the players trotted down the tunnel to the dressing-rooms. 'I've been watching you, Minnis,' he called, leaning over the barrier. Ahead of them, Fred Mort turned, grinning, and made a rude gesture.

As he knotted his tie he heard Boustead's voice in the corridor. 'Here comes the ringmaster, boys,' said Brian Campbell. The doctor was followed in by Mr Warnock and Billy McClenaghan. Boustead waved a benedictory hand. 'Dunno how bad the other lot were, men, but they made you look good.' Mr Warnock, leaning against the door with his hands in his pockets, smiled: 'The doctor's pleased with you. We're all pleased with you. Damn good start. Look after yourselves.' He signed to the manager to take over and went out leading Dr Boustead firmly by the arm.

'Lennox—' In the silence Billy McClenaghan sought among them for the faces he wanted. 'Mulhern, Minnis. I want to see you up on deck when you're ready.'

As he closed the door behind him everybody started talking.

Lennox, his big hands fumbling at his locker, shrugged. 'I dunno what he wants. Might be anything.'

'Could be a telling off,' said Sam McIlveen.

'Could be,' said the goalkeeper looking down his nose at the young upstart.

'Then I wish I was being told off,' said Peden, and David's heart quickened at the murmur of agreement.

They found McClenaghan leaning against the rails his back to the deserted pitch.

'What are you lads doing next Wednesday afternoon? You, Mulhern—'

'Me? I'll be in my shop, I s'pose.'

'Could you get anybody to look after it for an hour or so?'

'Sure. My mother.'

'Fine. You're turning out for the Seniors against Bogsend. What about you two?'

'You can put your shirt on me, Billy,' said Charlie Lennox.

'Good. Davie?'

'Well, I dunno. I work.'

'Oh . . . pity . . . Mulhern and you . . .'

Mulhern was staring at him open-mouthed. 'Sure,' David said hurriedly, 'I'll be all right. I can get off.'

As they crossed the cinders Mulhern said, 'You put the heart across me there. They would have shopped me, too.'

'Ah, what are you worrying about? They gave you a trial in the Seniors last year on your own—'

'This is different, Davie,' said Lennox. 'They're trying you as a partnership on the wing—'

'Well, I wouldn't like to spoil Mulhern's chances. But it's difficult for me. I work Wednesdays.'

'And what d'you think I do? I'm on a wee tanker down in the shipyard. But on Wednesday they can get somebody else to slap red-lead round the bulkheads! This is our big chance, boy. Wouldn't we be mad to pass it up?'

Yes, he agreed with Lennox, they would be mad to pass it up.

He was glad Peden had waited for him. He wouldn't have to suffer the curiosity of Collins, Taggart, Campbell and the other players still hanging round the ground. Lennox and Mulhern would tell them all they needed to know. As they turned out through the gates Peden said, 'S'pose I have to congratulate you?'

'How did you guess?'

'Oh, come off it! You turned in some nice stuff tonight.'

'Thanks, Bap.'

'Will the boss let you away?'

He laughed. 'I'm gonna take the afternoon off. It's the only thing I can do.'

Peden drove for a time in silence. 'S'pose it is, Davie.'

'Well, isn't it?'

'You know what you're up to, Davie. There's one thing. If you have to do it that way I wouldn't tell too many people about getting a run for the Seniors. They might start wondering how you can make it on a Wednesday—'

'I can see that,' he interrupted. Peden disapproved. So would the others, his mother, and Maureen. Here he was with one of the big moments of his life and he couldn't tell anybody about it.

But it was Maureen who had the surprising news when they met. They were strolling homeward in silence under the beech trees in University Road, where, for a few hundred yards, their vast market town took on the grace and elegance of a city. She had said little during their walk. It made him uneasy when she was silent. Perhaps it was his fault. Something he had said. Or failed to say.

'Bonar's left home.'

He stopped. 'You mean run away?'

'No, no,' she said pettishly. 'People the size of Bonar don't run away!'

'Don't they?' he inquired mildly.

'He just said he was tired living at home. He wanted to try somewhere else for a change. Another part of the town.'

It was absurd, but with a sudden pang he felt that Boney should have talked it over with him first. 'Has he got a job?'

The answer was almost inaudible in the dusk. 'He's got a start as a labourer.'

His sympathy was with her immediately, with her mother and Arthur. He had seen enough to know how desperately hard it was for kitchen-house people to clamber one step above manual labour and how easy to slip back. 'Surely he could have got something better'n that!'

'That was the way he wanted it.' She sounded bitter. He didn't tell her about the dark-haired girl. He should have told her long ago. It was too late to tell her now.

There was a cup of tea for him in Majestic Street. It was one of the perquisites of being engaged. Sometimes he liked this prolonging of their night out. It all depended on his mood and who was in the kitchen. Tonight Mr McFall was alone and sober. For David's benefit he explained why the house was so unnaturally quiet. Willie was in bed, Arthur was out, Mrs McFall was over at her sister's, Bonar . . .

'S'pose you've heard about Bonar?'

'Yes, he's got a job and he's living in digs somewhere.'

Mr McFall considered. 'You could say that. Yes, you could put it that way. But it would be doing him less than justice. Like the immortal Bazarov he has submerged himself in the life of the people. Ah, yes—' The little man blew on his pipe and waited. 'That name means little to you, Davie?'

He sat with his chin in his hand, his gaze on the modest autumn fire in the grate. 'Not a ha'porth, Mr McFall.'

'Ah, well, it doesn't matter,' he heard the little man say. It didn't matter because Bonar's absence mattered so much. It had been in that 'ah, yes'. His wife absent, no one to restrain him in his gleeful blethering, yet the father sat silent, his hands on his knees, his cold pipe laced in his fingers. He wondered should he tell him about the match for Glenbank Seniors, but that too didn't matter at this time in this place. With relief they turned to the girl as she brought in the tea and the inevitable, delicious toasted barmbrack scenting the air with its peel and fruit and melting butter.

4

ALEC RODEN offered him a piece of chocolate. He declined with just the appropriate trace of squeamishness in his smile. Alec flipped the chocolate into his own mouth.

'What's up? Your guts banjaxed?'

'I dunno. It's nothing really. It'll go away.'

'Hope so. You look a bit white round the gills.'

He wondered how he had achieved that but was thankful for the corroborative evidence. Alec discussed the storage of a new line of thornproofs, took another look at him and suggested, if he still felt bad after lunch that he should let the apprentice do the lifting and heaving. He didn't pursue the matter. The seed, he felt, was sown.

At one o'clock he went round to Joe Snax, had a stew lunch, collected his bag from behind the counter and caught a bus for the Glenbank pitch. Billy Thompson, the assistant trainer, met him at the entrance to the dressing-rooms. McClenaghan was to be told the minute he arrived. They were afraid, said Thompson, that he mightn't be able to turn up. Irritated, he said, 'Well, I'm here. You tell him!' As he moved away the trainer followed him and whisered, 'Don't get a big head, buster, we're crowded here as it is.' A minute later Thompson was back to apologize, to explain. He shouldn't have spoken like that. Unobserved, they squeezed hands. 'It was my fault, Billy. Tell you the God's truth I *had* to make up a story to get away.' Thompson insisted, 'No, it was *me*. Sorry again. We all have the shakes. It's always the same at this time.' And David glancing round the dressing-room sensed the fidgety excitement of the players as the murmur from the crowd filtered down to them. He couldn't share in it. What he had already done surfeited, for the time, his capacity for unrest. 'Come and meet the boys.' He took the round of introductions pleasantly and modestly. Then he changed with Lennox, Mulhern and Garland. McClenaghan came over to them. 'I'm saying little to you chaps. I don't expect anybody to bust themselves this early. Just remember if you do well for the Seniors today, you do well for yourselves. All serene?'

They trotted out before the usual mid-week crowd, half-day men, the workless, and three or four bus loads of supporters from Bogsend. Traditionally, the Bogsenders took the game seriously. Gathered in a dense clump on the unreserved banking, they were revealing by means of flags and loud cries how they had fused, over the years, the seemingly incompatible elements of their politics, their football partisanship and their theological certitudes.

The referee drew the captains together and the coin twirled in the air. From his place on the right David glanced over the lineout of the sides and for the first time his spittle thickened in apprehension. The Bogsend men hadn't a star in their side but they were eleven tough triers who, by the end of the season, would have thrust themselves up into third or fourth place in the League. He had the pace, he thought he might have the tricks, he didn't know if he had the nerve to prise into that rugged defence.

The whistle trilled and Garland pushed the ball back to Blair at left-half. From Blair it ran to the inside-left who parted with it hurriedly in a through pass back to Garland. The opposing centre-half intercepted, failed to control the ball and Mulhern was in to lift it on his foot. Instinctively, David moved into the open space but even as they sighted each other Mulhern was robbed and a stabbing ground pass was laid behind David's heels to the Bogsend outside-left who ran it into touch. As they lined up for the throw-in he was bewildered. This was almost a different game. In the few seconds since the kick-off, men and ball had travelled about twice as fast as in the type of football he had played before. It was no longer a question of whether he would dance through the defence but whether he could keep up with the run of play.

But although they were jolted and thrown back for a time, the Glenbank line began to move with more coherence. Blair, under pressure in his own goal area, slung a long pass ahead on the left.

Too far ahead. The Bogsend left-back turned and unhurriedly gathered the ball to clear. As he steered it round he sensed a danger that shouldn't have been there. In his last quick glimpse he had seen only orange and black shirts. He came round to face David closing in on him. Unprepared for such a swift and eager challenge he gave away a corner.

It led to nothing but Glenbank now raided with more boldness into their opponents' half. Speed in itself is exciting but the discriminating ask for more. The new outside-right gave it, outrunning the half-backs and pushing the ball into Mulhern's flight or across the face of the Glenbank line. Mulhern's short vigorous rushes drew pressure away from Garland, and the centre-forward was given the chance to show what a viperish foot he possessed. The seams began to show in the defence. The left-half came heavily at Mulhern, bounced off and stretched himself melodramatically on the turf. An outraged murmur rose from the Bogsend crowd sharpening into demands that Mulhern should be penalized. The referee would have none of it. The crowd on the banking yelled abuse at the Glenbank inside-right. The Glenbank supporters yelled at the crowd on the banking. The referee waved play on. Blair won the ball and dropped it in a long curve to Fitzsimons on the left. It came to Garland who flicked it to Mulhern crossing swiftly in his wake. The inside-right allowed the ball to bound from the side of his foot. Garland walked it round the defeated goalkeeper and into the back of the net. It was the sort of goal Glenbank supporters dreamt of on long summer nights.

As he trotted back for the restart David glanced up at the stand. Dr Boustead was cocked back in his seat, his knees drawn up to his chin in glee. McClenaghan leaned forward, grinning, still clapping slowly as if his applause would have to run itself out.

David was about to overtake Mulhern when a man craned over the fence as the inside-right passed him and said in a low carrying voice, 'G'wan ye fenian bastard!' Mulhern stopped, took a step towards the sideline, and thrust up two fingers in a derisive gesture. David saw a policeman move abruptly at the foot of the stand. Outraged, the man gaped at Mulhern, then began to scramble over the fence. Along the length of the pitch, like the breaking of a drab wave, men came tumbling and vaulting on to the grass.

'Run Mulhern!' he shouted. As he backed away he saw the Glenbank supporters in the stand leaping down from seat to seat. Mulhern, frightened but sullen, stood with lowered head. Two or three Bogsend players ran towards the intruders, waving them back. The mob swallowed them up. Too late, Mulhern started to move. He brought up his hands as they caught him. A man thumped him on the face and knocked him to the ground. David saw a boot swing back. Then the police were among them, purposeful in their stiff black waterproofs. Two constables hauled Mulhern to his feet. A frenzied youth rushed in to swing at him, a baton cracked, and the assailant danced out of the crowd in agony, calling for God's curse on his wrist clapped between his thighs. Amen, you swine, thought David, watching him with relish.

Escorted by McClenaghan, Thompson and two constables, Mulhern was helped away. Police and club officials were driving the smouldering crowd off the pitch. Here and there fights sparked up like small fires. A young constable herding in the players bore down on David. His face was pale and he spoke brusquely. 'Come on, now. What's holding you? Get in, get in, the lot av you.' Obediently they trotted before him. The dressing-room was crowded. Billy Thompson bent over Mulhern, staunching a trickle of blood from his mouth. As he took the sponge away Mulhern protested again: 'But I'm not a Catholic. I'm a Protestant. Sure, everybody knows that!'

' 'Course everybody knows you're a Prod,' said Billy cheerily. 'It was your name that foxed them. They're a simple-minded lota buggers round Bogsend.'

A young fellow flapping an open notebook asked, 'Is your man all right, Billy?'

'Sure he is,' said Thompson. 'He coulda got hurt far worse if he had been playing football,' and he bounced the sponge playfully on Mulhern's head.

Dissatisfied, the young fellow peered around. 'You Davie Minnis?'

'Yes.'

'You all right, Davie?'

He disliked the familiarity, the sharp inquisitiveness. 'What would be wrong with me?'

'Not the best introduction to senior football, eh?'

From the doorway McClenaghan said, 'I want this place cleared as soon as possible, please.'

'O.K., Mac,' said the young fellow slapping shut his book.

Changed and waiting for a lift to Colinvista Street he remembered the inquisitive individual. He turned to Lennox. The goalkeeper laughed. 'That was a newspaper man. Surely you knew that?'

He hadn't known that. The idea that newspaper reporters might be there had never entered his head.

5

He had never before looked through so many newpapers in the same day. They all carried a report of the match, even the cross-Channel ones. As Mulhern had been beaten up due to a rather comical misunderstanding the local press refrained from drawing any political conclusions from the incident. But their headings, he thought, were unnecessarily graphic: 'Batons Drawn at Glenbank, Mob Attack Player in Unfriendly Friendly', and so on. And apart from the team list his name was mentioned twice. One reporter drew attention to his clever partnership with the assaulted Mulhern. The second told his readers that 'another newcomer to senior ranks, Davie Minnis, remarked to me in the dressing-room that this wasn't his idea of a first introduction to big football.'

I didn't say that!

So there must be two people called Davie Minnis? You weren't there?

No, there's only one Davie Minnis. I was there . . .

Everything was much the same around the department except

that Alec forgot to ask him if he was better. That was ominous. And when Mr. Whaley handed him an order he detected a note of resigned hopelessness in the buyer's voice as if it didn't really matter whether he put the order together or not. It was four o'clock before the Chairman sent for him. He went down the stairs flat-footed and feeling as if his bowels were reacting to a sudden and violent purge.

'Minnis, were you playing football yesterday afternoon?' Mr Clarence would have looked away, doodled, studied his fingers. The Chairman stared straight at you, even began to tap impatiently as the silence lengthened.

'Yessir.'

'Without, of course, asking for permission?'

He allowed himself a moment to consider this astonishing suggestion.

'Minnis?'

'I'm sorry, sir . . . very sorry . . .'

'First we had the slight indisposition in the morning then the miraculous recovery in the afternoon. It wasn't very clever was it?'

'I didn't mean—'

'You meant it, Minnis. And you might have got away with it if I hadn't been shown the newspapers. Remember what I told you some time ago?'

It was such an unpleasant recollection that he could only swallow and nod.

'Have you looked for another job?'

'Well, no, Mr Hamilton. They're kinda hard to find.'

'That's unfortunate, Minnis, because we're dismissing you from this one. I don't think you can consider that either hasty or unfair. Mr Ankatell—'

'Look, Mr Hamilton, if you'll give me a chance—'

'Why? What use would you make of it? In the years you've been here you've shown no interest in the work. That means you're not very good at it. No, Minnis, you're not going to get another chance.' The Chairman closed the file and tossed it into the Out basket. 'Mr Ankatell will give you your wages and whatever else is due to you. If you need a reference no doubt Mr Ankatell can look after that, too. That's all.'

Had he given in too easily? Could he talk old Hamilton into changing his mind? Perhaps if . . . ? The Chairman had lowered his head. He looked down on that pale, inimical baldness. Appeal rejected. He closed the door respectfully behind his dragging feet. And what of those Few Parting Words that Boney and Fogarty and he had elaborated and polished against the day they would leave the employment of Messrs Hamiltons? His tongue lay as nerveless between his jaws as had Boney's when his day had come.

The assistants in the Mantles Department watched him with curiosity. He paused, took out his pocket-book and rearranged some papers. Suddenly he stuffed his pocket-book back into his pocket. Why the hell should he go on acting a part that meant nothing now?

They were waiting for him in the Cash Office. As he entered, Mr Ankatell, slick on his cue as always, called for 'those things of David Minnis'. His cards and pay packet were brought to the counter by the snobbish little blonde who had always pretended that it was an accident when her eyes dwelt on him.

'Cards stamped up to date,' said Mr Ankatell, adding delicately, 'You know that if you've no other employment immediately in mind you take them to the buroo?'

It was the first time he had really thought about that. He was unable to answer Mr Ankatell.

'And here,' added Mr Ankatell, shaking the pay packet gently, 'you'll find your money right up to the end of the current week *and* a full week in lieu of notice. Not ungenerous of the Chairman, I think you'll agree?'

'Do I sign for this?' he said harshly.

'Here.'

When he had signed the pay sheet there was a very high-class envelope with the flap tucked in. 'Your reference,' said Mr Ankatell, 'and I'm sure we all hope it brings you luck.' Mr Ankatell held out one hand as he scrabbled up the pay sheet with the other. No time to be lost by the employed. David felt the secretary shake off his surprised but sincere clasp. No time at all for the unemployed.

Mr Whaley was in his shirtsleeves, a handful of patterns fanned out on the counter before him. 'Yes, David, I know.' The tired, quizzical eyes considered him. 'What's going to happen to you, eh? I'm not sorry to lose you, but I'm sorry you're going, if you see what I mean?'

'Thanks, Mr Whaley.'

'Hope things go well with you, David. By the way, you needn't go looking for Alec. He had to go out.'

'Sorry about that, Mr Whaley. I'd like to have shaken hands with Alec. He took such a close interest in my football career.'

Mr Whaley looked at him calmly. 'Somebody has to have a sense of responsibility, y'know, David.'

He moved away in search of Fogarty. He found him deep in conversation with a young woman at the back of the stockroom. Fogarty often had these long intimate chats with pretty customers. This time he didn't retreat as usual, but hung around within earshot busily folding sheets of wrapping paper. Although he felt hollow in the stomach he grinned at Fogarty's mounting irritation. At last they came out from among the coat-racks, and Fogarty escorted the girl to the head of the stairs assuring her loudly that the order would be delivered that evening. He came back, scowling. 'What d'ya mean hanging round like that, Minnis? That woman thought you were snooping. You'll get yourself into trouble with Mr Hamilton one of these days.'

David leaned against the counter to laugh.

'It's not funny—'

'You'll never know how funny it is . . .' He sobered up. 'Or, at least, you will. I've had my trouble, Fogarty boy. I've just been sacked—fired—chucked out.'

'Aw, go to hell,' said Fogarty.

He showed him the pay packet and cards.

Fogarty shook his head. 'That's shocking, boy. What did you do this time—I mean, worse than usual?'

Suddenly he wanted to walk away from the whole mess. 'Ah. I'll tell you sometime—'

'Where are y'going now?'

'Out.'

'I'll come with you. You go on.'

When he was halfway down the stairs he heard Fogarty shout: 'I'm going over to McConnell's for those samples, Mr. Whaley. More'n likely be back before half-five!' He put his hand lightly on the carved pillar of the banisters. The last time I'll touch you. But mebbe not. Mebbe I'll go into the tick drapery. Come back and buy stuff here. The effervescence of the idea carried him past Mr Hamilton's office and into the open air. Fogarty overtook him and headed towards Waring Street. David stopped. 'I thought you were going to McConnell's.'

Fogarty laughed. 'What put that idea into your head?'

'Do you do this sort of thing often?'

Fogarty shrugged. 'Sometimes I step out for an hour or so.'

'I do it once and get caught on.'

'You're the mug. You get your name in the papers.'

They crossed the street. 'Where are we going?'

'A place I know.' Fogarty dived under the arch of a narrow court and led him down the worn cobbles until they stopped under a heavy lamp. 'The neatest wee pub in the city. Come on.'

As they sat down David glanced at the pub clock. 'I've a date,' he said.

'You've tons of time. You should always have a coupla drinks in you before you meet a dame. Mebbe it's not that sorta dame?'

'No, Fogarty, it's not that sort of dame.'

'O.K., forget it. What'll it be—a pint?'

The barman slid the cold, tawny-crested glasses in front of them. 'Hair on your chest,' said Fogarty raising his pint and because of its weight making a thick, clumsy flourish in the air.

'On yours,' responded David, and took a swig. He repressed a shudder at the taste of the porter. He wasn't sure whether he liked the stuff. But it had two virtues. It was cheap and somebody had told him it wouldn't hurt his wind.

'What are you gonna do now?'

'Oh, I dunno. Something'll turn up.'

'Mebbe Roden did you a good turn after all.'

'So it was Alec split on me?'

'Who else?'

He was silent for a moment, fingering the fair hair at his brow.

'And on Boney?'

'On all that lot. He was sent down to the meeting to keep an eye on who went.'

'I hope the blirt sleeps well at night.'

'What would hinder him? He was only doing his duty. Somebody has to have a sense of responsibility—'

'Aw, button up, Tits!'

'—and he hopes to get married soon.'

He took a slug at his pint. It wasn't bad when you got used to it. 'He's been getting married ever since I knew him. I hope he gets what he deserves.'

'You going with a dame?'

He eyed Fogarty warily. 'Could be.'

'Thinking of getting married?'

'It could happen.'

Fogarty eased back in his chair, reassuring him. 'Why don't you stick into the football? There's money there.'

'Thirty bob a week?'

'I don't mean in this dump. I mean across the water.'

'You have to wait till you're asked.'

He drained his glass. The cold liquid that tasted like a penny in the mouth was warming and soothing in the belly. 'Drink up,' he said. 'We'll have the other half.'

Fogarty laughed. 'Aye, the other half of the quart.'

He gaped. 'Gor, you're right, you know. Two pints one quart, four quarts one gallon—what's after that?'

'That'll do to be going on with. Hi, manager, something similar.'

'Two pints one quart, four quarts one gallon, two gallons one peck, pole or rod—'

'I see you're a man of some education. Take your drink.' He hadn't meant to have two drinks. Two made your breath smell. And he had to speak to his mother and Maureen this evening.

'Well, here's to you, Tits. I'll have to be on my way.' Honours were even. He had taken a drink from Fogarty and bought him one in return.

The pub was filling. Men with the evening edition under their arms were gathering at the bar. A flock of office girls ventured in. The barman shooed them into the lounge. He could see them through the open door. They were all pretty girls. Their excited voices fifed and fluted through the doorway and the service hatch. They were celebrating the departure of one of their number to be married.

'You'll go on the dole, I s'pose?'

'Yes.'

'You should try the tick business. You could always get appro from the ould firm.'

He took his eyes away from the girls. 'I was thinking of that.' He drank and set down his glass. 'Some of those tick men do all right, don't they?'

'I'll say. Stick hard at it for a coupla years and you'll be able to get married—'

'Don't keep on talking about getting married! Who said anything about getting married?'

Fogarty held up a restraining hand. 'O.K., I thought you were going serious. My mistake.' He peered over David's shoulder into the lounge. 'That looks nice in there. What say we order the third half and move in?'

'No.' He fumbled at the buttons of his coat. 'Time I was going. Where's the Gents?'

When he came back there were fresh pints on the table.

'Who ordered those?'

'Me. You just said no to joining the company in the lounge, didn't you? And they've gone.' He looked into the lounge. The girls had fled in his absence. A man sat at their table staring morosely into his whiskey. He felt cheated. 'Off they flew on their wee ports and sherries. And not a thing'll happen to them. Good liquor wasted,' said Fogarty. 'Don't waste yours.'

David folded his hand round the glass. 'I shouldn't be doing this,' he said weakly. He glanced at the clock. It was now almost half-past six. His date with Maureen was for seven. He could never get home, have his tea, get cleaned and be at Majestic Street on time. Simply couldn't be done. The realization brought relief. He settled down to his drink. As well be hung for a sheep as a lamb.

Fogarty perused him. 'Sure, you're in no hurry,' he said. 'We never get a chance to talk.'

'That's terribly true, Tits. It's years since I've seen you.' Would Maureen be angry? He had the answer. Big row at the place. Got sacked. Had to have a talk that night with one of the chief assistants. Chance of another job. Come home, all will be forgiven. He took a long drink. The same yarn might do for his mother. Had to talk to a man about work. And that wasn't really a lie. 'I'm sure you'd help me all you could, Tits?'

'After meself there's no one whose future prosperity I will keep a keener eye upon.'

'Thanks, Tits.' He stood up.

'Again?'

'Again.' He reeled a little.

'Jaze, you're not blootered on two or three pints a porter?'

He waved an admonitory finger. 'It's on an empty stomach. When you're in strict training you're not used to drink. I'll be back.'

'Bet your life you will. It's your round.'

'Oh . . .' He fumbled in his pocket and drew out a handful of coppers. 'No use?'

Fogarty shook his head.

'S'all right.' He drew out the envelope that Mr Ankatell had given him and tore it open. He took out a pound note and slapped it down on the damp table. 'There y'are.'

He looked up through the lavatory window. The glow from ten thousand lights couldn't wash away the cool stars over the city. He blew out his cheeks and shuddered. Lovely, lovely stars. Maureen would be waiting for him now. Beginning to worry. He had never let her down before. Dear Maureen. Gor, this would have to stop. This would be the last time. Here he was—lost his job, let his girl down, hurt his mother, getting drunk. Everything bad. A fella couldn't get much lower than this. But tomorrow would be a new leaf—a fresh start. The tough (but not too protracted) upward struggle from tonight would demand all his strength and resolution. He was impatient to begin. Swaying gently, he closed his eyes to see that well-ordered, happy and important life that lay ahead. From tomorrow, b'gor . . .

6

He had never known his mother so angry. After breakfast she swept swiftly and silently through her housework with abrupt gestures and icy face. Crouched at the fire, gingerly tasting his saliva, he acknowledged that she still had the power to frighten him. But last night's fuddled mumblings about being sacked made it necessary for her to keep open some channel of communication. Instead of the bleak silence that he feared she stopped occasionally to question him in curt unsmiling words. And as her morning wore on, his drunken homecoming was eclipsed by the realization that he was sitting there, workless.

He made no attempt to tell her the truth. Business was bad and he had got a warning when they refused to give him his full rise, hadn't he? She weighed him up in her quiet, shrewd glance and knew that he was telling her a lie. But what would be damaged in telling him so would be irreparable. She had to be content knowing that he was aware of what she guessed. On a small point she revealed her scepticism. 'Why Thursday? Thursday's no day to pay anybody off.'

'It suited their books. Their business books, I mean.'

There was a silence. He tightened the girdle of his dressing-gown and went upstairs. Half an hour later he came down dressed and shaved. 'I'm going out for a while.' There was no reply from the scullery. 'I've a fella to see. I'll be back for lunch.'

He closed the street door softly and sniffed the air. Pity he hadn't got out into this earlier. But, after last night's carry-on, he couldn't rush out too quick, even if his head and legs had felt up to it.

He approached the Labour Exchange with a feeling of sick excitement, tramping towards it in a roundabout way through unfamiliar streets. The Exchange, fittingly enough, was in the town's dreariest thoroughfare. The workless thronged the pavement in queues, crowds, small argumentative clusters. After a few inquiries among the initiated lounging against the wall he attached himself to a queue. Heaven knew what indignities he might have to endure. He winced as someone bawled his name. It was young Wilson, late of the Woollens. 'Joined the club, Minnis boy?'

He turned and replied with a sickly smile. He had never liked young Wilson at any time. 'You still outa work, Wilson?'

Wilson edged up beside him. 'Oh, in and out. Got a month at Christmas selling toys. What hit you?'

'Oh, I just got—paid off.'

'Give you a tip. There's nothing for our trade here. Tell them you'll do anything. Just to get the ould stamps on the card. Me, I hawked encyclopædias for a while.'

'Did you sell any?'

'One. It was always raining. I used to sit in cafes and read the bloody things. A coupla months ago I could've made you dizzy talking about ecology, codology and conifarry. I've forgotten it all now—I woulda made a professor or something, I think, if I had got the chance,' he added wistfully.

Young Wilson told him that he didn't have to wait in the queue. To sign on for the first time he should go straight in. He hurried away from Wilson through a doorway worn dark and shining by the leisurely polishing of a hundred thousand shoulders. To his surprise the man behind the counter was sympathetic and helpful. David's refinement increased as they filled in a form together.'

'Why did you lose your job?'

'Ah . . . slack work.'

They both smiled at the ambiguity. 'I mean—'

'That's all right.' The clerk jotted something on the form. 'What sort of job are you looking for?'

'I dunno . . . I suppose something the same.'

'Not much moving in your sort of work. Take a retail job?'

'Yes, if you think . . .'

'If anything suitable turns up you'll get a card. You're supposed to take it. Understand that?'

'Yes, thanks.'

'You sign on at Box 27, 11.15 a.m. Wednesdays, and collect your money same time Fridays. Hope you get fixed up soon. Sign here, please.'

'Yes, indeed. I'm very much obliged to you.'

He saw the clerk's slightly surprised look. Mebbe I sounded a bit too cut-glass there, he thought as he turned away. But I *am* different from the rest of this crowd. Outside, the same queues, made up of other men and women, crawled patiently through the same soiled doorways.

There was still time to see Maureen as she came out at lunch-time. By a more direct route he hurried to Donegall House, the city store where she worked, and stationed himself a few yards down the pavement from the employees' entrance. She was punctual. As she came opposite him he stepped out. 'Hello,' he said. She kept her head averted, and for a moment he thought she was going to walk past. Then she glanced at him, and paused. They allowed the hurrying eddies of the crowd to carry them into the refuge of a doorway.

'I'm sorry about last night,' he said.

She looked at him again, rocking one shoe over on its high heel, then glanced away without speaking. She would have acted like this he thought with growing irritation even if I couldn't have helped last night's broken date.

'I'll be late for dinner,' she said curtly. 'Is there anything you want to tell me?'

'There is. I dunno whether you'll think it important. I lost my job last night.'

'Important?' She touched his arm. 'Oh, David . . . And me worrying about you not turning up! How did it happen?'

'Well, I got paid off—'

'Yes, but why? Did you expect it?'

He straightened himself. 'To tell you the truth, Maureen, I took Wednesday afternoon off to play football.'

'Oh.' Her hand fell from his sleeve. 'Without telling them? That wasn't very sensible . . . I mean . . . at this time . . .'

Responsibility. You've no sense of responsibility, everybody says. 'I was asked to play for the Seniors . . .'

He followed her as she moved away. 'What are you going to do now?'

'Get another job. A better one, of course.'

'Yes. Of course. David, I'll be terribly late.'

'I meant to tell you why I didn't turn up. There was that fella Fogarty, he had some ideas—'

She glanced distractedly at her watch. 'David dear, I'll be losing *my* job. Tonight?'

'Then you forgive me?'

'Yes, yes. I forgive you. 'Bye.'

He watched her neat, blue, leaf of a hat until it was swallowed in the crowd. He wasn't sure how she had taken the news. Perhaps he had said too much. But if you couldn't be absolutely truthful sometimes with the girl you were supposed to marry, with whom then?

Not until he was turning into Colinvista Street did he remember that he hadn't told that nice fella at the buroo that he earned a few shillings playing football. Come to think of it, he hadn't heard from the Glenbank people since Wednesday. He swallowed and hoped that they hadn't heard of his frolic on Thursday night.

On the following morning he went out to the ground. Fred Mort was seated outside the dressing-rooms cleaning and relacing a heap of boots.

'I thought I would've heard from you, Fred,' he said sulkily.

Mort looked up with a smile. 'Davie, you don't have to hear

from us. You're always welcome round the old place. Here, make yourself useful and stick a lace in that, will you?'

He pushed the boot aside. 'Come off it, Fred! I want something more definite than that. Isn't there a public trials game today?'

'That's right.'

'Why amn't I playing?'

'Don't you read your papers? After Wednesday's carry-on Mulhern will probably be suspended for ungentlemanly conduct—'

'What's that got to do with me?'

Mort didn't look up this time. 'Well, you see, the Doc doesn't want the combination broken up, like—'

'So I'm victimized because Mulhern's an eejit!'

'*Victimized*. Ah, Davie, come it easy!'

'D'you know what Wednesday's trouble cost me?'

'No, what?'

He drew back. 'Can I see Billy McClenaghan?'

'Sure, you can.' There was a crunching of tyres on the cinder patch. 'Mebbe this is him, now.'

But it was Bap Peden who came round the corner, hands in pockets, sprucely dressed as ever, his face lighting up as he saw David.

'G'wan, tell me, what did it cost you?'

'Nothing,' he mumbled. 'Forget it. But there's one thing I want to know,' his voice fell to an urgent whisper, 'and I want it straight. Has the club anything against me?'

Mort looked up in surprise. 'What are you talking about, Davie? Nobody's anything against you. A coupla weeks time and you'll be out there in a Senior shirt—'

'Thanks, Fred, thanks!'

'Hullo, there!' called Peden. 'Heard you were in the wars on Wednesday.'

'Oh, *that*. The papers always make a song and dance outa that sorta thing.'

7

Maureen was unfailingly attentive and considerate. Even when he could pay their way to a cinema she suggested a walk. On Sunday afternoons it was a seat in the park. One evening a week he helped her carry the family's reading from the branch public library. To her this sufficed very well as courtship until he was earning again. He felt some impatience with these tame and frugal outings but her earnestness, so winning in that charming face, and her confidence in him never failed in their appeal.

His mother, he felt, would have liked to keep the wound green, but her anger and disappointment swiftly gave way to anxiety about his future. From the unanswered applications, the morose homecomings, she began to apprehend something of the invisible barrier that rose between the employed and the workless. It was a wall through which, as day dragged after day, there seemed to be no entrance. In his wanderings around the city, David got the unnerving impression that every warehouse, factory, office and shop was staffed to completion, that there was no flexibility or flux in the world of work and earning.

To his annoyance young Wilson got into the habit of waiting for him. In the queue he tried to keep their exchanges to the minimum. One drear morning as they joined the tail of the queue he examined the long lines of hats, caps and bare heads that stretched in front of them.

'Must take a mint of money to keep this lot in idleness.'

'Cheaper than a revolution,' said young Wilson sharply.

He glanced at the other with distaste. 'Where did you get that crack, Professor? From your encyclopædia?'

'From being on the dole. You've a lot to learn, Minnis.'

'Aw, go to hell.'

When he arrived next morning young Wilson had taken his place ahead of him in the queue.

Lounging around at home had become unbearable. If the

weather was dry he made his walk back from the Exchange a slow wandering maze through the city streets, gazing into the shop windows, watching from the stillness of a doorway the hurrying, purposeful crowds. That same morning in Fountain Lane he met Bonar. The girl he had seen at the Spinners Hall was linking his friend's arm.

'Hullo, Davie.' The smile was absent but the familiar voice was warm. 'How's tricks?'

'Could be worse.'

The knobbly forehead was smooth, the dank locks cut back short. The face above the dark, muscular neck was the firm, grave face of a man.

'You're taller!'

They both laughed, Bonar and the girl. 'It must be the hard work.' Bonar looked down at her, the smile still lingering at the corners of his mouth. 'I don't think you've met Rona?'

He stifled a tremor of anger, smiled, and ducked his head. Her face was pale, with long, delicate cheekbones, and her hair that he had thought black was touched in the movements of her head with secret colours, like the wing of a bird. He could consider her face with a prim dispassion. Such colour and contours were alien to him. He remembered Harry Peebles' claim that he could tell three out of every four Catholics that he met in the street. And they could do the same with us. It's born into us to be able to do that, Peebles had said.

Bonar was genial, ready to respond, but his eyes wandered continually over the crowd, scrutinizing the approaching faces with a strange, alert wariness. It was only when the girl spoke that his attention was fully engaged. They're in love, he thought, and saw how she leaned close to the hard, muscular flank of the man. He'll soon have trouble remembering my name, he thought bitterly.

On the point of parting he said, 'Ah—will I mention at Majestic Street that I saw you?'

Bonar paused and turned back. He considered the other for a moment. There was contempt in his voice when he spoke. 'If you remember and you think it's worth while.'

A woman forced her pram between them. The crowd swirled in driving them apart. When he looked back Bonar and the girl had disappeared. He hurried away with his head down. Roast him, I meant it all in good faith. You'll wait a helluva long time before you catch me even thinking of Bonar McFall's name again.

There was no message from McClenaghan awaiting him at Colinvista Street. On Saturday the Seniors had a home game. McClenaghan would expect him to be there, playing or not. Show them you're as keen as mustard, had been Lennox's advice But on Saturday afternoon he sat in the house listening gloomily to a broadcast commentary on another match. Glenbank lost their first League game by three goals to one.

On Monday morning resentment and boredom drove him out to the football ground. He felt he would welcome a chat even with Collins, the footballer with the paintbrush. As he entered the ground Fred Mort left the groundsman and came across the pitch towards him.

'The very man, Davie! McClenaghan wants to see you—'

'Why?'

'He'll tell you. I think he's down with the painters at the big stand.'

He was glad he had run into Mort first. Whatever it was that McClenaghan wanted to see him about he must be careful not to show too much enthusiasm. He met the manager near the track.

'Feeling fit, Davie?'

'I'm all right, Mr Mac.'

'Good. You're out for the Seniors against Barnsmore on Saturday.'

'With Mulhern?'

'With Mulhern—' The manager paused. 'Well, good news?'

'Only kind of, Mr Mac. It seems I've been hanging round all this time waiting on Mulhern's convenience—'

'Now, don't get sour, Davie! It hasn't made all that much difference—two matches.'

'Except that I'm outa work.'

'Why didn't you tell us?'

He shrugged. 'What would be the use?'

'Lift your cards and bring them to me tomorrow morning—'

'Not painting or driving in nails round the ground?'

The manager laughed. 'No, not that! Bring your cards and I'll give you a receipt—in the shape of a professional form.'

'That—that's great, Mr McClenaghan.' His eyes smarted as he stuttered his thanks. 'You know I—you know how it is—'

McClenaghan didn't clap him on the shoulder but just said in a quick, business-like voice, 'When you come along to the office make sure you know your own mind.'

'I know it now, Mr Mac.'

By the time he had got down to the Exchange, over to the Glenbank ground, and back home he was late for his dinner. He brushed aside her questions and ran upstairs. In the privacy of his room he laid out the money that McClenaghan had given him. Forty pounds for his mother. Ten pounds he folded back into the envelope which he slipped between the spring and the mattress of his bed.

As he sat down he pushed the roll of notes across the table to her. 'That's what kept me late. Football money. I've signed again for another year.'

She looked at it distrustfully. 'That's far more than anything you've had before—'

'That's right. I'm far better than ever before.'

As she hesitantly leafed the notes a dozen small bills vanished from behind the clock. The amount seemed generous, extravagant. Was she fit to judge whether or not her son was giving fair service for such an amount of money? With a feeling of unease she turned her back on the query.

'Forty pounds, gracious! Won't you have to tell the buroo people about this?'

'They've been told.'

'This—won't interfere with your getting a real job?'

He noted the hesitation and kept his voice restrained and level. 'Not in any way, mother.'

She leaned over and kissed him on the head. 'I'll buy you a new sports jacket. You're a good boy, David.'

'You're a good mother,' he said looking up with a smile.

Maureen was very glad. She could see that that was expected of her. They had walked up into the Castlereagh Hills and now stood in a grassy gateway looking down on the glowing beadwork of the city streets. In a low, excited voice he talked of what this chance meant to him. A good season with Glenbank and he might get an offer from one of the bigger clubs, Glentoran mebbe, or Linfield. Then, who knows, a transfer to an English side. That's where the big money was, and a player's life was short. As he talked, moving precipitately from one point to the next, he contrived with almost conscious recklessness to sketch a future that included himself alone. Her silence dragged him to a standstill. 'I'm telling only you about signing professional. I didn't tell my mother. She would only fuss. D'you think I did right?'

Grave, reproachful, he held her out at arm's length in the darkness. 'Are you bored by all this?'

'No—no—' To his horror she was sobbing. He drew her into him, soothing her with a tenderness that he frantically tried to feel in his heart.

Afterwards they were subdued and rather frightened. But on their way down the hill they began to laugh at themselves, like the first timid blink of sun after a shower. By the time they reached the tram terminus they were swinging along, hand in hand, happy in each other's company.

At Majestic Street she brought him in for a cup of tea. The kitchen was crowded. Pat Rogan was there with Arthur, Sadie Monteith had dropped in bringing with her a package of fish and chips. Willie had been allowed downstairs for his share.

It was Maureen who told them (with his permission) that they had a senior footballer in their company. Observing that Arthur was impressed the women showered him with congratulations.

'I'll be there on Saturday, Davie,' said Arthur.

'Thanks. Hope you'll be there too, Mr McFall.'

The father shook his head. 'Not even for you, Davie. Not even for you. I've seen too many workless streaming out of football grounds fighting about things that had damn all to do with them. "One way of getting an idea of our fellow-creatures' miseries is to go and look at their pleasures."' The little man glanced around at their discomfited faces. 'Well, is nobody going to ask me who said that?'

Willie, his mouth shining with grease, looked up. 'You did, Da.'

Mr McFall tried to take the interjection in his stride but the sage's identity was lost in laughter. Mrs McFall clapped her youngest on the back. 'Bully for you, love! Here we've been suffering for years and nobody thought of that answer!' She pushed her gleeful face into her husband's. ' "Out av the mouths av babes and sucklings—" Can you tell me who said that, y' ould cod, ye?'

He settled back in pleasure to take in the bright fire, the smell of appetising food, the laughter, the alive comic expressions of these friends around him. It was almost like old times.

8

TIME was hard to kill. He learnt, very quickly, how priceless was a job, almost any job, to a man. Most days he went across to Glenbank. But he had to be careful. When a training session was finished he cleared out. It was too easy to become a Collins, an odd-job man, or worse, one of the anonymous crowd that hung around during the day content to breathe the air of a big football pitch. Mort warned him against these insolent, obsequious characters, lounging about in track suits, who had lost heart and fibre to take them on to the track and pitch.

He did his best at home, whitewashing the yard, fixing the roof of the outside larder, helping with the cleaning. She was appreciative, but managed somehow to convey that she would be better pleased if he was out hunting for work. And because he hadn't told her the truth at the beginning he had to conceal from her that his future livelihood would be earned on the football field. It was difficult. His disciplined physical life made him as taut as a drawn bow. A flattering press report, or the suggestion that cross-Channel scouts were interested in him, filled him with such exuberance that he had to press his lips together as they sat facing each other across the Saturday evening tea table.

To please her, and without telling McClenaghan, he picked up the occasional job. For a day he unavailingly hawked trade jugs and pencils around pubs and at six o-clock was told not to come back again by the hard-faced little Welshman at the top of the dirty flight of stairs. He carried a case of assorted brushes to a hundred suburban doors. At the end of a week he had sold three toothbrushes and had fled from an avid matron leaving a pot scrubber clutched in her hot fingers. Mr McFall appointed him his unofficial lieutenant. On the mornings when the little man was overcome by melancholy he sped lightheartedly round the city rousing out the cherished favourites of aldermen and councillors to guard holes in the roadway. Always he refused the few shillings Maureen's father pressed him to take. It was worth it, he said, just to get out of the house.

Ever since that evening on the Castelereagh Hills he hadn't talked about football to Maureen. She wasn't really different from his mother. They both wanted him in a warm, safe job. That's how they built him into their future. Neither of them understood he had the makings of a great footballer.

It was a pity that he couldn't tell her what he knew. But he was becoming quite adept at keeping secrets from those who loved him; that is, the people who might claim a right to influence or even curb his future. And he knew that if something hadn't turned up yet, it lay just below the horizon. At half-time on Saturday, as they took a breather in the dressing-room, someone had come in with the news that there was a representative of an English club in the stand. They had all heard that story before. When the football scribes ran out of chit-chat they brought English and Scots talent scouts over the Channel like a flock of rooks. But this time the players noticed a jumpy excitement in the Glenbank officials. There was a tantalizing smell of transfer money about the place. Nobody dared to ask McClenaghan. Billy Thompson said he knew nothing. Mort advised them to keep their minds on the fact that they were a goal down. Then, last night after training, Thompson had told a handful of the Seniors that a director and the manager of an English Second Division club would be at Glenbank on Saturday.

'The same boys that were here last Saturday?'

'Could be.'

'Are they coming back on spec or have they spotted somebody?' asked Kinnear.

'That's all I can tell you,' said Thompson firmly. 'If you ask any more questions you'll make me sorry I opened my mouth.'

As they dressed the players whittled down the possible attractions to four: Charlie Lennox, Garland, Mulhern or Minnis.

'Mulhern *and* Minnis,' said Kinnear.

He stared resentfully at the speaker. 'Why? We're not bloody Siamese twins!'

Mulhern laughed. 'For your sake I hope not. Because I'm not leaving here.'

He sidled up the bench to Mulhern. 'Not even if you got a chance across the water?'

'Not on your nelly.'

'Why?'

'I'm running a nice wee cash business with my mother. I would hardly have my foot on the Heysham boat before my brother would be out of the shipyard and into it like a ferret.'

They all had a card up their sleeves; Lennox was a tradesman, Peden had his agencies, Mulhern his grocery business. He had nothing but his football. The time was past when he could afford to worry about other people's susceptibilities.

Billy Thompson glanced round to make sure that he couldn't be overheard. 'I can tell you one thing, fellas. Whoever gets the offer to go our directors'll be generous with him. Give him a cut of the transfer money—'

'Whadya mean "generous" Billy? A quarter?'

'A third?'

Waving his hand Thompson extricated himself from the chattering mob. 'Now, you know as much as me . . . I only overheard that . . . come on boys, get redd up. I don't want to be here all night.'

He sat apart from his excited team-mates. Say these Englishmen offered to buy him for a thousand quid. That wasn't too big a figure. Say the Glenbank directors gave him a quarter. Two-fifty quid. Gor, *that* was money! With that amount of money he could . . . With that amount of money he would have to be very careful, very discreet, very quiet. 'Coming, Billy . . .'

9

THERE were mornings before big matches when a good digestion, warmth, peace of mind, filled him with a pervasive sense of calm. This is Saturday he would remember as he came up out of the depths of sleep. I've nothing gnawing in my mind. Nothing bigger than a man's hand. As he lay in bed he would tense and relax his limbs restraining the tremor that ran through his body. Calm, calm. I'll need that knife-edge of excitement, that detonation, before the day's out. After breakfast he had to be particularly careful how he moved through the house. A difference with his mother had to be avoided at all cost. He knew, in those mid-morning hours, that she was aware of his hidden eagerness. Even against their wills, it sparked off a resentment. To take the string bag from Freddie's lax hands and run a few messages was the best safeguard. It was a dutiful act and took them out of each other's way.

He was ready for the game when he joined his team-mates under the Glenbank stand. Earlier in the season their opponents, Linfield, had defeated them in the City Cup. But the kaleidoscope of success had been nudged since then. The new names in the Glenbank forward line promised a different outcome today. If the English visitors were interested in him he could wish for no more exhilarating test than this.

The first shadow of uncertainty came to him early in the game. Too often he was losing touch with Mulhern, his inside man. The incisive partnership that the crowd and the opposing defence expected was sluggish and erratic. Once, when he glanced the ball to Mulhern and sped away, expecting the ball to drop as usual into his flight in the open space, he found himself running alone. The crowd chortled. When he looked back the ball had been worked across to the other side of the field. A few minutes later he fed Mulhern again, and watched him as he moved obliquely away. His inside man, usually so thrusting, fiddled with the ball, almost lost it, recovered, and turned it back to Kinnear at centre-half. To his anger and horror he realized that Mulhern was starving him out. So did Kinnear and his half-backs. They fed the ball more and more to the left-wing and David found himself acting as rebound for crosses that swung too far beyond the goal area.

The spectators began to take Mulhern's fumbling under their notice. Their early astonishment turned to derisive yowls. They watched the inside-right secure the ball and turn upfield. Once again David raced hopefully into the open space where the pass should fall. It didn't arrive. He relished the crowd's growl of sympathy and annoyance as he trotted to a frustrated standstill. 'D'ya want him to send ya a diagram, Mulhern?' someone howled from the unreserved side.

As the players came off at the interval he overtook Mulhern. 'What goes on? I haven't had a clean pass from you all afternoon—'

'Sorry, Minnis. I'm just not busting myself.'

'I can see that. But what about me?'

Mulhern scowled. 'If you're all that keen on the bloody ball go after it yourself. McClenaghan and his English pals will think all the more of you.'

Mulhern's play improved a little in the second half. He had decided that he had done enough to deter any possible buyers. But David had still to fetch and carry for himself. And he discovered that Mulhern had been right. The crowd were with him as he went back time after time to work the ball up the field. In the last minutes of the game it was evident to the ten thousand people in the ground that if Glenbank were to force a draw the only man likely to do it was their outside-right. A trickle of spectators was moving towards the exits before his persistence was rewarded. He leaped high in the air for joy as Garland deflected his through pass into the back of the Blues' net. There was no time left to centre the ball. The applause for the goal merged into the chatter of the drifting crowds. His back was thumped as he dived down the passage to the dressing-rooms.

Mr Warnock appeared in the doorway, grinning, giving them the thumbs-up sign. 'Splendid work, boys,' he called. David answered with a bright smile and a wave of the hand. He felt he had played too big a part in the game to pretend that he wasn't due to a big part of the praise. But Mr Warnock's genial appraisal covered them all. When David looked again the Chairman had gone. That was that. Another sports-writer's fairy story. Mulhern, smoothing down his collar, was beside him.

'Well, backwoodsman, satisfied?'

The other looked at him for a moment. 'Minnis,' he said, 'use your loaf. I've told you before that nobody's putting *me* in a packing-case. But if they want you they'll ask for you. After all you're the fella that was talking about Siamese twins.'

'Mebbe there's nobody up there at all.' he mumbled.

'Then what are you bellyaching about?' Mulhern's expression changed. 'Hullo, Billy,' he said backing away.

McClenaghan was standing beside them. 'When you're ready, Davie, the doc and me want to see you in the boardroom.'

Open-mouthed he watched the manager leave the dressing-room. Then he turned with an uncontrollable giggle to Mulhern. 'Seems I was wrong,' he said.

The other shrugged and grimaced. '—And the besta luck, Minnis.'

He tapped at the boardroom door. Dr Boustead turned as he entered. 'Ah, here's your man.' The idiom defeated the tall elderly man beside him with the whiskey glass in his hand. 'Not yet,' David heard him murmur. There were five of them standing round the table: the doctor, Mr Blackie in a mustard Harris coat, McClenaghan, the tall individual, and another man unknown to

David who had been reading the inscription on a tarnished cup on the sideboard.

'But it *is* the boy you mean?' asked Dr Boustead in mock anxiety.

The tall man smiled patiently. 'Nice game, Minnis,' he said.

Dr Boustead cut in swiftly. 'Minnis, I want you to meet Alderman Hemphill and Mr Tusson, two gentlemen from—ar—*will we tell him*?' He turned to the others and suddenly went into a running hiccup of laughter, the whiskey jibbling in his glass.

McClenaghan drummed irritably on the table 'That's the general idea,' he said. 'Davie, these gentlemen are—'

'Davie!' roared Dr Boustead throwing an arm round David's shoulders. 'This is Alderman Hemphill, Chairman of Maitland Park, top of the English Second Division—'

The tall man smiled coolly.

'—and Mr Tusson, Manager. They were in the stand this afternoon. Watching you play, m'boy. Gentlemen,' the doctor stepped back with a flourish, 'he's all yours—barring a signature, of course.'

Alderman Hemphill's mouth smiled again. The rest of his face remained impassive. 'The impetuous Irish, eh, Doctor? Well, Minnis, I wouldn't say we came all this way to see you, but we watched you play and rather liked what we saw. Agree, Mr Tusson?'

Mr Tusson leaned his back against the sideboard and examined David over his glass. He'll ask to feel my muscles, he thought. The others waited. 'It seems your club's agreeable to you making a move, lad,' said Mr Tusson at last. There was a further pause. 'If we were able to find a berth for you could you come to Maitland Park?'

'Well, I—I think I could. I believe I could—'

'We're not pushing you,' said Mr Tusson carefully, 'but we'll need a firm answer, sometime.'

'You'll want to discuss this with your family, of course,' suggested Alderman Hemphill.

He hesitated and saw Mr Blackie make an involuntary gesture of impatience.

'Well . . . thanks, sir. I know it'll be all right.'

'Anyway, talk it over with somebody, Minnis.' Then to the room at large the alderman said, 'Tusson and I are staying over this weekend. We'll meet again on Tuesday. Any matters to discuss—terms—'

' 'Course terms would be discussed between the managements,' said Mr Blackie.

He felt some faint surprise that it was Mr Blackie and not Dr Boustead who was handling the affair. He looked round the circle of amiable faces and took heart. 'I would have to have a say,' he blurted out. 'I've a mother and a young brother—' Chuckling, Dr Boustead slipped an arm round his shoulders again.

'If you come to Maitland Park,' said Mr Tusson, 'you'll have no cause to worry. We look after our lads.'

Alderman Hemphill offered his hand. 'Glad to have met you, Minnis. Let's say three o'clock, Tuesday, at my hotel. Until then . . .'

Mr Blackie followed him outside and closed the door behind them. 'Pleased, Davie?'

'You bet, Mr Blackie.'

'We want you to give this offer serious thought, Davie. Like to see a good lad get his chance.' The man drew closer. David could smell the whiskey on his breath, the strangely nostalgic odour of his tweed coat. 'And I can tell you that if all parties agree there's a fair share for you in any money that's going. Know what I mean, Davie?'

He knew what Mr Blackie meant. But his good luck seemed so improbable that he kept to himself the source of his information.

'But, remember, mum's the word, Davie.'

'Mum's the word, Mr Blackie.'

The ground had emptied. The last wisp of Glenbank supporters drifted around the door of a pub opposite the tram stop. An old man among them looked up and saw David seated in the tram. He raised his arms, fingers outstretched. The rhapsodic cries of the afternoon found their way again to his black, taciturn mouth. 'Minnis, me lovely, lovely man! Me dazzling boy!' His companions turned at his shout, the boredom slipped from their faces, they waved and shouted too. He jerked his thumb in response, screwed up his face and winked back at them, desperately did all he could not to look like Royalty in the news-reels. The tram groaned, shuddered, and started to move. He glanced over his shoulder to make sure that he was alone on the top. Then his cheeks exploded in a crow of excitement and delight. As the tram swayed and clicked down the long road he drummed his feet in time with its song.

10

THE curlew's cry betrayed its passage high above the house. He strained his hearing to follow the bird in its midnight flight to the dark hills that ringed the city. As a child he had snuggled into his mother's flank as it had passed over in its mournful pursuit. Now he followed the sound, his lips framing silently the liquid keening. There might not be hills and birds encircling Maitland.

In the room below his mother lay asleep, as unaware of her coming loss as she was of the flight of the bird over the roof. Far across the city the Albert Memorial sounded one o'clock. He would tell her on Tuesday when everything was signed and sealed and there could be no drawing back. And he would be able to put down a hundred pounds or more on the table as he told her the news. That would be an answer to all her questions and misgivings, wouldn't it? He rearranged his pillow, smiled, and slid farther down under the bedclothes. An hour later when the deep notes of the clock sounded across the streets and squares he was still awake to hear them.

On the following morning as he tightened his tie he felt a sudden urge to see Bonar again. Why? asked his reflection. Well, I'm going away. Bet you he never gives you a thought. He's moved about a million miles from you. Remember how he acted last time you saw him? His head full of that wee papish bit and the odd bunch of characters he's in with. He turned his back on the mirror.

He spent most of the afternoon puzzling how he might find his friend. He daren't ask Mr McFall. It would be unbearable if the father had to admit that he didn't know of his son's whereabouts. Then he remembered the Spinners Hall.

DON'T BE VAGUE ASK FOR HAIG said the neon sign over the Serbia Bar. VAGUE flittered and blinked in its lighted tubes like an imprisoned moth. He wondered was that intentional or just a lucky accident. Hope the luck holds for me, he thought, as he crossed the rough, dark street to the Spinners Hall. Children swarmed over the railings in front of the hall, squeezing their agile small bodies between the iron shafts, swinging from the few pompous, ineffectual spearheads that time had left. Gingerly he stopped a small girl. 'D'you know anybody called McFall?' The cunning, soiled little face was green in the neon light. 'He comes to the Hall,' he added. She turned and shouted, 'Is there a McFall about the Hall?' Her companions took it up, flinging themselves at the railings, tumbling over the worn wall. 'Is there a McFall about the Hall!'

The noise brought a man in a duncher cap to the doorway of the Hall. He spoke to the children without heat. 'G'wan away home before you get your backsides broke. Looking for somebody, mister?'

'A fella called McFall—Bonar McFall.'

The man took a butt from his vest pocket and put it between his lips while he examined David.

'Well, d'you know him?'

'Sure. S'pose you wouldn't want to tell me what it's about?'

Nettled, he also took time to reply. 'That's right,' he said with acid geniality. 'It's personal.'

'Would he recognize your name?'

'Tell him it's Davie Minnis.'

The man's face remained expressionless. Not a Glenbank supporter, anyway, thought David with an angry smile.

'I'll send one of the kids for him. You wait over in the bar.'

It was early yet. There were only two truck men up at the counter. He slipped into the snug where he had sat with Boney's father and the others listening to old Shriberger. He shook his head as the boss came over. 'I'm waiting for somebody,' he said.

Bonar was standing at the snug entrance. David glanced up to see a wary curiosity slip from his face.

'Bould Davie. It's yourself!'

'Bould Boney! Take a pew. Hope you don't mind me sending for you?'

'S'pleasure.' His friend was looking at him. He felt a tightening at the heart as the old familiar smile widened. 'You look good, boy.'

'I feel good. What'll you have?'

'Nothing much. A glass a light. What brought you to this wilderness?'

'I'm going away—'

'Should I have read about it—Court and Personal?'

'It's not in the papers, yet,' he said huffily.

Bonar's grin widened. 'I know—football!'

'That's right. I've got a transfer to Maitland Park.'

'Well, well!' David winced inwardly at the harshness and power of the hand that gripped his. 'I'm delighted to hear it, Davie.'

'Thanks, Boney.'

'I used to go and watch you in the odd game—'

'And never came near me!'

'What hell use, Davie? Anyway I don't have the time, now. I don't even follow the game in the papers.'

'Are you working?'

'Still getting the odd turn.'

He considered the open, collarless shirt, the hard white hand curled round the glass. 'Not at the old trade?'

'I'm labouring. I'm one of the fellas that digs the holes for my old man's flying squads to put their red lamps round.' With his head lowered Bonar whirled the dregs of his glass until he had raised a thin white foam. 'Ever run across him?'

'Yes. He's fine.'

'My mammy?'

'She's fine. They're all fine.'

The other touched David's sleeve as though acknowledging a gift. They sat silent for a time. The pub filled around them.

'Remember the last time we sat here?' said David.

'Old Shriberger!' and Bonar laughed.

'D'you still hold the same views, Boney?'

'Yes. I've seen nothing to make me change my mind.'

He laughed lightly. 'Sure we all see the same things.'

'Do we?' Bonar indicated the crowded pub; the old man fondling the greyhound's head, the drab, clean men on the benches, the truck men growing morosely drunk up at the counter. 'What are those to you?'

'Just—ordinary fellas.'

'To me they're *extra*ordinary fellas. They're the pile-drivers of the richest civilization in the world and this is all it has to offer them at the end of the day—'

'They don't *have* to come here.'

'Where else would they go? The pictures? The dogs? To see you playing football?'

'That's the sort of thing they want.'

'Aye. Oddly enough that's what they get. Even when they're outa work it's fixed so that they can still get the pictures, the dogs, drink—'

'You're the only one that's worrying. They think it's good enough.'

'What do you think?'

He lifted his shoulders. 'It serves its purpose.'

Bonar laughed harshly. 'By Christ, you're learning the language, all right. But you wouldn't like to come down here and share it?'

'Me? Why should I? I'm—'

'Different?'

He flushed. 'If you like.'

He should have known better than to come back here. He should have known that McFall's subversive concern with these men who went through life as ciphers would grow and swell in the back streets. And he felt no shame in regarding himself as different from them. He, too, had had to start from near the bottom, but his ability was winning him a place among important people. Down here they might wonder if they would have a pay packet next week and fight like dogs for an extra twopence an hour. He was going, by right, to where men paid honourably and handsomely for his considerable skill. He stared back coldly at the heavy face of his companion.

'You'll never change it.'

'I don't want to change it. I want to sweep it right away.'

For some reason this made him laugh. 'Ah, for God's sake, Boney! By violence?'

'If need be.'

'Well, let me out of the country before you let fly.'

Bonar grinned slowly. 'I'll watch it.'

They seemed almost back on their old footing. 'Care for the other half of the pint, Boney?'

'No thanks. If you don't mind. Time I was pushing back home.'

'Home? Oh, sure, sure.' But he settled back into his corner wishing desperately for the courage to ask a point-blank question. Bonar stirred restlessly.

'Ah—how's the girl—Rona?'

The other looked up. 'Rona? I forgot you met her. She's fine, thanks.'

'Nice girl.'

'Not bad.' Bonar got to his feet. 'Coming?'

Ah, well, he thought as he followed him to the door, I did my best. In the street, Bonar fumbled for his hand. 'Thanks for taking the trouble, Davie. Besta luck, boy.'

'Besta luck, Boney.'

He stood for a moment, flexing his tingling fingers, watching the other disappear and reappear under the lamps until finally he sank into the tunnelled darkness.

II

THEY called for him early on Tuesday afternoon. As he opened the door to Billy McClenaghan he was surprised to see Mr Warnock's car waiting at the kerb.

The manager spoke quickly and quietly. 'How d'you feel, Davie? Are you ready to come with us?'

He frowned. ' 'Course I'm ready to come with you.'

'Sure you wouldn't like me or Mr Warnock to speak—?'

'No, no . . . I told you that was all right . . . wait till I get my coat.' He called into the living-room that he was going downtown and without waiting for an answer hurried out of the house.

Mr Canty, a director that he had met once or twice before, sat with Mr Warnock in the front seat. He nodded to them both and looked round in bewilderment. Mr Warnock watched him in the driving mirror. 'Expecting Doc Boustead, Davie?'

'Yes. Or Mr Blackie. I thought, mebbe—'

'They're sorry. Neither of them could make it, today.' As he pushed the gear lever with the heel of his hand the club's chairman added, 'But don't worry, Davie. Mr Canty, Billy Mac and I know all about it. We'll be able to talk to the Maitland Park men. Hercules Hotel, isn't it, Billy?'

'That's right.'

He had often glanced into the chrome-and-glass portal of the Hercules without any great desire to enter it. The display of expense and knowingness on the other side of its revolving doors had no meaning at all in his existence. And now this world, hostile to the moneyless, had sent for him. It was like entering enemy territory. He followed the others inside hoping that his heart would fall into step with his breathing before he had to speak to anyone.

The air of the reception lobby, laden with the odours of food, chrysanthemums, and cigar smoke, hummed with voices. Quiet restrained voices. Even the elevators rose and fell and the doors opened and shut with muted hisses and thuds. The people who hurried to and fro padded over thick carpeting. At the reception-desk two young women collected and dispensed keys and letters with durable charm. As Mr Warnock reported the arrival of his party David looked about him with cautious interest. He had never before seen so many well-clad, self-possessed men together at the one time. Some of the women were good-looking, all were expensively clothed. Their anglicized voices filled him with resentment and pleasure. He swelled a little under his clothes. This, he decided, was the life. His roving glance stopped abruptly. Something had jarred on his eye. He turned carefully and looked again. A small man in shabby, sausage-shaped clothes had somehow got in and was standing close to the door. He had an ordinary, pale, worried face. The sort of face that David found deplorable in these surroundings. To his annoyance, the shabby man was staring straight at him. He responded with a glance of aloof boredom, perfectly executed, and turned away. The young woman at the desk, having listened carefully to Mr Warnock, crooked her finger and a brightly buttoned ancient with smooth hair appeared at her elbow. Conscious of the scrutiny of the shabby man at his back David watched intently. He suppressed a giggle of astonishment as the buttoned individual burst into a high chant of 'Pyging Mr Hempill . . . pyging Mr Hempill . . .' and vanished into the throng. Gor. The only time he had ever seen that happen was in a comedy film.

There was a furtive pluck at his sleeve. The shabby man was beside him, talking from the corner of his mouth. '. . . a friend . . . I know why you're here . . . don't sign anything . . .'

David freed his arm sharply. 'What's the idea? Who are you?'

'A friend . . . tell you sometime . . . right now don't sign . . . I'm on the phone with Lincoln County . . . wait . . . mebbe get you better terms . . .'

'Wait? I've been waiting for a year—'

'Tell you . . . don't do a thing . . . I'll be back . . .'

The intruder was slipping way when McClenaghan turned and saw him. For a moment David thought he was about to spring on the wearer of the shabby raincoat and drag him to the ground. Then the manager recovered himself, glanced around, and hissed in a low, choking voice, 'Beat it, Creaney—'

'It's a free country,' said Creaney scowling and backing away. McClenaghan took a step towards him. 'G'wan before I break—before I—'

People were turning to look at them. A group of business and professional gentlemen replete from their weekly fraternal lunch drew aside in humorous distaste. A maroon-and-gold porter, not too clear what was happening, moved ominously in the wake of the retreating Creaney. Just to be dressed like Creaney was an offence in itself. Mr Warnock looked back and said irritably, 'What is it, Billy?'

Briefly, Billy told Mr Warnock and his fellow-director. With low cries of alarm they gathered David into their midst. He was sheltered and walled-in among them. 'Isn't Mr Hemphill to be found?' said Mr Warnock impatiently to the receptionist. Another buttoned boy was summoned and took flight with the same monotonous cry.

'What did that character say to you, Davie?' asked Mr Warnock.

David told him as best he could.

'Better terms, eh?' The three men looked at each other with expressions of pain and incredulity. Mr Warnock shook his head. 'Would you believe a man could *do* a think like that?'

'That man could,' said McClenaghan.

'Gor, it beats anything,' said Mr Canty.

'Who's Creaney?' asked David. 'A scout, or something?'

'Some people call him that,' said Billy McClenaghan. 'I've another short name for him.'

Alderman Hemphill and Mr Tusson appeared from an elevator. Their faces shone as if they had just washed for their visitors. 'Sorry, gentlemen!' the alderman cried pressing forward with outstretched hand. 'Sorry for the delay. Boy said he couldn't find us—'

He led them towards the cocktail lounge. It was pink and soft like the inside of a woman's mouth. David hung back at the entrance drawing McClenaghan to a hesitant stop. 'Nobody's said anything to me about terms, Mr Mac.'

McClenaghan clapped him on the shoulder. 'It's in the hands of the big boys now, Davie. Wait till Hemphill's finished with us, and then Mr Warnock and Mr Canty and you can have a chat.'

He knew that McClenaghan was to be trusted. But he didn't know enough about the business himself. Perhaps he had been a bit of a big-mouth suggesting to Hemphill and Boustead and the rest that he made his own decisions. Yesterday, he should have looked up somebody who knew about these things, instead of lounging about at home. Peden would have kept him right. Alderman Hemphill was waving them to chairs, in a secluded corner of the lounge.

'Well now,' said the alderman clapping his hands, 'what about a gargle? Mr Warnock?' The choice was made, the waiter called, and until he returned with the drinks they discussed a trip the Englishmen had made to the Glens of Antrim and the weather, and when they fell silent examined each other smilingly. David tried to work out which managerial group had decreed that he was to have a shandy.

'Now,' said the alderman, glass in hand, staring at him. 'Made up your mind what you want to do, lad?'

'Yes. I would like to go to Maitland Park.'

'Good. Then we can get down to business.'

From a slim leather case Mr Tusson took a handful of papers. The glasses were pushed back and the forms spread out on the table. David set down his name where he was instructed. 'And that's yours.' He looked up questioningly as Mr Tusson handed him the sealed envelope. 'Your signing money.'

As he tried to read the contents through the envelope with his finger tips his hand was grasped by Alderman Hemphill. 'And our wish for a happy partnership, Minnis.' He had to relinquish the envelope to his pocket. Everybody shook hands with everybody else. More drinks were called for. Then, between them, Mr Tusson and the alderman told him what they expected from him and what he might expect from them.

'Mr Tusson, here, will be looking out for you coming off the midday train at Birmingham on Friday.'

'You mean . . . *this* Friday?'

'Yes. No time like the present, lad. Is there anything to hold you up?'

'No . . . no, nothing. I'll be there.'

'Good. We'll arrange your tickets and berth with Mr McClenaghan before we leave.'

'Thanks,' he said, and smiled weakly at the alderman.

The talk drifted to football, to business, to football again. No one asked his opinion. He scarcely listened, anyway. This meant that he would have to leave home on Thursday. He couldn't imagine what it would be like to live anywhere else but at home. To end one's journey in any other street but Colinvista Street. He was now a fully-fledged professional signed for an English club and he had never before felt so miserable. But he daren't show it under the watchful eye of Mr Tusson. If the break had to come, the sooner the better.

Mr Warnock stood up. 'All right with you if we handle the newspapers, Hemphill?'

'Of course. You know your way around.'

'Well . . . ' Mr Warnock held out his hand. 'Hope we've done a good stroke of business for each other.'

'I'm sure we have.' Mr Tusson echoed his director. Is this the time to ask my question? he thought. Mr Canty and Billy McClenaghan were also on their feet. With him in their midst the football executives patted and chaffed each other out of the lounge, down the lobby, into the reception hall. Alderman Hemphill and Mr Tusson came to a halt. 'See you Friday, Dave!' Mr Tusson called after him as he went out into the flat, grey light of the street. Mr Warnock hurried ahead of them twirling his car key.

As they drove along Donegall Place he said, 'There was no word of money for me, Mr Warnock.'

'I thought I saw Tusson giving you your signing-on-fee?'

'Yes, but I'm talking about the transfer money. I still haven't heard what that was.'

'No secret about that, Davie,' said Mr Canty. 'You cost Maitland Park fifteen hundred quid.'

'That's the money I'm talking about. My third.'

There was a silence in the car. Then Mr Warnock, as he slowed up at a crossing, said carefully, 'I didn't quite get that, Davie. Something about a third?'

'My third of the money. Mr Blackie told me about it.'

Mr Warnock looked at Mr Canty beside him, stole a glance back at Billy McClenaghan. His expression was very grave. 'I think we'd better go somewhere quiet and talk this over.'

'You could use my place, if that'll do,' suggested Mr Canty.

'That'll do,' said Mr Warnock. They drove round a couple of blocks and parked the car.

Mr Canty was a furrier's agent. He occupied a salesroom and a small office on the third floor. He led them through to the office. A girl working at a filing cabinet cleared out smartly at their entrance. She's seen a lot of Glenbank's business settled here, David thought. They settled themselves on chairs and the corners of show cases.

'Now,' said Mr Warnock, 'tell us about it, Davie.'

He told them what Mr Blackie had said to him outside the boardroom door on Saturday.

'Did you hear this, Billly?' asked Mr Warnock.

Billy shook his head. 'No, I never heard money mentioned.'

He kept his voice level. 'Billy didn't hear it. Billy wasn't there when it was said. I've told you how it happened.'

Mr Warnock spread his hands. 'Davie, I'm not doubting your word. But you're mistaken. Blackie—no one—could promise you anything like that.'

'Well, he did!'

'What actually did he say?'

'Something about "a fair share of any money that's going".'

Mr Warnock looked puzzled. 'I understood you to say something about a third of some money—'

'That's right,' said Mr Canty, 'that's what you said. Did Norman Blackie say "a third of the transfer money"?'

He thought. No, Mr Blackie hadn't used those words. Then he burst out, 'I remember now. It was Billy Thompson that put the idea of a quarter or a third into my head!'

Mr Warnock smiled patiently. 'Ah, now, Davie, be sensible. Dressing-room gossip—'

'That's it,' said Mr Canty. 'You've got it all mixed up—'

'But that's what I understood!' He looked at the three men. They were watching him with an expression of perplexed sympathy. 'I did it for the money! If I had known I wasn't going to get it I wouldn't have signed!'

'Oh, ho!' said Mr Canty.

The three men sounded each other. 'Mebbe it's not too late,' said Mr Warnock. 'Mebbe we could still get Hemphill on the phone—'

'Leave Hemphill out of it!' he shouted. 'It's Blackie. Why don't you get *him* on the phone?'

An edge came into Mr Warnock's voice. 'We've already told you that Mr Blackie couldn't have promised you this, Minnis.' He paused and then cast aside prudence with a shrug. 'But I'll tell you what we'll do. We'll give you a gift of twenty-five pounds. I think you'll find that rather more generous than the Maitland Park fee—'

'Fair enough, fair enough,' murmured McClenaghan.

He turned on the manager. 'D'you think so? Fair enough for what should've been three or four hundred quid? You think it's fair enough?'

'You don't have to take it, Minnis,' said Mr Warnock.

'And we don't have to give it to you,' said Mr Canty.

When the voices ceased in the office the typewriter in the next room broke into a guilty chatter. Hope you got an earful, you bitch. From the rushing street below, the clamour filtered in through the two windows that stretched Mr Canty's name and calling in gold letters across their width. The gold was dull to him from where he sat. As were the eyes of the men watching him incuriously. They could sit out a hundred of me. They know I'll go anyway. They have me chinned. He thrust out his hand. 'Gimme the money.'

The gesture surprised Mr Warnock into slapping his pocket. Mr Canty slid lightly off a display case. 'I think I have that much in the kitty outside,' he said. No one spoke. Mr Canty came back flittering the five fivers through the air, holding them up before his audience like a conjurer.

'There you are, boy. Best of luck.'

'Best of luck,' said Mr Warnock.

'Best of luck, Davie,' said McClenaghan.

He took the money in silence. In the outer office he remembered his coat. They were still standing as he had left them. No one had spoken. He felt that they had expected him to come back. This time he closed the door behind him as he left.

He was in his room when he heard the rattle of the letter box and the plop as the evening paper fell on the hall floor, then, after a time, Freddie's slow step mounting the stairs towards him. His brother tossed the paper on the bed and pointed to a paragraph on the sports page. 'Seen that?'

He glanced at it. 'Not yet. But I expected it.'

'You didn't tell my mother at tea-time.' Freddie was growing big and was afraid of hardly anybody now.

'No. No, I didn't. I don't know how the hell I'm gonna do it.'

Mollified, Freddie sat down. 'You'll have to.'

'I know.'

'It says you're going to Maitland Park straight away.'

'Yes. Well, aren't you gonna congratulate me?'

'Ah, that's all right, David, but you shoulda told her—'

'I know. I'll go down and do it now.'

'Where is Maitland Park?'

'I dunno. Have you got your school atlas?'

They searched until they found it in Warwickshire.

'It should be warm down there,' said Freddie.

He laughed. 'Slap up against the equator.'

Freddie grinned, and got up. 'You'd better tell her.'

She was working at the sink. He leant against the door frame and watched her. 'I've got news for you.'

She looked up quickly. 'Yes?' He was smiling. 'Yes?' she said relaxing.

'I've got a job—in England.'

'Goodness, David!' She dried her hands and followed him up to the living-room. 'England?'

'In a place called Maitland, in Warwickshire—a football job.'

Suddenly she looked old and defeated. 'You mean being paid to play football?'

'That's it.'

'How long will that last?'

'Just as long as I can play football.'

'What sort of people are you going amongst?'

He had to be careful here not to betray himself. Before this afternoon that question would have been so easy to answer.

'They're all right. One of the officials that came over to see me is an alderman—'

She turned away. 'When are they taking you?'

He laughed nervously. 'Nobody's taking me anywhere, Mother. But I have to go soon. This week.'

Her face was hidden but he saw her head sink a little. 'You don't give a body much notice.'

'I'm sorry. I only heard this evening, myself.'

'I suppose the time's past when you would discuss these things with me?'

'What good would it have done, Mother?'

'Very well, David. I'll try to get your things together in time. You'll need some new clothes . . .'

Not very nice, he thought, as he went upstairs. Not very pleasant. Imagine another house where there would be no joy at a fella being asked to play for a big English club! But at least there hadn't been a fight. All she could think about, apparently, was new clothes. And I can pay for them. And pay her something for herself. And give Freddie a quid or two. There had been ten pounds in the Maitland Park envelope. He added them now to the money that Canty had given him and encircled the roll with his finger and thumb. It should have been thicker. Much, much thicker. But there was always the future. He had thought it over since leaving Canty's office. A lot of money now would have meant entanglements, irrevocable commitments. He glanced at his watch and ran a comb hastily through his hair. By this time the McFalls would have seen it in the paper.

Maureen answered his knock at the door. He saw in her face that she knew.

'It came quicker than I expected,' he said.

She put out a warning hand then stepped back and took her coat from the hall. 'I'm going out for a minute,' she called over her shoulder. Going up the street he helped her with her coat. 'What happened, David?'

'More or less what you read in the paper. It all happened this afternoon.'

'Had you no idea it was coming so quick?'

'I met them on Saturday, but there's been so many false alarms I had to wait until today before I could be sure. It's in the bag now. They have my name in ink—'

'But you're going away so soon!'

She was looking up at him. The pain in her voice couldn't be ignored. He caught her hand. 'I know, sweetheart. But I've got a job, haven't I?'

'Yes, you've got a job.'

'Let's go up to the embankment.'

Huddled together on a bench they gazed out over the dark curve of the river. Streets of small houses, Majestic Street and its neighbours, ran down to the opposite bank, spilling light and distant noise onto the whorled surface slipping past to the lough. Over and beyond the humble roofs the city lifted its bronze shoulders out of a sea of light. Pale river mist crept past their bench to gather in the playing-fields of the Park.

He told her about his meeting with Alderman Hemphill and Mr Tusson, and how the shabby man had tried to waylay him in the hotel. After a time his voice trailed away into silence. She waited and then in a small, courageous voice she said, 'And what does this mean to us?'

'Us? It means that our wedding day is nearer.' She moved closer and his arm tightened about her. Then he picked moodily at an overcoat button until she asked softly what was wrong. He came back with a start. 'Ah, it's not worth talking about. My usual luck when it comes to money. On Saturday one of the Glenbank directors hinted that if I got the chance to sign, a third of the transfer money would be put my way. This afternoon a different bunch of directors turn up and say they never heard of any such arrangement. You saw in tonight's paper what Maitland Park paid for me. By rights a third of that's mine. We could have started with something like five hundred pounds—'

'Oh, David—'

'—and all I got out of it was the usual few quid for signing on. Most of that will have to go on odds and ends of new clothes to take with me, I suppose.' His voice, he felt sure, sounded bitter.

He took her ungloved hand in his. 'And no ring yet for this sweet finger.' He lifted it to his lips and kissed it.

The smarting tears rose, and she closed her eyes. Neither she nor her boy wished anything but good to people and yet these cruel things kept happening. Perhaps she was asking too much. But it was hard not to feel cheated.

She turned her face to him. In the dim reflection from the river he could see that she was smiling. 'Oh, well,' she said.

He caught her hands, and crushed them against his body as though trying to thrust something into his heart. 'I love you, Maureen. My god, I love you. You're a million times too good for me—' His voice was hoarse and for a moment its sharp agony seemed to startle rather than reassure her. 'I love you.'

'I know.' She caressed his head and whispered, 'I love you, my love,' playing with the words joyfully, tenderly. 'My love, I love you, my love.' She raised her head and looked deep into his eyes. 'That's better than anything, isn't it?'

'Yes.'

For a time they sat locked in each other's arms, watching the river, lost in their thoughts. In the distance a car swung onto the embankment. Its glaring headlights rushed towards them piercing the river mist. Light sped along the dusting of frost on the rail of the bench. Maureen shivered and drew her coat more tightly around her. 'It's time to go home,' she said.

12

SHE looked up in surprise as he rose from the tea table. 'Are you going out, David?'

'Have to, Mother.'

'On your last evening at home?'

He paused in the hall. He had forgotten that it was her last evening, too. 'I won't be late—and I'll be around all day tomorrow.'

'It must be important.'

He closed the door gently behind him.

They had laid it on for him in style at Majestic Street. Mr McFall had managed to get a collar on and Mrs McFall her apron off. But not so long ago, he thought, glancing into the scullery where heaped plates were carefully covered with bits of muslin and linen. It was his evening. He was touched by their gaiety, their kindness, and delicacy. No one wondered where Bonar was, no one cracked a joke at the expense of Maureen and himself. Perhaps that should worry me, he thought.

Shortly after ten o'clock Mrs McFall said, 'I don't want to hurry you, Davie, but this is your last night at home. Your mother'll want to see a wee bit of you, won't she?'

'Yes,' he said. 'I'll have to go. She'll be waiting.'

In the hall, as she helped him with his coat, Maureen said, 'Your mother'll be going with you to the boat?'

'—and Freddie.' He shrugged. 'I don't know why. I'm not going away a million miles.'

She looked at him strangely. 'But people always do it, David . . . I'd like to have seen you off.'

'It's difficult, darling.'

'I know.' They were both speaking quickly and quietly.

'And it's a cold dirty place.'

'Still . . .' Her head was stubbornly lowered. He put his hand gently under her chin, and smiled into her eyes.

'Please yourself, sweetheart. There are more important things. The moment I arrive I'll send you a telegram—'

'David!' Holding her in his arms he wondered did he detect a note of panic in her voice and her embrace.

Almost twenty-four hours later he leaned over the ship's rail looking down on the clustered faces on the quayside. His mother and Freddie stood near the shed door. They had run out of words to shout back and forth. Occasionally he would lift his hand in salute and they would respond. They would go on doing that until the gangway was pulled in and the ropes cast off. Suddenly he saw Maureen. She stood half-hidden in the shadows. Without moving his head he could see these two women who meant so much to him, there with the one purpose, and yet separate and unknown to each other. Slowly, almost furtively, he raised his hand and waved to her. She made no response. Perhaps from where she stood it was impossible to make out the faces under the loading lights. A couple of deckhands were unlashing the gangway ropes. He saw her turn slowly and move away. 'Maureen!' he shouted. 'Maureen!' His mother looked up inquiringly. The girl had vanished. He gave his mother and Freddie a last salute and drew back. His place at the rail was filled immediately. As the vessel crept out into mid-channel and the figures on the quayside became indistinct blurs, he felt he was receding from an insoluble problem. Now he was going where relationships could be started afresh. Simple, honest and uncomplicated. A chill wind blew in from the lough. He drew his coat around him and went down to find his berth.

13

THE post office clerk ran her pencil swiftly over the words. ' "Miss McFall ninety-three Majestic Street Belfast arrived safely love David"—That will be two shillings, please,' she said.

Only two shillings to send a handful of words back over the night's throbbing journey across the sea? He took another form and pencilled the same words to his mother. 'And this one,' he said, pushing it under the grille. He turned away with a feeling of relief and of guilt. The message seemed a last signal at parting, a final farewell, rather than an intimation of arrival.

Mr Tusson had met him at the train and was waiting now in the car. As they moved into the traffic rattling and fuming between the ancient overhanging houses Mr Tusson said, 'We'll go round by Mrs Compton's. You can meet her and leave your baggage. But not before we've had a cup of tea in the Sceptre. That'll save time. Then we'll run out to the Park.'

'Whatever you think, Mr Tusson.'

'You'll like Mrs Compton's. Comfortable house. Good food. She's a widow. Her husband, Joe, used to play for the Park.'

'Sounds as if I'll be happy.'

'If you're not, let me know.'

'I'm sure I'll be all right,' he murmured.

The car slowed and for a moment he gazed with surprise and pleasure into a court of black and white, timbered houses. 'Are those real—those houses?' he asked as they drew away.

'S'pose so, lad. Not that I know much about that sort of thing. You can get a history in the library. In the summer there's quite a tourist trade. But that's not what keeps the town going. Over the river is Beadles Aluminium Works and a couple of big housing estates. That's where the hard cash comes from—and the supporters that fill the Park's ground.'

After tea and hot buttered scones in the antique dusk of the Sceptre Mr Tusson drove him and his luggage to 5 Regent Place. It was a street of big, florid, redbrick houses. Mrs Compton had an air of professional motherliness that promised comfort and competence. A fire twinkling beyond a heavy mahagony door drew his attention. She pushed the door wider. 'The dining-room,' she said with a friendly smile. He stepped in, and ran his eye over the spotless cloth and gleaming electro-plate on the table, gently sniffed the pungency of sauce and furniture cream. 'If you and Mr Tusson step in here I won't be a moment—'

'Thanks, but I had breakfast on the boat—'

'—and we've had a cup of tea at the Sceptre,' added Mr Tusson. 'Could his bags be taken up to his room? Right now I want to get him out to the ground. Alderman Hemphill's waiting for us.'

Mrs Compton shrugged in disappointment. 'All right. But come straight back, Mr Minnis. I'll have something waiting for you.'

As he clambered into the car beside Mr Tusson he said, 'You're right. I think I'm going to like it there.'

The close turf, he noticed, ended precisely at the edge of the red sand running-track. The woodwork and metal of the barriers and great overhanging stand were freshly painted. Not even a discarded cigarette packet blemished the vast sweep of the unreserved banking. Everything about Maitland Park Football Club looked fresh, business-like, prosperous. At the town end of the pitch half a dozen sweatered figures tipped and punted and headed a ball among themselves. The manager followed his glance. 'You can meet the lads later. Let's go down and see who's in the office, first.'

There were three men in the office under the big stand, Alderman Hemphill, Mr Verney, a fellow-director, and the trainer-coach, Henry Sharples. Sharples, he remembered, had worn the royal blue shirt of Everton. As he returned the trainer's handshake he exclaimed, 'I know you. You used to play with Dixie Dean!'

The others laughed. Sharples, pleased, held his hand for a moment. 'Hope you'll have as much luck as I've had, Minnis.' The trainer crossed to the door. 'Send him out to me when you're finished.'

Alderman Hemphill lit a cigar and settled himself comfortably on the edge of the desk. 'Glad to see you here safe and sound, lad. Henry wished you luck. So do we.'

'And a happy football career here,' said Mr Verney.

'That's right. That's important. A happy player does well by his club. In a manner of speaking,' continued the alderman, 'your luck starts from now, Minnis. We've only to keep up our average for the next half-dozen games and we'll be in the First Division next season. That means you go up with us. Provided, of course, you make a steady berth for yourself in the senior side. But whether you do or don't, keep trying out there, and remember you're now a member of Maitland Park Football Club. That goes for you and all the other lads you'll meet with Henry. That's what you are first of all.'

'Yes . . . I'll remember . . . thanks, Mr Hemphill.' His attention had been distracted and he stumbled over his reply. Whether or not he made a steady berth for himself? But he had been brought here to play for the Seniors. Ever since he had put his foot on the boat he had never thought of any other possibility! Surely they hadn't brought him all this way without telling him the truth. In angry panic he watched Alderman Hemphill and Mr Verney leave the office.

'Well, that's that,' said Mr Tusson.

He turned. The manager was bent over the desk searching for something. He let out a long breath. Yes, that was that. Directors' bull. Everybody knew about it. The people to pay attention to were the footballers, Tusson, Sharples, the fellas out there on the pitch. He smiled charmingly 'Who did you play for, Mr Tusson?'

Mr Tusson's bald spot slid back as he looked up. 'Maitland Park. In the Midland League nearly forty years ago. A bit before your time, eh?'

He grinned weakly. Well, he wouldn't ask *that* question again.

Mr Tusson found what he sought, an insurance form to be signed. 'Now,' he said shuffling his papers together, 'I'll take you out to Henry and you can meet some of the players.'

They walked towards the cluster of mobile figures in the middle of the pitch. The elasticity of the grass under his feet tingled upwards through him in a surge of excitement. He looked from side to side over the unbroken turf. Gor, he thought, I could fairly skim over this place. I could fly like a bird!

Mr Tusson handed him over to Henry Sharples.

'Dave, I want you to meet first—Jimmy Rusk, your skipper.' And Scotland's, he remembered, as he smiled back at the bow-legged, little inside-left.

'You're from Glenbank?'

'Yes.'

'Ever meet up with Pony Douthart?'

'Pony? Sure. He taught . . .' He stopped, afraid of sounding boastful.

'Me too. In the old days at Ibrox.'

'Now, Stan Ellis, Eddie Betmead, Bobby Milner, Cliff Barton, Ret Hayward . . .' He recognized all the names, or most of them. He knew the stories they had drawn after them across the sports pages; Rusk, Ellis, Hayward, the scoring machine that had carried Maitland Park to the top of the Second Division; Cliff Barton, who had held the Welsh defence together in a score of international matches. He felt confused as he tried to fit unfamiliar faces to familiar names.

'. . . and meet Chris Tunney. Plays for Ireland—the other Ireland.'

'I know.'

Sharples looked from one to the other. 'You two ever met?'

Tunney was black-haired, sharp-featured and florid in colouring. He confirmed David's impression of what a Southerner should look like. Tunney shook his head. ''Fraid not, Henry. Ireland's bigger than you think.' His voice, David noticed, had taken on an English inflexion.

'Then why do you blokes keep leaving it?'

'Because you blokes keep sending for us. Come ye over . . .' He released David's hand with a handsome grin. 'Glad to meet you, Minnis. You should like it here.'

Mr Tusson joined them. 'Met the boys? Good. I'll run you back to Mrs Compton's as soon as you're ready.' He saw David hesitate, and added, 'We intend to rest you this weekend. That'll give you a day or two to shake down—'

'But I'll want to see you tomorrow,' said Henry Sharples. 'Early. I'll have my hands full in the afternoon.'

The players had moved onto the track. As he left the ground with Mr Tusson he saw them jogging round in twos and threes at the far end of the pitch. Three internationals among that lot. And the makings of at least three others. He swallowed. Wonder have I really got what it needs to live in that company? A groundsman flicked his cap to them as they drove out. Less than twenty-four hours ago he had been looking down on his mother and brother from the boat-deck. It seemed a lifetime ago.

When Mrs Compton led David into the dining-room, a small thin man, seated on the fireplace side of the table, was mopping up the last of the gravy on his plate with a crust of bread. 'Mr Common meet Mr Minnis,' said Mrs Compton. 'Mr Minnis has come to play football for the Park,' she added. Mr Common, chewing steadily, looked up at the newcomer with a lack-lustre expression. Nettled, David drew out the chair at the head of the table. Mrs Compton, with a smile of reproof, took it from his hands and set it back. 'No, *there*, Mr Minnis,' and she pointed to a place laid opposite Mr Common. 'This is Miss Gibbon's place because she likes looking out of the window. And that,' indicating the other end of the table, 'is Mr Plinter's because he doesn't. Miss Gibbon and Mr Plinter are away at weekends.' She was about to go when she thought it advisable to add, 'And Mr Common *always* sits with his back to the fireplace.'

As the door closed behind her he sat down heavily and watched Mr Common pour himself a cup of tea. Thinning hair, seamed face, stiff collar, drab clothes, he looked as if his surname had taken possession of him. It fits him too well, thought David, he must be a comedian or something. Listlessly he examined the table and its furnishings. As spotless as his room upstairs. But this sit-here-and-don't-move stuff wouldn't do. When you're independent you just don't take anything. Tomorrow he would start looking around. Mebbe Tunney could put him on to something. He became aware that Mr Common had risen from the table and was speaking to him.

'I said "they don't go together".'

'Sorry . . . they . . .?'

'Gibby and Plinter. Not weekending together. None of that sort of stuff here, Mr Minnis.'

He stared at the small man indignantly. 'What're you talking about? I—'

'Just wanted to keep you right. Might make a joke at table. Well-meant, but embarrassing. Mrs C. would blow up.'

As David pushed his chair back his fellow-lodger sidled up to him, and whispered, 'Wouldn't put the idea past Plinter. But, Gibby!' Mr Common opened his eyes wide, ballooned his cheeks, and then let his breath out with an explosion. 'She would blow up!' With an extraordinarily agile skip Mr Common vanished shutting the door behind him. David subsided and looked around angrily. It was a nut-house, too. He would start looking for somewhere else right after he had finished his meal.

The door opened again and Mrs Compton brought in the meal. He watched in silence as it was set before him. Grilled steak dressed with mushrooms, and tomatoes on the side. A dish of fried potatoes. A rack of toast and a plate of brown bread. He glanced at the place vacated by Mr Common. The same utensils were there, empty. This must be the usual evening feed. Mrs Compton stepped back, fingers curled appreciatively. 'Now,' she said, 'if there's anything more you want, don't be afraid to call.'

'Thanks, Mrs Compton.' He picked up his knife and fork. 'I can't think what it would be.'

When he had finished he sat back with a sigh. He hadn't realized how hungry he had been. He looked at the litter before him. If all the meals were like this he felt he could put up with Mr Common's vagaries, even the worst that the unknown Gibby and Plinter had to offer. Before he left the house he called his thanks into Mrs Compton's sitting-room. Her smile assured him that he had done the right thing for once in his life.

At half-past eleven the next morning in the company of a dozen or so youths in sweaters and track suits he was jogging round the track at the Park. In a busy morning Henry Sharples had introduced him to a couple of club directors, the assistant trainer, Bertie Peplow, and the men he was now training with, most of them members of the Reserve side. Between times Sharples and Peplow had taken him round the players' quarters, told him something of the training routine, and fitted him out with boots, training kit and the black and yellow hooped shirts of his new club. In the dressing-room Peplow tossed him a club blazer to try on. It was several sizes too large.

'That doesn't fit him, Bertie.' They looked round. Mr Tusson was standing in the doorway.

'No, but it will,' said Peplow jocularly, gathering up a handful of loose cloth at the back.

Mr Tusson didn't smile. 'See he gets it right, Bertie—'

'Sure, sure,' said Peplow indulgently.

'Have a look at yourself, lad,' said Mr Tusson. 'That's the crest of the best club in English football.'

He looked at himself in the mirror, and at Mr Tusson's face over his shoulder. There came a time when you had to admit that something represented the best for you. This was probably it. 'I think so too, Mr Tusson.'

The manager clapped him on the shoulder and left the dressing-room.

Henry Sharples brought them off the track. He beckoned to David. 'I've fixed a seat for you there, Minnis.' He waved to the benches beside the tunnel that led to the dressing-rooms. 'Be back here at half-past two. Right, lads, that'll do for now.'

A bit abrupt, that wave, a bit too much of an order, he thought, as he sat over lunch with Tunney and Ellis in the Sceptre. A smile wouldn't have cost Sharples anything. You're being a fool, he told himself. You're doing nobody a favour. You're being paid for being here. He remembered what Fred Mort had said to him when he had failed to turn out one morning for training. 'Tell you what you've got to watch, Davie boy. This gifted amateur act. You're an incorrigible bloody amateur at heart. Watch it, boy. Pro football isn't blow football.'

Ellis was grinning at him across the table. 'What's biting you, cock? Wish you were turning out this afternoon?' He straightened up in his chair. 'Something like that, Stan.'

But when he got back to the Park he understood the reason for Sharples' peremptoriness. A herd of empty buses sporting the claret and blue of Burnley stood outside the ground. The banking was already full, the stand on the other side of the pitch was rapidly filling. The turnstiles were clicking like clockwork. It was with a feeling of being privileged that he clambered up to his reserved seat.

For the first ten minutes of the game he followed intently the play of Butler, the outside-right drafted up from the Reserves. Had he been out there would he have let that half-back beat him? Could he have turned in that pass with more precision? Would he have been swifter after that loose ball? Could he . . .? Then his attention widened to take in the whole swing and run of the game. He joined in the roar of voices when Rusk put the Park ahead, groaned when Burnley equalized, was swept to his feet when Ellis flicked in the third and winning goal of the game.

As he waited for Ellis and Chris Tunney to change, Mr Verney and Mr Tusson came out of the dressing-room. They looked pleased with themselves. The manager stopped to speak to him. 'Enjoying yourself, Dave?'

'You bet. A great game.'

'It was.' Mr Tusson rubbed his hands together. 'I hope to see you in action, now. We've a mid-week match with Crewe Alexandra. I'm putting you in—'

'Ah, thanks, Mr Tusson—'

'Work hard for Henry Sharples. Shape yourself in with Ret Hayward. Got to know any of the lads, yet?'

'Yes, Tunney and Ellis. We're going out together, tonight.'

'That's the order. Best of luck.'

In the evening, as they sipped a discreet beer together after the cinema, his companions congratulated him on his luck.

'An away game against a Third Division side?' said Ellis 'Why, it's a piece of cake!'

'Does it make all that difference?'

'It depends,' said Tunney, 'on whether you've got what the newspaper boys call the Big Match Temperament. How are you off for that, Dave?'

He drained his glass and set it down with a laugh. 'I dunno. I've never had a big match yet!'

When he came down to breakfast on Monday morning the other three places at the table were occupied. Mr Plinter, a young man with a canary pullover and a small, neat moustache, greeted him with the newspaper and a cheery 'Good-morning'. Miss Gibbon examined him sulkily through a lock of blonde hair. He wasn't accustomed to such treatment from pretty girls. The smile died on his face, and he turned his back to her. 'Sure you're finished with this?' he said to Plinter indicating the paper.

'Positive, old boy. Time I was away, away. Coming, Gibby?' But Miss Gibbons had folded her napkin and disappeared.

As the door closed behind Plinter, David looked across suspiciously at Mr Common. 'Miss Gibbon didn't seem too pleased at my arrival.'

'Oh?' Mr Common opened his eyes wide. 'I didn't notice anything.'

'Nothing was said before I came down to make her—ah, "blow up"?'

'Nothing. It's probably Monday-itis.'

'What does she do?'

'She calls herself a librarian. That is to say, she stands behind a counter punching dates in grubby books.'

He didn't pursue this. 'And Mr Plinter?'

'He calls himself a banker. That is, he's an underpaid clerk who puts in his day counting money—other people's.' Mr Common stood up, and dusted crumbs from his waistcoat.

'Your own work must be very important, Mr Common.'

Mr Common looked at him distantly. 'You would think I was bragging,' he said, and left the dining-room.

Mrs Compton came in. He thanked her as she set his sausage and egg on the table. 'What does Mr Common do?'

'He's a senior draughtsman in Beadles. I heard you talking a moment ago.' She smiled. 'What do you make of him?'

'Well . . .'

'He *is* a card, our Mr Common, isn't he?'

He, hesitated not at all sure what meanings this unfamiliar epithet carried. Mrs Compton smiled guilelessly down on him. 'Yes . . .' he said doubtfully. 'Yes, I expect he is.' Then suddenly he asked, 'Mrs Compton, your husband played professional football, didn't he?'

'Joe? Yes, for the Park.' She rested her hand on the table. 'And I'll tell you something. It's great to have a footballer in the house again. Like old times—'

He snatched up his knife and fork and grinned his thanks. 'That's all I wanted to know, Mrs Compton.'

An hour later he was in an atmosphere where men talked, breathed, lived football. A world that had at its core a hollow ball. He was not without some experience of the workings of a professional club. But the routine activities that had been carried out often in a casual manner at Glenbank were heightened here to a purposeful discipline. With his team-mates he sat in front of a board while Mr Tusson tried to anticipate the strategy of Wednesday's game. Ellis and Tunney might make light of their opponents but by the time the manager had finished his blackboard campaign David felt that he knew every member of the Crewe defence intimately. Out on the pitch his acceleration and bewildering change of pace was noted and approved. But he betrayed some clumsiness in the control of the ball.

'O.K., Dave,' said Henry Sharples. 'You've got speed. That's in your body. Providence gave you that. Now get back onto that ball and make it look like it was tied to your toe.'

On Wednesday as he was about to leave his lodgings the midday mail tumbled through the letter-box. There were two envelopes for him. One was from his mother, on the other he recognized Maureen's handwriting. He stuffed them into his pocket and hurried out to join his team-mates and the coach to Crewe.

I don't want an easy game he said to himself as he trotted onto the turf at Gresty Road. Just let things be fair to me; the run of the ball, my speed, the opposing guile, a clear-eyed ref, no cracked bones. He was brought into the play in the first five seconds. A lozenge of curt passes from Ellis to Rimmer, Rimmer to Hayward and the inside-forward cast a long shot upfield. To the observant watchers in the stand he seemed to spring from the ground in pursuit. He brought the ball round with the inside of his right foot, then turned too abruptly into the Crewe defence. As the trap of half-back and back closed in, his confidence wavered and he drove the ball fiercely across his advancing forwards. Even the sure-footed Rusk failed to tame it and fumbled it away to Bobby Milner, his fellow-Scot on the left wing. Milner, off-balance, ballooned the ball harmlessly forward and out of play. This opening of darting speed and uncouth play amused the Crewe supporters. A surf of amusement rose from the banking. 'Hi, Minnis, the rest o' your mates are playing up and down the pitch!' shouted a voice.

In the stand Peplow said, 'If the posts were on the touch-lines he would've scored.'

Mr Tusson lifted his chin from his hand. 'Leave the jokes to the wags, Bertie. Let us see if the lad knows where he went wrong.'

As he moved back for the kick-out Milner grinned across at

him and shook his head in mock despair. He felt the blood rise in his cheeks. A hand gripped him firmly by the elbow. Jimmy Rusk was trotting past. 'Use your side-line a wee shade more. You'll make it, Davie lad. Don't worry.'

For the remainder of the first half he was given few chances to stretch his legs up the side-line. The Railwaymen, with the vigour and courage of giant-killers, held the game around the Maitland Park goal. Time after time he was drawn back to help stem the onslaught of the scarlet shirts. There was no score at the interval.

In the dressing-room Mr Tusson looked a bit depressed.

'Careful with those crosses, Dave.'

'Sure, Mr Tusson. Sorry.'

'And move about a bit. You're not on rails.'

'I'll do that.' He waited, hardly daring to hope that he was going to get off so lightly. It seemed that he was. Mr Tusson turned away from him and raised his voice. 'That goes for you all. Let's see a bit of life up there in front, boys. It may be a friendly but you don't have to make it a love-match.'

About ten minutes after the restart he tracked a pass into the Crewe penalty area. The back covered up confidently, then seeing David's hopeful spurt, hesitated, uncertain whether to clear or tap back to Hesketh in the Crewe goal. His tardy clearance rebounded from David's shins. Before he could recover David had raced round him, steadied the ball, and slammed it past the aggrieved Hesketh.

It was a chance goal. There had been no strategy laid deep in the Park half, no cunning interweaving of passes; an optimistic boot ahead, an opportune follow-through—and the Park were one goal ahead. But it was good enough for the phalanx of Park supporters who waved their arms and hooted for joy, and for his team-mates, who embraced him, thumped his back, wrung his hand. He tried to impress the scene on his memory. The applause and movement from the terracing. The signals of congratulation from the group in the stand. The pleasure of his team-mates. This is my first goal in English football. Take a good look at it. It can't happen again.

His success drew a bolt in the Crewe defence. In the next thirty minutes Ellis scored twice. Rusk nodded in a fourth from a corner-kick. Towards the end Tunney, Hayward and he ran through an exhausted defence to give Ellis his third goal and the fifth of the match. This was the form and style of a team of champions. Mr Verney came down to tell them so. Jimmy Rusk told them so. Even Mr Tusson seemed surfeited. The forward line he had dreamt of was now complete.

He was undressing to go to bed when he remembered, with a small start of guilt, the letters in his pocket. His mother's he read first. It was brief and much as he had expected; full of concern, affection, and some news of Freddie and herself. He sat on the edge of the bed to savour the bitter-sweet emotion of home-sickness. I'll write her at the weekend, he thought, laying her letter on the mantelpiece. The other he opened slowly, with an inexplicable feeling of reluctance. As he read, he saw behind the words the firm delicate outline of his sweetheart's face, the candid clearness of her eyes. She possessed the elemental gift of writing in her own voice. And in her words he heard a restrained ardour, the joyous acknowledgment of a bond between them. When he had finished the letter he closed his eyes and rested his head on his hand. She'll have to be written to tomorrow. He felt a dull resentment at the thought and anger with himself for feeling it. He fumbled through the litter on his dressing-table until he found a picture post card. He stuck it upright in the bristles of his hair-brush. I'll think of something to say tomorrow. In bed he thumped and folded the newspaper to read for the fourth time the report of the match. At each mention of his name a smile came on his lips.

Part Four

I

'YOU'LL have to get steel shafts,' said Plinter.

'You think so?'

'A must, old man. The old hickory sticks are all right for the Bank Holiday type of golfer. You don't quite come into that category, eh?' Plinter stroked his small moustache and surveyed him with a genial smile.

'Well, I dunno . . . how many clubs will I need?'

'Say four to begin with—a brassie, a couple of irons, a putter. You add to that as you go along—get better at the game, and so on. I could introduce you to a bloke in Stone's Emporium, tomorrow—'

Plinter's eyes glowed with goodwill. Knew everybody. Cars, games, clothes, knew everything. 'For a pal I can get them almost wholesale. Know a bloke . . . .'

David shook his head. 'Thanks, but there are one or two things . . .' Those small forebodings on the edge of his mind. No news yet as to whether he was in Saturday's senior team. Neither Mr Tusson nor Sharples had been at the Park. With the others he had taken his training instructions from Bertie Peplow. No one had mentioned his performance at Crewe. Chris Tunney had said everything was all right and then turned the talk to golf. Too quickly perhaps, he thought gloomily. Then there was that picture post card now well on its way across the Irish Sea. He saw her picking it up from the worn green linoleum in the Majestic Street hall and winced at the memory of its meagre, cowardly words. This was no time to think of golf, of trivialities. 'Thanks, Plinter. Awfully good of you. When I get round to it I'll ask you again.'

But next morning as he rode out to the Park some of his despondency lifted. He had bought a couple of papers at the bus stop. The football columnist of the *Midland Echo* peering into the morrow thought that the Park were unlikely to upset the forward line that brought them five goals at Crewe. His fellow-seer of the *Maitland Herald* went one better and confidently printed the team: Drewry; Barton, Snowdon; Rimmer, Betmead, Tunney; Minnis, Hayward, Ellis, Rusk, and Milner. He lowered the paper on to his knee and looked down on the hurrying citizens of Maitland Park. How much, he wondered, do these football fellas really know?

He hurled himself from the bus before it drew into the sidewalk, sprinted through the enclosure gates and eagerly scanned the sheet pinned on the notice board. Drewry; Barton, Snowdon; Rimmer, Betmead, Tunney; *Minnis* . . . He looked around sheepishly, fearful that somebody might have seen him running to the board like that. What does it matter, he thought, I've achieved something great at last. He went down to the dressing-rooms with a light step, one of the elect.

For the next two days so many demands were made on his intelligence and stamina that he had little time to think of anything else. Mr Tusson made it evident that his new young winger was to be taken in hand and in the short time before Saturday's kick-off the manager coaxed more cunning and fire from David's head and feet than their owner thought was secreted there. On Saturday Maitland Park held Leicester City, their rivals for promotion, to a draw. For the first time David faced a vigorous and crafty defence and moved creditably in the space allowed him. For the first time, too, he played before the home supporters and the crowd liked what they saw, and said so.

Then, as the weekend's exhilaration dwindled, the memory of Maureen, never quite absent from his mind, came back. Throughout a sleepless night the inexorable approach of her letter filled his thoughts. He watched over her shoulder as she wrote it, followed her light step as she carried it to the pillar box in the Ormeau Road, retreated before it over the sea, waited for its rustle in the letter-box of Regent Place.

After lunch on Monday he sat on at table until Mr Common

and Gibby and Plinter had gone back to work. When the dining-room was empty he opened the letter. 'Dearest David (it began)—Thank you for the card. Leamington Spa looks nice. How are you getting on. I was looking forward to your letter so much. Perhaps you were too busy to write at length. I hope I didn't say anything wrong in mine. (You must excuse me because I have never written a love letter before.) You must help me. To me it seems so simple . . .' There was small talk of what she had been doing day by day since he had gone. And through it all the vibrant confession of her yearning for him, the love and trust that she nursed in his absence.

He grasped the marble mantelpiece and stared into the fire. He could read no further. He need read no further. This was not the answer he had awaited. Expecting reproaches, he had intended, coldly and deliberately, to quarrel with her, and see to it, as time went on, that there was no reconciliation. But she had failed to reproach him. To her, the bond between them was stronger than ever. He stooped and put the letter in the fire. It lay for a moment on the blazing coals, crisp, shapely, unsmirched, offering him a last opportunity. He stood motionless. A tongue of flame flickered up, the smooth page withered suddenly into scorched ugliness and was drawn down into the heart of the fire. As he climbed the stairs to his room he was assuring himself that what he had done was not irreparable. I can still answer her without knowing all that she had written.

'I'll have a look at those clubs today,' he told Plinter at breakfast a couple of mornings later.

'Good man. Come into a bit of lolly?'

He smiled mirthlessly. 'No, it's not that. I just—'

'That's the only reason Plinter knows,' said Gibby disdainfully from the end of the table.

To his surprise, Plinter, who never failed to rise to anything the fair-haired girl said, flushed, and mumbled something unintelligible into his cereal.

For all Plinter's comic affections he had come to like him. He didn't much like Gibby. But Gibby was right this time. To poor Plinter everything in life seemed to turn on a coin, or come wrapped in a bank-note. Mebbe it was because he worked so much among the stuff. He glanced half-pityingly at his fellow-boarder. There were so many things more important than money. But you didn't know that until you had lost them. Peace of mind, for example. Freedom from the guilty thought that three hundred miles away a happy girl was soon to suffer unjustly. He closed his eyes in pain and shame. How many times must the postman pass ninety-three Majestic Street before she knew what a blow had been dealt her confidence and hope? There had been times, since he destroyed her letter, when he had struggled, angrily demanding from himself why he should have to give up this happiness. Then, when he had laboriously conjured up their days together, the memory of her good looks, her charm, her sincerity, filled him with revulsion. God, he thought, nobody's ever gone through anything like this before. There must be something wrong with me.

At midday, in the sports department of Stone's Emporium, Plinter and the bloke he knew were swinging golf clubs knowledgeably before David's bemused eyes. With a sigh Plinter relinquished a gleaming steel shaft into his hands. 'Try that for balance, Minnis.' He wiggled the club obediently. 'Seems all right, Farrington?' Farrington agreed. Plinter rattled it in beside the others in the new bag. 'That's the lot, Farrington. See what your boss can do for my friend Minnis.'

David chuckled. He suspected Plinter was playing truant from the bank for this outing. He liked Farrington too. They had fussed around him as if he had a thousand pounds to spend. Differing in build and colour yet they looked alike. The same nervous chirping speech, the same urban pallor, identical rugby ties peeping over the canary pullovers, the same rolling gait of Third Fifteen regulars. Their feet, he noticed guiltily, were affixed at the wrong angle for even a semblance of pace. They were the sort of fellas, he thought, who would slip almost unobserved through a life of small pleasures and small pains.

A short, bald man was hurrying towards him with beaming smile, and outstretched hand. 'Mr Minnis. Dave Minnis. Glad to meet you. Seen you at Crewe last Wednesday. Grand display. Welcome to Stone's Emporium!'

'Ah . . . thanks, Mr Stone.'

'Peabody. Stone's dead. Now, what's the problem, Mr Farrington?'

Mr Farrington started to explain. Mr Peabody waved him to silence.

'Give Mr Minnis the lot. Driver, spoon, irons, number—'

'But look, Mr Peabody!' David expostulated.

'Mr Minnis, these are on loan, with the compliments of Stone's Emporium. Anything more you need, call in. All we ask is that you tell your friends that you go to Stone's for everything. Bargain?'

'Well—'

'Mr Farrington, where's that new number with the zip hood?'

He left the store feeling like a circus caravan. Plinter followed him, impressed and rather crestfallen. As he sidled along the crowded pavement he glanced over his shoulder at a highly coloured object dangling from the bag.

'Plinter,' he said irritably, 'do I really need that bloody bedsock thing?'

'I say. Take it easy, old lad!' said Plinter, shocked.

'All right. Would you like to carry 'em?'

Plinter brightened at once. The contents of the bag made a rich, expensive sound as he slung the loop on his shoulder. For a time they threaded their way through the lunch-time crowd. David noticed that his companion had grown unusually gloomy.

'Too heavy, Plinter?'

'No, not at all.' Almost audibly Plinter plucked up courage. 'Minnis, what do you think of Gibby?'

'Gibby?' He stopped in surprise and they were immediately elbowed into a doorway. 'Gibby? Oh, I suppose she's all right.'

'I'm in love with her.'

He breathed a small prayer of thanks that he hadn't said what he really thought. 'Oh, great. That's all right, isn't it?'

'No. You see she won't have me.' Plinter raised his face and

David winced at the misery he saw there. 'It's not because she doesn't like me. It's because I've no money.'

'Oh well . . .' He blustered a bit. 'If that's the type—'

'No, it isn't like that. You see, she had bad luck once before. He turned out to be no good. Now she says that if ever she gets married *everything* will have to—'

'Plinter!' As he raised his voice he grasped the other by the arm. 'I dunno what you're going to say. But don't. If it's advice you want, don't ask me. I know nothing about girls.' He smiled in an effort to soften his words. 'You've been very decent to me this morning, Plinter. Before you go back to the bank let me stand you lunch. Come on, we'll go to the Sceptre.'

Maureen's third letter arrived on Monday. He thrust it into the fire without opening it and watched until it was a pulsating transparency falling apart in feathers of ash. He had held it in his fingers for such a brief time, its destruction was so swift and complete, that an hour later he felt as if he had never received it. There was nothing further he could do. Already she seemed a great distance from him.

If you kept yourself occupied, he reasoned, there would be no time to feel guilty, no chinks in the waking hours where remorse could seep in. He worked at full stretch during training spells at the Park. With Tunney and Ellis he spent an hour or so on the links every morning swinging his new clubs. Plinter took him to a party where he sat on the floor sipping draught cider and listening to music that reminded him of the shipyards at home. He mentioned football to a pretty girl in blue slacks. She gazed at him uncomprehendingly. A dull evening, but every hour, he felt, was an hour stretching towards forgetfulness for both of them.

His mother's letter at the weekend was filled, as usual, with the small happenings at Colinvista Street. He skimmed through it with amused impatience his attention held by nothing until he read: 'A girl called at the door last night. She wanted to know if you were still at the same address. She said she was a sister of your friend Bonar McFall. When I said Yes she didn't answer: She seemed almost distracted. Then she ran away up the street without a word of thanks. It was growing dark, and I didn't call her back. You know David if your friend has written to you . . .'

He folded the letter slowly and put it into his pocket. What was I doing a couple of nights ago when it was growing dark? Getting ready to go out with the boys. As I put on my Park tie I remember thinking she had never seen it, that she had no further interest in what I wore or said or did. It made me feel a bit sad in the heart for a minute or two. But it's all over now, as the song says. I thought I had got out of it without doing too much damage. I was wrong. At that very moment she still had some belief in me. Enough to force herself to walk down Colinvista Street and knock at my mother's door. He considered his reflection in the mirror. You don't amount to much, do you? Well, you've got your freedom now even if you had to kill a girl's heart to get it. Take what joy you can out of that, you poor bastard.

Mr Tusson demanded from his players everything they had to give in energy and talent. He didn't always get what he wanted. But being by nature tolerant and having spent most of his life among men who earned their livelihood by the delicate combination of wits, courage and nimbleness, he didn't always expect to be satisfied. After the Leicester City game he watched David closely. He had seen too many young footballers lying back after a good Press report. For a day or two he thought he detected an indifference, a slacking-off. Then suddenly young Minnis was never away from the place. Indoors, he followed the tactical discussions eagerly and intelligently; on the pitch, Henry Sharples had no more willing pupil. Mr Tusson was highly pleased.

In their struggle for promotion Mr Tusson reckoned that the Park could afford to drop one game in their half a dozen end-of-season matches. They had a run of successes in February and March against Barnsley, Norwich, Aston Villa and Chesterfield. The one permissible defeat was inflicted by Spurs at White Hart Lane.

It was David's first visit to London. Tunney, Ellis and he got permission to stay overnight. Ellis, the Londoner, was their guide. His first job he told them had been as a London telegraph messenger. He boasted that he knew every street, square, lane and alley between Paddington and Peckham. To David, as he followed his companions on Sunday morning, each great thoroughfare seemed the innermost centre. Together, they seemed not parts of one city, but a constellation of cities.

On the Embankment he stopped before a news-bill. 'Look, Chris,' he said. Tunney read out the crayoned words: 'SOLDIER DIES IN ULSTER BORDER RAID'. He turned to David. 'Well, what about it?'

'What about it? It's started again.'

'It makes news, doesn't it?'

'Is that all it means to you?'

'That's all it means to anybody. Ireland, north and south, the smile and the tear, is a bloody bore to the English. Ask Stan.'

'Don't ask me,' said Ellis resting his arms on the parapet. 'I just don't like hearing about a bloke getting shot—'

'You buy yourself a paper, Dave. You come from there. You're interested.' The jibe in Tunney's voice angered him.

'So do you! You know what it means!'

'I've forgotten.'

He stared unbelievingly at his companion. 'You mean to tell me that what happens in Ireland doesn't interest you any more?'

'Not much. Why should it? This is my country now.'

'And you'll never go back?'

'Mebbe. To see my folk. To play a match. On a holiday. That's all.'

He leaned on the cool rough stone beside Ellis and looked across the river to the massive façades on the other bank. It wouldn't be difficult for a stranger in this vast city to believe that his prejudices, tongue, history were of no significance. Particularly if you set your mind to it, like Tunney. He rebelled against the idea. He was going back. But not now. He had no desire to be seen on the streets of Belfast for a long time yet. He suddenly realized that he was going to spend the summer in England. He would have to find something to do. And break the news to his mother. He reckoned he could get his way gently but firmly in the three or four letters he would write before the end of the season.

There was nothing momentous or heroic in the Park's final League victory at Doncaster. With Leicester City they were already assured of promotion. But the citizens of Maitland Park decided that this was the occasion on which to fête their champions. They stopped the motor coach in the outskirts of the town at the end of its journey from Yorkshire and drew it to the market square. The players were pulled out, pawed, pinched, thumped and carried on the shoulders of the mob to the Town Hall steps. The Mayor, his words and hair tossed about by the wind, read them an address of congratulation. David saw Mr Hemphill at the top of the steps. Under the festooned lamps his face, like the faces of his fellow-councillors, glowed with joy. A team in the First Division meant bigger business next season in the cafés, pubs and stores of Maitland Park. The mayor thrust his notes into his pocket and threw wide his arms to announce that the council had decided unanimously to entertain the team to a dinner and dance at the Sceptre. The Aluminium Works' band struck up a march. Enthusiasts took a firmer grip on the calves, thighs and buttocks of the hapless men on their shoulders. David, too mortified to complain, suffered agony as he was carried with his team-mates in a last triumphal circuit of the square.

His mother didn't take kindly to the idea of him not returning home. The Belfast papers, because there was an ex-Glenbank player in the team, gave more than usual prominence to Maitland Park's success. Freddie read the news to her. Reproachfully she wrote asking what there was to hold him in England 'now that the job was done'. Because he had no intention of going back he chuckled good-humouredly. To hear her you'd think I was an Irish navvy that had come over to work on the last mile of a railway line. Then towards the end of her letter she told him that Mr Rankin, defeated once again by the world, had been brought back to the harbourage of Colinvista Street. He had seized on the chance eagerly. There would at least be the shadow of a man about the house.

It was impossible to go home, he wrote. The off-season wages were too small to live on. He would have to find a job for the summer. Perhaps he might manage a few days before the autumn. Meantime, he had just heard of something he couldn't afford to miss. I wonder what that would be, he thought as he sealed the letter.

He partnered Stan Ellis's sister-in-law to the Celebration Dance. At one time he had thought of asking Gibby but the prospect of having to face Plinter's reproachful and gloomy despair was too much. And he wasn't sure that he wanted to take a chance on that taciturn young woman's answer being a refusal. Ellis's sister-in-law wasn't bad-looking. Fellows who didn't have a girl handy always took her to the club dances. She was a good sport. But she didn't play straight with him. To his silent fury she kept leaning her forehead against his chin, getting her hair into his mouth, clinging yearningly to his arm as they left the floor. Without seeming downright rude to Stan Ellis and his party he pleaded occasional business at other tables where indeed he was slapped on the back by His Worship the Mayor, toasted by Mr Verney and his cronies and was cajoled into a dance by Mrs Rusk. He was returning her to her husband when he was asked to sit down and have a drink.

'What are you going to do with yourself, Davie?' asked Rusk as he filled the glasses. 'Go back home?'

'I dunno. I don't particularly want to.'

'Take a job?'

'It depends. Anything in mind?'

'Before I was married I worked two or three summers at a holiday camp on the Clyde. Duncan Ingram, the manager, wants me back this year. Jeannie won't hear of it. But it's nice money, nice grub, nice work. If you like I'll mention your name to Ingram when I'm in Glasgow next week.'

'What's the job?'

'Sports Organizer. Look after games, organize walks, jolly up the old 'uns, impress the young 'uns with your club blazer.'

'Well, if you're sure you don't want to go—'

'He's positive,' said Jeannie Rusk.

'Thanks, Jimmy. I'll try it.'

Ten days later he was on his way to Scotland.

2

THE voices and music fell away behind him as he climbed the rutted lane. On the brow of the hill he stood upright in starlit silence. Only by looking back could he assure himself that he hadn't clambered up from an empty moor. The camp lay below him, a pattern of lights; the gapped row of chalet windows, the roseate flush from the Auld Plaidie Tavern, the white, naked light behind the kitchens, the coloured glare that leaked from the Auld Ceilidh House where the Saturday night hop was warming up.

There was no courting couple on the bench below the Auld Bogle's Thorn. Everybody was at the dance. He took a seat under the long-suffering boughs and watched the ships' lights glide down the Firth of Clyde. This was his last evening at the Clachan Holiday Camp. Tomorrow he would be returning to Maitland Park. Slowly and with care he imprinted the scene on his memory; the midnight bulk of the hills around him, the dark luminosity of the Gare Loch and beyond the moving ships the far-off powdered glow from the Clyde towns. The shape and colour of these hills was nearer to those of his own country than the genteel horizons of Warwickshire. He had enjoyed the three months among them. Out of the hundreds of men, women and children who had holidayed here, only a few faces, a few incidents, remained with him clearly. There had been the nimble-footed Glasgow schoolboy whose name and address he had noted for Tusson. The young couple who had been married in the camp. The angry American who had reported him to Ingram for refusing a tip. But he was richer by a hundred pounds and a second-hand car that he had bought in Greenock. Tomorrow, and he swallowed at the thought, he would set out to drive it all the way to Maitland Park. A hundred quid. I can buy her and Freddie all the clothes they want . . . They're just over the sea beyond those hills. I wonder what they're doing now? A stone rattled on the path below him. A girl came round the corner. He jumped to his feet.

'Gibby!'

'Hello, Minnis. They told me I might find you up here.'

'Where did you come from?'

'Off the eight-thirty bus from Helensburgh.'

'Yes, but—'

'I had a long weekend left. I thought I'd come up and see how you were getting on at what's-it Holiday Camp.'

'Clachan. It means—'

'Don't trouble.' He scowled in the darkness. There she goes already. Taking no interest in what I say.

'Aren't you going to ask me to sit down? Or have you a date?'

'Don't be silly. Sit down.'

He made room for her on the bench. She cupped her chin in her hand. Her face was hidden by the falling wave of hair.

'Come up here often?'

'Pretty often.'

'Alone?'

He laughed. 'Sometimes.'

'It's nice.' Her voice sounded indifferent.

'I like it. This is a last look for me. I'm going back tomorrow.'

'Oh . . .'

Then she said. 'Have you ten pounds, Minnis?'

He turned in the darkness to look at her. 'I could raise it, I suppose. Why?'

'Plinter's in trouble. He's taken money from the bank.'

'Gor, how much?'

'Over forty pounds. Mrs C. has divvied up a tenner. I've divvied up a tenner. We want you to divvy up a tenner.'

'Sure, sure. What about Old Man Common?'

'He went round to the bank and paid off the lot. That's how we kept Plinter out of court.'

'Well—' he collapsed. 'Well, I dunno . . . put me down for a tenner.'

'Thanks, Minnis.'

'Where's Plinter now?'

'Gone home. Somewhere in London.'

A night moth blundered out of the foliage. She shrank back against him striking out with her hand.

He laughed. 'It's only a moth!'

'I hate beasties!' She drews wiftly away from him, her voice angry as if she had been caught off guard.

'Well, let's go down. The mist's rising from the lough.'

They stumbled down the path in the darkness carefully avoiding any contact with each other. 'So you're going home, tomorrow?'

'Yes, practically got my bags packed.'

In the light from the Auld Ceilidh House they stopped. The music of a waltz slid out and curled around them. He bent his head to see what she was thinking.

'Put your hair up, Gibby, will you!'

After a moment she brushed back the glistening hair. He failed to understand what he saw in the grave watchful eyes.

'Care for a hop?'

She drew up her shoulders in the smallest shrug. 'Thanks, why not?' As she turned he felt again the soft, unpremeditated touch of her body.

Rather less than twenty-four hours later he steered carefully into Regent Place, braked firmly opposite No. 5, and switched off his engine. His eyes burned, his arms ached, the hinge had gone out of his right ankle. But it was worth it, he thought, as he clambered out and stood uncertainly on the pavement. I wish some of the boys back home had seen some of that driving today. He picked up his bags and limped into the house.

After supper he gave the ten pounds to Mr. Common. Politely he waved aside Mrs Compton's thanks. He had been fond of Plinter, too. He felt especially magnanimous as he handed over the money. At that moment all he could remember of Plinter was his silliness.

Next morning, as he came off the track, Mr Tusson was waiting for him at the entrance to the dressing-rooms.

'Nice to see you again, Dave,' said the manager. 'Have a nice holiday?'

'Grand, thanks, Mr Tusson.'

'They must have worked you hard up there. I thought you looked tired in that work out.'

'Ah, it's nothing. Still a bit stiff after last night. I drove my car down from Scotland.'

'You did?' Mr Tusson waved towards the car park. 'That yours—the Wolseley Hornet?'

'Yes. Looks all right, doesn't it?'

'Very nice. Get rid of it, Dave.'

'Get rid of it?'

'That's right. Sell it.'

'Why?'

'Because it makes you sluggish and stiff. It might,' and Mr Tusson laughed rustily, 'make you stiff for good. I don't like my players driving cars.'

'Hell, Mr Tusson, I bought it with my own money!'

'I don't doubt that. I hope you don't lose anything.'

'I'll have to think about it,' he muttered.

'Don't think about it too long. Don't bring it back. Don't let me hear about you driving it. That's an order.'

Ellis and Tunney, to his chagrin, refused to sympathize with him. Ellis, who had a wife and two small children, thought he was dense not to have noticed that even the family men in the team hadn't cars. He said that he couldn't see what had that to do with him. If he kept the car he was only standing up for his rights.

'Ever got hurt in a game and been laid off, Dave?' asked Tunney.

'Only for a week or two at Glenbank.'

'What happened?'

'What happened? I went back on to the team when I was fit again.'

'Know what would happen here? You would go down to the Reserves. Butler hasn't given up hope of getting his place back. Then there's this new boy they've signed from Birmingham. You would have to fight to get back. Of course, if you were hurt in a game you would have Tusson's sympathy. Get yourself hurt in a car after what you've been told and you haven't a hope in hell of making it again. Tusson would see to that.'

'Or,' said Ellis, 'you can stand up for your rights. Say, you weren't told you couldn't own a car. Make it difficult for Tusson and the club. Get your name in the papers—'

This dire recital of possibilities tickled him into amusement. He held up his hand. 'O.K., Stan, I've got the idea. If it's going to be half as bad as that I'll get rid of the car. I had never any hankering to be a martyr.'

The trees at the end of Regent Place gently relinquished their leaves. A keenness had come into the morning air. As a small compensation for the loss of the car he bought himself an overcoat and a couple of suits with some of the money. He was gratified when the assistant in the shop recognized him. By the end of September a hundred small boys in the town had his name on autograph books, bits of paper, fragments of cigarette packets. Ret Hayward, Jimmy Rusk and he were invited to a tea-party in the local Children's Hospital. One evening as he and several of the players and their wives sat in Rusk's house they discussed a dance to be given by the Maitland Park Supporters' Club.

'I suppose,' said Jeannie Rusk, 'we'll have to find Dave a girl, as usual?' Ellis's wife, he noticed, kept an ominous silence.

He straightened up in his chair. 'You needn't bother, Jeannie,' he said. 'I don't need anybody's help. I gotta girl—'

They crowded round him, laughing. Tunney punched him in the ribs. 'You gotta girl?'

'Of course I've gotta girl!'

'Well, where is she? Why haven't we seen her? What's she like?'

'You'll see her all in good time,' he said. And they failed to draw him any further.

The next evening at supper he crumbled a biscuit on his plate and watched Gibby from under his brows as she sat reading at the fire. The clock struck eleven. He cleared his throat, and said, 'Are you busy next Thursday evening?'

She didn't look up. 'I don't think so. Why do you ask?'

'There's a football dance in the Sceptre. I thought you might like to go with me. Only to make up the party . . .'

Her book closed with a little snap and she rose, smiling sweetly. 'How could anyone resist such an invitation?' Without another glance she stepped lithely past him. At the door she paused. 'What are the women wearing?'

He swung round. 'I dunno . . . I never thought . . . I could find out.'

'Do. It would be helpful.' Her 'Goodnight' came to him from the hall.

It was raining on the night of the dance. He had a taxi waiting at the door. It had been waiting there for ten minutes and yet from upstairs there had been neither sight nor sound of Gibby. Surely if she had gone to dances before she would have been ready long ago? He looked at himself once again in the hall mirror. His scalp tingled from repeated combings, his nervous fingers had ironed out the last pucker from his dress-tie. There had been moments in the past week when he had been both relieved and exasperated to see that her attitude towards him was precisely the same as at any other time. These cuff-links were inclined to nip him. But you could never tell. Heaven knows into what secret flurry of unreadiness his invitation had thrown her. He should have played safe and asked the wee nurse from the Children's Hospital. He hoped Farrington had been right in advising him to buy a soft-fronted shirt. But he had told Ellis and Tunney and Rusk and their womenfolk that he was bringing her.

His eye rather than his ear sensed her approach. A slim, silver figure descended from the darkness of the tall house. Her hidden feet stepped noiselessly on to the hall. He never thought she could own such a dress. That she could move and look like this. Her face, as ever, was grave, but it was impossible not to see the slight colouring in her cheeks, her grey eyes watching him.

'I'm sorry. I hope I haven't kept you waiting?'

He got rid of the croak in his voice. 'No, no . . . you're splendid . . . we've plenty of time.'

She paused to draw a scarf over her head. Diffidently he offered to help her across the slippery pavement.

After that evening if one or other of them needed a partner they went out together. She asked him to a cocktail party given by the chairman of the town Library Committee. He took her to another club dance and to a charity matinée in Birmingham. Their attitude to each other was friendly and rather detached. She showed no desire that he should grow fond of her. It was an admirable arrangement. If there were moments when he found himself silently and quite unreasonably rebelling against it, common sense prevailed. He wasn't unhappy. Keeping out of love wasn't so difficult. It was like going to a party, he told himself, and making up your mind not to get drunk.

As the early weeks of the new season passed he played himself firmly into the Park senior team. Since last year he had gained weight, power and speed. Henry Sharples and Tusson disciplined his fondness for showy and useless running on the field. 'A forward running hard without the ball is a man with a bad conscience,' Sharples told him. 'He knows that he should have been somewhere else at that time.' In the relentless grind of First Division play he learned that Sharples was right, that speed was a poor substitute for a sense of anticipation. He began to emerge as the footballer of craft and intelligence that the knowledgeable ref had discerned on the cinder pitch in Ormeau Park years ago.

The first hint that he might be considered for his national side came in a cutting from a Belfast paper sent him by Freddie. Then, during the interval in a League game against Preston North End, he was told that there was an Irish selector above in the directors' box. That afternoon Hayward and he could never shake off the formidable Preston defence and the Park went down by three goals. There was no news for him in the dressing-room after the game. He had forgotten the rumour before he left the Deepdale Road ground. On the following Tuesday he was told to go to Mr Tusson's office. The manager tossed him a letter across the desk. 'The I.F.A. want to know if we can release you as a reserve for their game against Scotland.'

He stared blankly at the sheet of paper. 'That's great—that's terrific, Mr Tusson.'

Mr Tusson retrieved the letter in silence. David, fearful of a refusal, blundered on. 'I can hardly believe it after what happened at Preston.'

'Oh, I don't know,' said Mr Tusson. 'Even an Irish selector could hardly expect you to go on the rampage against one of the top sides in the English League. Still, he must have seen something to please him.'

'And what's the answer?'

The manager leafed laboriously through his desk calendar. 'Your game's on the third of October. We play Grimsby that day. Jimmy Rusk will be away with the Scottish team.' Mr Tusson looked up and smiled. 'I think we can do without the two of you for an afternoon. Yes, Dave, you can go, it's all right with us.'

'Many thanks, Mr Tusson. And, of course, the directors . . .'

'That's all right. I'll tell 'em. If we can manage it the Park never stands in the way of a lad playing for his country. Who's the man in possession?'

'Billy Hanna of Stockport.'

'A nice player, but not growing any younger. If you don't get it this time, you'll get it soon.' As they left the office the manager said. 'You didn't go home last summer, did you?'

'No, I got a job.'

'Why don't you get away from here after the game on Saturday and spend a few days with your people before you join the rest of the Irish boys on the Tuesday?'

'I will. I'll do that, Mr Tusson. And thanks for everything.'

It took good humour and time to get away from the Park dressing-room on Saturday. Rusk held his hand and shook his head despondently over him. Rimmer and Ellis wanted to take him for a beer. Henry Sharples had some last-minute advice about a thigh bruise. He escaped from them at last to his taxi.

As he came down the stairs at Regent Place he saw Gibby in the dining-room. He stood for a moment in the hall, then set down his case and went in, closing the door. She was gazing into the fire, her arms resting on the mantelpiece. The soft fall of her hair, illumined by the flamelight, hid her face from him.

'I'm away, Gibby.'

'Oh.' She turned with a quick smile. 'Well, goodbye.'

'Bye. I'll bring you back a leprechaun.'

He moved closer to her and she looked up questioningly.

'You haven't wished me good luck.'

'I'm sorry. Good luck.'

He shook his head. 'That's not how it's done.'

'No?'

'No. It's done like this.' Her fingers brushed his shoulders as he drew her towards him and kissed her on the mouth.

3

He had fallen asleep to the beat of distant engines and the fitful creaking of woodwork. He awakened to a heavy thudding on the deck above, cries, and the hurried tread of feet. In the watery light he saw a timber baulk framed in the cabin porthole. It was motionless. Muttering, he swung his legs out of the berth. There was a tap at the door and the steward came in with a squat teapot and a cup and saucer on a tray.

' 'Morning, sir.'

'We've arrived?'

'Just tied up. Fast run across last night.'

David glowered at him. 'I wanted to see the Antrim hills as we came in.'

'Wouldn't have seen nothing, sir. Black as a sweep's hand as we came up the lough.' The man set down the tray and with a grin drew a folded newspaper from his pocket. 'With the purser's compliments, Mr Minnis. He thinks you won't have heard the news yet.' As he held out the paper the man traced a headline with his finger. David read: 'MINNIS TO PLAY FOR IRELAND SAYS I.F.A.' Slowly he took the paper from the steward and read what followed: 'Stockport County have informed Hanna their Irish outside-right that they cannot release him for the game against Scotland. At I.F.A. headquarters our correspondent was told that D. Minnis of Maitland Park will fill the vacancy. This will be his first "cap". . . '

He dropped the paper on his knee and stared at the steward. 'Thanks . . . and thank the purser. I'll want a taxi in about half an hour.'

The door had barely closed when he crushed the paper into a ball and kicked it exultantly around the narrow cabin. Then he wanted to read again what had been read last night by Dr Boustead, Roden, Hamilton, all those whose names brought back unpleasant memories. He rescued the paper and smoothed it out. A few words between his outstretched fingers held his attention. They read like a fleering parody of what he sought: 'He Died for Ireland,' says I.R.A. The gunman injured in the raid on Derryarb police barracks on Tuesday morning is now known to have died of his wounds. It is thought that he was a native of Belfast. The Irish Republican Bureau, Dublin, has issued the following statement. 'Bonár Lách Mac Phóil a member of the Republican Army died following an engagement with Occupation forces at Derryarb on the 22nd September. Fuair bás ar son na hÉireann.'

He examined the dead man's name incuriously. It was a sentimentality not a disguise. What contempt Boney would have had for that thought! Their last encounters returned vividly to his mind. Each time they had met he had seen his friend more hopelessly drawn into the grip of his fanaticism. He should have known that he would die like that in a Fermanagh ditch. Because of this he experienced neither astonishment nor horror, only a guilty intermingling of pity and aversion. A capricious urge made him twist the paper to make the headings lie side by side. The page tore. There was a knock at the door and the steward's voice said. 'Taxi for you in about ten minutes, sir.'

He had never seen the Sunday morning city before. The streets were silent and wide and empty save for a windblown newspaper, a policeman pacing slowly, a shirtsleeved caretaker rinsing a blotch of vomit from office steps, a string of wome like black beads, hurrying to early devotions. At the ends of long wheeling streets he saw again the rath of blue hills that surrounded this place.

Freddie opened the door to him. They danced a wild bear's-hug down the hall. She was watching from the doorway of the living-room. He was surprised again at the firm wiry strength of her arms as she embraced him. She held him out at arm's length. There was more grey in her hair, more fine wrinkles at her eyes as she smiled.

During breakfast, while she tried to save him from Freddie, he could see that she herself was eager to question him. He described Maitland Park, told her a lot about Mrs Compton and a little about his fellow-lodgers. Yes, he said, yes, he went to church sometimes. Superlatives, he discovered satisfied Freddie. It was terrific playing with men like Rusk and Ellis and Tunney, shattering when you first trotted out against a side like Spurs. They were amused when he told them that he hadn't known he was in the international team until the ship's steward had shown him last night's paper. After that he was silent.

'You're tired,' said his mother.

'No, no. Tell me all about what's been going on here.'

'Oh, well . . .' they both began. The Emmets had gone south. Malcolm Tweedie across the street had joined the Navy. Old Moore's Almanack had broken her leg . . .

'And Mr Rankin's back?'

'Yes. He goes to friends every weekend. You'll see him this evening. He comes back about tea-time.'

'Are you glad he's living here again?'

She shrugged. 'I don't need his money so much, if that's what you mean. But he needs the quiet of this house.'

'I hope he doesn't make too much work for you,' he persisted.

She looked up quickly and laughed. 'Mr Rankin? Sometimes you wouldn't know he was in the house.'

'Except when he scrapes that blown-up fiddle,' said Freddie.

Impatiently she said, 'Oh, that's nothing. It makes a nice sound.' She was unwilling to have her elder son's concern for her frittered away. It was the first time she believed that he had taken any notice of how hard she worked. 'No, David dear, he's no trouble.'

He smiled warmly in response. 'That's good, Mums.'

Pleading weariness he stayed in the house all day. He knew that Freddie wanted to be seen with him, to show him off to his pals. It hurt him to disappoint the boy but the fear of whom he might see in the street, even at a distance, kept him indoors. Some time after tea he heard Mr Rankin's key in the door. He went out to the hall. Under the lamp, Mr Rankin looked smaller, a little stooped, the hair of his head sparse and silvery. But his eyes were clear and candid. The shy, evasive smile was gone. His clasp was firm on David's hand. If this was a man defeated he had taken trophies from his enemy.

Mr Rankin ate with the family. After supper they sat for a time talking at the living-room fire. They insisted that he sit in the old, fat, leather chair. To rest up his legs for Saturday, Freddie said. Saturday? Saturday's a hundred years away. I can't remember, he thought to himself, ever feeling so free, so untroubled. Then Mr Rankin said goodnight and left them. As they talked the vibrant notes of the 'cello sounded in the room above. He found himself listening expectantly, as he had listened when a child, for the mounting liquid sounds to take off into melody. Then the break, the silence that had always filled him with a vexed discontent, the deep, tremulous note as the poignant ascent began again. He was about to turn to his mother and say 'He hasn't changed,' when it struck him how untrue that was. He sat upright in his chair. 'I should have gone out today!'

'You should,' Freddie agreed glumly.

'Right. We'll make up for it tomorrow. What time do you come from school?'

'About four—' Freddie was watching him cautiously.

'I'll be there.'

'Can I bring my pals?'

'Two—three, mebbe. No more. And—' he looked at both of them, 'tomorrow evening we go to the theatre or something.'

'Oh, David,' she said raising her hands, 'I've never . . . I haven't been in a place like that for years!'

When Freddie had gone to bed she took down her knitting and they drew their chairs closer to the fire. He lay, legs stretched out, lulled by the warmth and the whispering of the needles. 'Will you ever live in this house again, David?'

He opened his eyes. 'Why not? You can't play football for ever, you know.'

'Then what'll you do?'

'When the time comes for me to hang up the boots I might come back here and start a business.'

She was attentive to her needles, her voice was low as she proceeded. 'Would you have the money, son?'

It was the first direct query she had made about his material well-being. He leaned towards her. 'I seem to be doing all right, Mother.'

'Yes . . . yes, David, I'm glad.' Every week his money had arrived, punctual, generous. A gift of twenty pounds lay in her handbag in the scullery. Her conscience was fettered.

When she stood up he said, 'Gimme a glass of milk and a biscuit before you go.'

She smiled, puzzled. 'Are you still hungry?'

'No, but I'd like that.'

She understood. 'Just like old times?'

'Just like old times.'

Familiar sounds came back to be recognized; the sporadic protest in the hot water tank, the people next door raking out their fire, the bubbling of a motor bike in the alley. He sipped his milk and stared into the fire. She had so few questions to ask me. Mebbe I've changed more'n I think. Mebbe she sees me as a man at last? No questions about having a girl. But then she might still not want the answer to that. He smiled gently, tapping the glass with his nail. I mustn't forget that leprechaun. The smile went slowly from his face. No questions about the girl who called at the door. No questions about her brother . . .

He set down the glass gently on the table. He hadn't mean't to think about Boney. Not that he had put him deliberately out of his mind, just sidled away from any uncomfortable thoughts that came up. No one could blame him for that. Indeed, respectable people would *expect* him to forget such an acquaintance as rapidly as possible. Keep your mouth shut and pass by on the other side. The family in Majestic Street would learn that he was back in the city. No matter how numbed they were, Arthur would open a newspaper, old McFall would talk to somebody. Would they really be surprised if the friend of their dead son kept away from them? In the tragedy that had overtaken them would they notice his small act of faithlessness?

On the following afternoon he went downtown, booked theatre seats and met Freddie outside the school. The two or three pals stipulated had grown to a dozen. But seeing the pride on Freddie's face as he introduced his friends, he was willing to overlook the misunderstanding. He wrote his name for them on jotters and bits of paper and then took them into a fadgee's for a feast of ice-cream and hero-worship. One by one, on the way home, the boys left them. At the top of Colinvista Street he said, 'You go down home. I've a job to do.'

He was about to turn away when he saw the troubled look on his brother's face. He paused. 'What's wrong with you?'

'Where are you going?'

'I told you.'

'Majestic Street?'

'Could be. Why?'

'That McFall crowd?'

'He was a pal of mine. Now go home.'

'That was before you really knew him. He was no good, David.'

'Let me look after this, will you?'

The boy moved closer so that no one could pass between them. 'He wasn't even a decent rebel. He was a traitor. He lifted a gun to his kind and ours—'

'You're getting mixed up in things you don't understand. Go away home, schoolboy!'

Freddie pushed his face closer to his brother's. His lips were quivering. 'Who the hell d'you think you're talking to? A child? This is the sort of thing I was taking care of when you were away in England! Keeping m'mother from reading about your pal in the paper. *We've* got to go on living here, y'know!'

David fumbled at a button. 'But he's dead now . . .'

The boy saw the irresolution in his brother's face as he turned away. 'David, don't go—' he called after the figure crossing the road.

He wasn't quite sure what he had meant to do. Perhaps go straight down to the house. His steps grew more uncertain as he approached Majestic Street. A large Union Jack fluttered from the gable. It flew there as a protestation, a symbol of anger and abhorrence that these streets should ever have spawned a Republican gunman. *We've got to go on living here.* How many peeping eyes were watching for those who still approached number ninety-three as friends? He plunged across the street and through the side entrance to Barney Harkin's. The pub was cool, and deserted. Behind the counter a youth was polishing glasses. David waved aside his nod of inquiry. 'Nothing, thanks. Know a Mr McFall at number ninety-three?'

The polishing slowly ceased. 'Sure.'

'Would you ask him to come up. There's half a dollar in it for you.' He tossed the coin on the counter.

The other didn't trouble to look at it. 'What name would I give, mister?'

'A friend.'

The youth's gaze never left his face. 'That wouldn't bring him up, mister.'

'All right. Say Minnis—Davie Minnis.'

'You Davie Minnis the footballer?'

David slapped his hand on the coin. 'That's right. Want to see my birth certificate?'

'No . . . sure, Mr Minnis . . . I'll go.' He whipped off his apron, shouted into the darkness behind the bar, snatched the half-crown and ran out. He was back almost immediately. 'The ould fella's coming.'

Five, ten minutes passed. Perhaps he's thought better of it. Perhaps his wife has stopped him. Perhaps . . . He heard the slippered feet, the side door crept open and Boney's father stepped in uncertainly.

'Hello, Mr McFall.'

The man touched his outstretched hand, looking round for refuge. David guided him to the gloom of a snug. They sat down facing each other across the scarred leaf.

'A drink, Mr McFall?'

'No . . . no. You've heard.'

'I saw it in the paper.'

'They didn't give him back to us. Did you know that?'

'No, you see, Mr McFall, I've been away for a long time—'

'—but Arthur found out where they were burying him. He went to the funeral. That took courage. I didn't know my sons had so much courage . . .'

Was that courage? He saw Arthur's pale, book-keeper's face, his prim, spotless clothes, as he searched his enemies out and joined himself to them for that last journey with his brother. Listening stonily to their condolences. Hating the voices, the beliefs, the aspirations that had brought destruction to his brother and mourning to his family. Would he not have done as much for Bonar himself?

'It's a lonely house now, Davie boy.'

'Mrs McFall, how is she?'

'She goes about her work. She never complains.'

'And . . . Maureen?'

'I thought you knew. She's away from Majestic Street. She's married.'

He didn't speak.

'In the spring. She hardly told us before it was all over. A fella called Bob Kane . . . a nice big fella . . .' He thought the old man smiled. 'They tell me she's gonna have a baby . . .'

He didn't think that that could still have hurt him. After a moment he said, 'And yourself, Mr McFall? You'll have to keep yourself busy. What about your work, the Almanac?'

He felt a shiver go through the man opposite. 'That cursed thing? It's scattered, burnt, destroyed! If it hadn't been for that kinda fooling my son would be alive today!'

'Ah, now, Mr McFall, I talked with Bonar. Don't blame—'

In the dusk the other had risen to his feet. David felt the gnarled, feverish fingers searching for his lapel. 'Don't say anything. I know. They never complain, the others. But I know. I talked to him about destroying things that I wouldn't have dared to lift a finger against. I didn't know what I was doing to him. I didn't know my son.' The hand was withdrawn. The old man crumpled back into his seat. He seemed to have forgotten David. He began to rock gently, his voice coming in a mumbling sing-song: 'I sacrificed him to my own vainglory. I led him into the land of Moriah. But there was no ram caught in the thicket for me . . .' He began to sob. Fearfully David stretched out his hand and touched him. 'Mr McFall,' he whispered, 'Mr McFall, I'll have to go now. Are you all right? Can I leave you? I'm sorry . . . sorry . . .' He stumbled to his feet, shrinking from the old man's pain, and ran from the pub.

Freddie was standing where he had left him. Without speaking, without looking at each other, they fell into step. Nearing their door Freddie said, 'You liked him more'n any other pal?'

'Yes.'

'I'm sorry about what I said.'

'That's all right.'

Freddie gave an irrepressible skip of excitement. 'Are you gonna take us to see a play or something, David?'